REGENCY
CHRISTMAS WISHES

Carla Kelly
Christine Merrill
Janice Preston

MILLS &
BOON

Published in Great Britain 2017
by Mills & Boon, an imprint of HarperCollins*Publishers*
1 London Bridge Street, London, SE1 9GF

REGENCY CHRISTMAS WISHES

© 2017 Harlequin Books S.A.

ISBN: 978-0-263-92612-5

The publisher acknowledges the copyright holders of the individual works as follows:

CAPTAIN GREY'S CHRISTMAS PROPOSAL © 2017 by Carla Kelly
HER CHRISTMAS TEMPTATION © 2017 by Christine Merrill
AWAKENING HIS SLEEPING BEAUTY © 2017 by Janice Preston

Our policy is to use papers that are natural, renewable and recyclable products and made from wood grown in sustainable forests. The logging and manufacturing processes conform to the legal environmental regulations of the country of origin.

Printed and bound in Spain
by CPI, Barcelona

CONTENTS

CAPTAIN GREY'S CHRISTMAS PROPOSAL

Carla Kelly

To all who believe in the magic of Christmas

Dear Reader,

All my life I've noticed that the Christmas season is a time when people everywhere seem to become a little better, perform kindly deeds, think of others more and act upon good promptings. It's almost as though Christmas gives us permission—as if we needed it—to bring out our better natures and the better natures of those around us.

We become more susceptible to the possibility that glad tidings of great joy can become a reality. Maybe we're more willing to believe in impossible things because at Christmas all things feel possible.

In that vein, I bring you the whimsical tale of a post captain in the Royal Navy—a careful man swept into an adventure made possible by the receipt of a years-old letter that went astray. The Peace of Amiens (1802–1803) becomes a window of opportunity that takes him from Plymouth, England, to Savannah, Georgia, in the new country of the United States—a place he remembers well from his childhood and has never quite forgotten.

There's a touch of magic, too...or maybe it's more than magic. Maybe it's the grace that can shower down upon us all if we're willing to let the spirit of Christmas and St Nicholas step in and make things right.

Reader, whatever your faith or creed, I invite you to consider the possibilities of this season of wonder.

Carla Kelly

Prologue

This wasn't a story shared widely. After some thought
and a few laughs, New Bedford shipbuilder James
Grey and his wife, Theodora, decided to tell their little ones this odd Christmas tale of how they'd met,
or re-met, after years apart. They thought it wise to
tell it before those same children reached maturity
and no longer set much store by St Nicholas. Later,
if more adult scepticism took over—well, that was
their worry.

It was Christmas story to tell around the fireplace,
drinking Papa's wassail and gorging on Mama's pecans nestled in cream and caramelized sugar she
called pralines. None of the children's New Bedford
friends ate pralines at Christmas, even though many
of them had seafaring fathers who travelled the world.

None of their friends had a mother like Mrs Grey,
or for that matter, a father like James Grey. If their
parents' origins were shrouded in mystery, everyone
in New Bedford appreciated the solidity of Russell

and Grey Shipworks, whose yards employed many craftsmen at good wages. More quietly whispered about was the boundless charity of Mrs Grey, who assisted slaves to freedom in Canada, or helped free men and women of colour find work in New England.

From the first, a deckhand out of Savannah, to the latest, a young couple fleeing Mississippi and a brutal owner named Tullidge, she and her network of volunteers provided food, lodging, employment and hope.

She was a woman of great beauty, with the soft accent and leisurely sentences heard in the South of the still new United States. James Grey spoke with a curious accent that placed him not quite in Massachusetts, but not quite in England, either. He had a mariner's wind-wrinkled face, and the ships he and his partner built were sound and true. That James adored his lovely wife was obvious to all. That the feeling was mutual was equally evident.

Something about the Christmas season seemed to reinforce this tenacious bond even more. Their oldest friends had heard the pleasant story of how they met in a distant Southern city, after years apart. There always seemed to be more to the story than either party let on, but New Englanders were too polite to ask.

Chapter One

❧

'Captain Grey, please excuse what happened. I found this under a box in my officer's storeroom.'

Mrs Fillion held out a letter most tattered and mangled. James Grey set down his soup spoon and picked it up. He squinted to make out some sort of return address. Stoic he may be, but he couldn't help his involuntary intake of breath to see a single word: Winnings.

'What? How?' was all he could manage as he held the delicate envelope as though it were a relic from an Etruscan tomb. Mrs Fillion, owner of The Drake, was kind enough to allow her Plymouth hotel to serve as an informal postal and collection station since the beginning of Napoleon's war. He motioned her to sit down at his solitary table, wishing she didn't appear so upset.

'What happened was that I set a box with some poor dead officer's personal effects on top of the letter, which I was saving for you,' she said, apologising. 'Unfortunately, I haven't seen you in years.'

'That's because I've operated on the far side of the world for several voyages,' he said. 'Don't let this trouble you.' He stared at the envelope. 'Any idea how long it might have been there?' He found himself almost afraid to open such a fragile document.

He couldn't help wincing when she said, 'It's been there since 1791, because the box I set on top of it had "1792" scribbled on the side.' She sighed. 'Eleven years, Captain. I hope it wasn't something terribly important.'

Likely not. When he never heard from Theodora Winnings after he proposed by way of pen and paper, James Grey, a first lieutenant in 1791, understood a refusal as well as the next man. Since his career seemed to keep him on the far side of the world for much of that decade, he had felt a little foolish for proposing to sweet Teddy Winnings in the first place. Then he dismissed the matter, except when he stood a watch, the perfect time to reflect on so much charm, goodwill and charity in a lovely frame. He stood a lot of watches. Still, Mrs Fillion needed to be jollied.

'I wouldn't worry, Mrs Fillion,' he said. 'I was a brand new first luff and I proposed to a fetching young thing in Charleston, South Carolina. Did it by letter, so you see how callow I was.' He laughed, and thought it sounded genuine.

Mrs Fillion smiled, which relieved him. 'Captain, would you be brave enough to propose in person now, providing the right fetching young thing happens along?'

'Unlikely. I'm a ripe thirty-seven, and serve in a dangerous profession. Why inflict that on a woman?'

'You underrate females, Captain,' Mrs Fillion said.

'I have long been fortune's fool.' He picked up his soup spoon again, giving Mrs Fillion liberty to continue circulating among her other guests.

The dining room was less busy, mainly because of the Treaty of Amiens, which meant most warships were in port, with officers uncomfortable on half pay and scrimping, and crews dumped on shore to starve. War was almost guaranteed to break out again, but until it did, this meant tight times in ports like Plymouth and Portsmouth.

Jem waited until she was engaged in conversation with another officer before picking up the mangled letter. Eleven years was a long time to expect a letter to rule in his favour. Whatever the fervour of the moment, it was long past, whether Teddy's reply had been yea or nay.

He had already finished reading his newspaper, and there was still soup to be downed. Might as well see what she wrote all those years ago. He slit the letter open carefully, dismayed to see water damage inside.

'Yes!' The word leaped out at him. *My God*, Jem thought, *she loved me*. The rest of the letter was mainly blotched and illegible. He stared hard, and fancied he made out the phrases, '…but you need to know…' and then farther down the ruined page, 'I should have…'

The box Mrs Fillion set on top of Teddy's letter must have been damp. He could decipher nothing else.

His soup forgotten, Jem leaned back in his chair, staring out the window where autumn rain slid down the panes. His first glimpse of Theodora Winnings was through a fever haze, as though he gazed up at her from the bottom of a pond. That was his second relapse from malaria. Since the frigate *Bold* was peacefully moored in Charleston Harbour, the post surgeon had taken him ashore and left him to the tender mercy of the Sisters of Charity.

He had recalled nothing of the first week except the stink of his sweat and his desire to die. Toward the end of that week, he vaguely remembered a visit from his captain, who announced the *Bold* was sailing to Jamaica, but would return in two months, hoping to find him alive. At the time, he had preferred death. Even in his addled state, Jem knew that was nothing to tell his commander.

By the second week, he could get out of bed for a call of nature, if someone clutched him close around the waist. The Sisters of Charity were tough women who manhandled him so efficiently that any embarrassment quickly vanished.

By the third week, life's appeal returned, especially when Miss Theodora Winnings sat beside his bed to wipe his forehead and read to him. He was still too wasted to pay attention to the words, but he enjoyed the slow molasses sound of Miss Winnings' Southern diction.

By the next week, he spoke in coherent sentences and silently admired the loveliness of her ivory skin, dark hair and eyes and full lips, not to mention a bountiful bosom.

'Captain, your soup must be cold. Would you like more?'

'Oh, no. I'm done.' He looked down at the letter with its nine legible words. 'Mrs Fillion, she said yes eleven years ago.'

He shouldn't have told her, she who set the box on his letter in the first place. He knew Mrs Fillion had been through much, with children of her own at sea, and bad news when her lodgers died in the service of king and country. Her eyes brimmed with tears.

'Look here, ma'am, don't weep on my account,' he added hastily. 'As it turned out, once the *Bold* picked me up and revictualled, we left the Carolinas and never returned. I was a foolish lieutenant. Our paths were destined never to cross again.'

Mrs Fillion wasn't buying it. 'Love doesn't work like that,' she argued. She dabbed angrily at her tears. 'If you had known her answer, you would have found a way.'

'Poppycock and humbug, Mrs Fillion,' he stated firmly.

He misjudged the redoubtable owner of the Drake. 'Listen to me, Captain Grey,' she demanded.

Unused to being dressed down, he listened.

'I think you should go to the United States,' she

said, lowering her voice so the other Navy men couldn't hear. 'Find Miss Winnings.'

'What is the point, madam?' he said, exasperated, more with himself than with her.

'She said aye eleven years ago,' Mrs Fillion replied.

He knew he was wearing his most sceptical expression, but she touched his sleeve, her hand gentle on his arm. 'Have a little faith, Captain.'

He had to laugh. 'Madam, I am as profane a captain as you will find in the fleet, as are most of my associates. We rely on time and tides, not faith.'

'I don't believe you.' She looked around the room. 'I doubt there is a captain or lieutenant in here who doesn't rely on faith, too, say what you will.'

What could he add to that? He wasn't up to a theological argument with a hardworking woman he had long admired. 'I'll think about it,' he muttered, then leaned over and gave Mrs Fillion a whacking great kiss on her cheek. For both their sakes, he chose not to continue the narrative. He could pretend he had reassured her, and she was kind enough to think so, too. That was how polite society worked.

He knew it would be wise to leave the dining room then, and spare Mrs Fillion from more discomfort. He looked in the card room, not surprised to see the perpetual whist game about to get underway. He couldn't remember who had named it that, but during wartime, there was always someone in port to make up a whist table. Some of the officers preferred backgammon, and there was a table for that, too.

Lieutenant Chardon, his parents French *emigrés*, was looking for a partner to sit in the empty chair opposite him. The other two partners, good whist players, were already seated.

'Captain Grey, would you partner me?' the luff asked.

Jem considered their chances of taking sufficient tricks from the proficient pair looking at him with similar calculation. He knew the state of Chardon's purse—his parents dead now, and Auguste Chardon living from hand to mouth, thanks to the Treaty of Amiens. Jem knew they could defeat their opponents, who were post captains like himself, with ample prize money to see them through the irritation of peacetime. Chardon needed a big win to support his habit of eating and sleeping under a roof.

'I'd be delighted,' Jem said, and sat down.

'Our Yankee captain,' one of the opposing captains said, and not with any real friendship.

Jem shrugged it off as he always did. There were worse things to be called. Hadn't his older friend Captain Benjamin Hallowell, also a Massachusetts Yankee, managed to become one of Sir Horatio Nelson's storied Band of Brothers after the Battle of the Nile?

'Aye, sir,' he said, broadening his relatively unnoticeable American accent.

Jem motioned for Lieutenant Chardon to shuffle the deck.Ninety minutes later, he had the satisfaction of watching the captains fork over a substantial sum to Chardon. A note to Mrs Fillion had brought sandwiches and beer to their table. Jem wasn't hungry, but he suspected Chardon was. How nice to see him eat and play at the same time.

After the captains left, grumbling, Chardon tried to divide the money. Jem shook his head. When the lieutenant started to protest, Jem put up his hand.

'I have been where you are now,' he said simply. 'This discussion is over, Lieutenant Chardon.'

And it was; that was the beauty of outranking a lieutenant. He invited Chardon to join him down the street at a fearsome pit of a café serving amazing sausages swaddled in thick bread. He ate one to Chardon's three, bid him goodnight and returned to the Drake, before the lieutenant, not so poor now, could go in anonymity and without embarrassment to his meagre lodgings. In due time if Chardon survived, once war resumed, he would have his own prize money earning further income in Carter and Brustein's counting house.

'You may prefer me not to say this, Captain Grey,' Chardon told him as they parted company. 'You are a man of honour.'

Jem Grey returned the little bow and made his way back to warm and comfortable quarters at the Drake. He could unbutton his trousers, kick off his shoes, lie down on a bed that did not sway with the current, and contemplate his next step, now that he knew Theodora Winnings had loved him eleven years ago.

Chapter Two

After a beastly night worrying how long Teddy Winnings had waited for him to reply to her letter, James scraped away at the whiskers on his face, slouched downstairs to the dining room, and settled for a coffee and a roll, which didn't please Mrs Fillion.

'I really hope you're not still troubled over that unfortunate letter,' she said as she poured him a cup. '*I* worried enough for both of us.'

'No, no,' he lied, then repented because he knew Mrs Fillion was intelligent. 'Aye, I did worry some.'

'What are you going to do about it?'

He looked around the dining room, wishing there were someone seated who had more courage dealing with Mrs Fillion. He saw none, and he knew most of the room's occupants. Men could be such cowards.

'I don't know,' he said frankly.

Honesty appeared to be the best policy with Mrs Fillion. She declined further comment, to his relief passed on to her next customer, coffee pot in hand.

He had a headful of things to do, but lying awake nearly all night had pushed one agenda directly to the top of his mind's disorderly heap. His jaw ached. A man feeling as low as he did could only take the next step, which he did. He drew his boat cloak tight around him and walked to Stonehouse Naval Hospital.

Unwilling to face the nosy clerks in Admin, Jem walked directly to Building Two, where an orderly met him at the door.

'Where away, captain?' the man asked, in proper navy fashion.

'Surgeon Owen Brackett,' he said. 'Tell him James Grey would like a word, if it's convenient.'

The orderly touched his forehead and gestured to a sitting room. It must not have been convenient for Owen, because Jem sat there for at least thirty minutes. Still in a dark mood, he read through the obituaries in the *Naval Chronicle*, remembering the time he was listed there when his frigate had been declared missing after a typhoon in the Pacific. When the *Nautilus* finally made port in Plymouth a year later, there had been surprised looks from the harbourmaster. He smiled at the memory.

'Jem, what brings you here?' he heard from the doorway.

If Jem had thought he looked tired when he stared into his shaving mirror this morning, he was a bright ray of sunshine compared to Owen Brackett.

'I thought this damned peace treaty would turn

you into a man of leisure,' he said to Owen as they shook hands.

'Hardly. Why is it you deep-water sailors have so many ear infections?' Owen asked.

'Too many watches on deck in storms,' Jem replied promptly. 'If you don't have time…'

'I do. What's the matter?'

Everything, Jem thought. *A proposal of marriage I tendered was accepted eleven years ago but I never saw it.* 'My jaw aches,' he said instead.

Owen gestured for him to come down the hall to his office. 'Have a seat and tip your head back,' the surgeon said. With skilled fingers, he probed, asked a few questions with his hand still in Jem's mouth, and nodded at Jem's strangled replies.

'Tense jaw is all. You've been gritting your teeth for years,' he pronounced. 'It's a common complaint in the navy.'

'Surely not,' Jem said. 'I don't grit my teeth.'

'Probably every time you sail into battle,' Owen countered.

Jem opened his mouth for more denial, then closed it. The surgeon was probably right. 'What's the cure?'

'Peace. Maybe a wife,' Owen replied with a smile. He consulted his timepiece. 'There is a shepherd's pie cooling below deck in the galley. Join me for luncheon? The ale is surprisingly good here.'

They walked downstairs together, the surgeon talking about gonorrhoea with an orderly who stopped him on the stairs with a question. It was more information than Jem wanted or needed, but he couldn't interrupt a friend with no spare time, peace or war. Good thing Owen already had a patient wife.

Owen was right about the shepherd's pie, which had the odd facility of both filling his stomach and loosening his tongue, although that could have been the fault of the ale. A fast eater from years of necessity, he decided to ask Owen's advice about the letter, while the surgeon served himself another helping.

'Here I am, the proud possessor of a letter in which a young woman I love, or at least loved, accepted my proposal,' he concluded. 'I'm curious to know how she has fared through the years.'

'You say she is pretty.'

'Quite, but that's not the half of it. She was so kind to me.'

Even now Jem clearly remembered the loveliness of Teddy Winnings' creamy complexion, and the deep pools of compassion in her eyes at first, followed a few weeks later by lively interest when he was coherent and—he hoped—charming. Young he may have been, but he was a gentleman. He had known he was enjoying the company of a young lady properly raised, and behaved himself.

'Her father ran Winnings Mercantile and Victuallers, a few doors down from the hospital and convent,' he told Owen Brackett. 'It was a substantial business, and I imagine she had plenty of young men interested in her.'

'She's likely long-married,' Owen said.

'Aye.' He hesitated to say more so Owen filled in.

'But you're going to cross the Atlantic and find out, aren't you?' the surgeon asked.

There it was, laid out before him, the very thing Jem wanted to do. Owen knew.

'Better see a tailor right away and get yourself a civilian wardrobe,' Owen said as he stood up and held out his hand.

Jem shook his hand. 'Don't tell anyone. I'm ashore on half pay, but I'm not certain Admiralty House would be happy.'

'Why not?' Owen asked as they headed to the main floor again. 'We're at peace, and that unpleasantness with the colonies is long over.' He took a good look at Jem. 'You want to go back, don't you, and not just for Miss Winnings.' It was a statement, not a question.

'I don't know what I want,' Jem replied frankly. 'I liked living in Massachusetts Colony, but when you're ten years old and your parents pull all the strings...' He shrugged. 'Don't say anything.'

'I'll be as silent as an abbey of Trappist monks,' Owen assured him. 'Bon voyage, friend. Let me know at what longitude your jaw ache ends.'

James took himself to his tailor in the Barbican, who opened his ledger to Jem's previous measurements and congratulated him on maintaining an enviable trimness.

'It's easy enough to do in southern latitudes, when you sweat off every ounce of fat,' Jem said.

Of nightshirts and smallclothes he had an adequate amount. Shoes, too. He assured his tailor that three suits of clothes would suffice, and he could use his navy boat cloak. He reconsidered. As much as he loved the thing, one look would give him away immediately as a member of the Royal Navy, which was perhaps not so wise. He could store his Navy uniforms with Mrs Fillion.

His order complete and promised in two weeks, Jem went next door for a low-crowned beaver hat which struck him as faintly ridiculous, even though the haberdasher assured him he was now *à la mode*. He knew he was going to miss the added intimidation of his tall bicorn, but as Teddy Winnings had told him once—how was it he was starting to remember their conversations?—he was already tall enough.

He paid a cautious visit to the harbourmaster to inquire about any outbound ships headed for the United States. He knew the harbourmaster as a garrulous man. To his surprise, George Headley didn't even blink when he mentioned wanting passage to a former enemy country.

Headley leaned closer. 'This is a special mission, isn't it?' he whispered. 'My lips are sealed, of course.'

'Good of you,' Jem said in the same conspiratorial tone, hoping the Lord Almighty wouldn't smite him dead for deceiving a good, if chatty, man. 'The less said, the better my chances are that none of Boney's spies will hear.'

The harbourmaster nodded, his eyes grave, and gestured toward a fair-sized vessel at anchor in the harbour. 'Captain, the *Marie Elise* is headed to Baltimore, I believe. Would you like me to hail a waterman to take you out there?'

A mere half hour later, he sat in the captain's cabin, drinking Madeira and then forking over passage money.

'We'll sail for Baltimore on or about the middle of October,' Captain Monroe said. 'We're looking at a seven-week passage, give or take.' The Yankee gave Jem a shrewd look. 'You're a seafaring man.'

'I am,' Jem said. 'Royal Navy. It's private business.'

The captain nodded, obviously not believing a word of that, and sounded remarkably like the harbourmaster. 'My lips are sealed. You'll only be a short distance from Washington, D.C. How is it you already sound slightly American?'

'Many people on the Devonshire coast have a similar accent,' Jem hedged, 'but you are right. I was born in the colony of Massachusetts.'

'We two countries need to get along, eh?'

'Indeed we do. I'm lodging at the Drake. Send a boy around when you're ready to lift anchor,' Jem said.

'You've been away a long time from Massachusetts?' Captain Monroe said as he walked topside with a fellow captain, showing him all the courtesies.

'Twenty-seven years,' Jem replied, as he sat in the bosun's chair to be swung over the side to his waiting boat. He wouldn't have minded scrambling down the chains, but he couldn't ignore the American captain's kindness.

'A lot has changed, Captain,' the Yankee said as he motioned for the crew to swing him over now.

I hope not everything. Or everyone, Jem thought as he went over the side and waved to his American counterpart. *Is it too much to hope that Theodora Winnings remains the same?*

Chapter Three

James made a note in his log—personal logs were a habit not easily broken—to let Owen Brackett know when next they saw each other that his jaw stopped aching at Latitude North thirty-eight degrees, four minutes, Longitude West forty-eight degrees, forty-six minutes, roughly the middle of the stormy Atlantic.

The passengers aboard the *Marie Elise* were a disparate lot, some Americans heading home, a French *emigré* or two and Englishmen who were no more forthcoming about their reasons to travel than he was. He had a private chuckle, thinking that some of them might have been what the harbourmaster thought of him, spies or government emissaries.

The crossing was rough enough to keep many of the passengers below deck during the early days of the voyage. Jem had no trouble keeping down his meals, and less trouble standing amidships and looking at oily, swelling water hinting of hurricanes.

He only spent two days in the waist of the ship before Captain Monroe invited him to share the quarterdeck. Jem accepted the offer, scrupulously careful to stay away from Captain Monroe's windward side. From Monroe's demeanour, Jem knew the Yankee appreciated the finer points of quarterdeck manners.

Captain Monroe apologised in advance for some of his passengers. 'Hopefully they'll stay seasick awhile and not pester you with gibes about Englishmen who couldn't fight well enough to hang on to the colonies.' He laughed. 'And here I am, making similar reference!'

'I'll survive,' Jem said, and felt no heartburn over the matter. 'We need to maintain a friendship between our countries.'

'From what you tell me, the United States might be your country, too,' Captain Monroe pointed out. 'D'ye plan to visit Massachusetts during this visit?'

'Perhaps. We'll see.'

Mostly Jem watched the water, enjoying the leisure of letting someone else worry about winds and waves, especially when it proved obvious to him that Captain Monroe knew his ropes. He felt not a little flattered when Lucius—they were on a first-name basis soon—asked his opinion about sails and when to shorten them.

Even better than the jaw ache vanishing was the leisure to recall a much earlier trip in the other direction. He stared at the water, remembering that trip when he was ten years old; he'd been frightened because so-called patriots had torched the family's comfortable Boston house. He remembered his unwillingness even then to leave the colony where he had been born and reared and now faced cruel times.

Looking around to make certain he was unobserved, Jem leaned his elbows on the ship's railing, a major offense that would have sent one of his midshipmen shinnying up and down the mainmast twenty times as punishment. Most painful had been his agonized goodbye to his big yellow dog with the patient, sorrowful eyes and the feathery tail always waving because everyone was a friend. 'I want another dog like you, Mercury,' he said quietly to the Atlantic Ocean.

Papa had named Mercury, because he was the slowest, most good-natured creature in the colony, even after some Sons of Liberty rabble caught him, tarred and feathered him. If Jem's tears could have washed the tar away, Mercury would have survived. He never asked Papa how he put Mercury down, but at least his pet did not suffer beyond an hour or two.

Here he stood, a grown man of some skill and renown among his peers, melancholy over a long-dead dog. As with most complicated emotions that seem to surface after childhood is gone, James wasn't entirely sure who the tears were for.

Contemplating the water through many days of the voyage, Jem found himself amazed at his impulsive decision to bolt to the United States, after reading a mere scrap of a decade-old letter. He knew himself to be a careful man, because he understood the monumental danger of his profession and his over-arching desire to see all the officers and seamen in his stewardship as safe as he could make them. Quick decisions came with battle, but this hasty voyage had been a quick decision unrelated to war.

In the cold light of this Atlantic crossing, he justified himself, convinced that the Peace of Amiens, while a fragile treaty, would last long enough for him to make sure all was well with Theodora Winnings and return with Admiralty none the wiser.

Or so he thought. Anything seemed possible, now that his jaw didn't ache all the time and he was sleeping eight hours instead of his usual four. Until this voyage, he had forgotten the pleasure of swinging in a hammock and reading.

As the journey neared its end, he spent a pleasant evening in Lucius Monroe's cabin, drinking a fine Madeira; maybe he drank too much. However it fell out, he told the Yankee skipper about Theodora Winnings and the long-delayed letter.

'Am I a fool for this expedition?' he asked Lucius.

'Probably,' the Yankee replied. 'She helped nurse you back to health from a malaria relapse?'

'Aye, she did. I was a stinking, sweating, puking, pissing, disgusting mess.'

'Then it must be love,' Lucius Monroe joked. 'More?'

Jem held out his glass. 'I never had the courage to ask her why she was even there. There were other women in the ward besides the nuns, but they were all slaves.'

'Who can understand the ladies?' Lucius said. He leaned back and gave a genteel burp that he probably would have apologised for a few weeks earlier, before theirs turned into a first-name acquaintance.

Lucius broke the comfortable silence. 'I've been curious about this since you came aboard, James. You tell me you were born in Massachusetts Colony and spent your first decade in my country. How do you feel about it now?'

'I liked Massachusetts,' he said finally. 'I liked the dock people who didn't mind my chatter, and my friends who took me fishing. My father was next in authority after Benjamin Hallowell, Senior, then serving as Admiralty High Commissioner. Papa let me roam all around the docks.'

He saw by the way the American nodded, that his own childhood had been spent much the same way. 'You understand, Lucius, don't you? There is a freedom here that I cannot explain or understand.'

'Did you come back for another glimpse of that, or of Miss Winnings?' Captain Monroe asked.

'I wish I knew.'

When the *Marie Elise* docked in Baltimore, James walked down the gangplank, took a deep breath of United States' air, realised it smelled the same as it did in Plymouth, and laughed at himself. With instructions from Captain Monroe, he arranged passage on a coasting vessel to Charleston, South Carolina.

After an evening of good food with Captain Monroe at the curiously named The Horse You Came In On Tavern at Fell's Point, and a night at the inn next door, James boarded the *Annie*, a vessel that deposited him in Charleston a day and a half later, none the worse for wear, even though the vessel was less sound than he liked and the crew even more dubious.

He had stuffed his effects in his old sea bag, which still naturally fit the curve of his shoulder. After a short walk, spent trying to divest himself of the seagoing hip roll, he stood in front of the Magnolia Tavern and Inn, took a deep breath and wondered again what he was doing.

He didn't bother with luncheon. After dropping his duffel in his room that overlooked magnolia trees with their heady blooms, he walked the route from the dock to Winnings Mercantile and Victuallers. At least, he walked to where it should have been, and stared up at a swinging sign that read South Carolina Mercantile. He reminded himself that things change in eleven years, and opened the door.

The smells remained the same—dried cod, pungent tobacco, turpentine. Jem fancied he even recognised the man behind the counter, a fellow with an outmoded wig and a big nose.

'May I help you?' the man behind the counter asked.

Jem relished the soft sound of his speech, wondering how it was that an English-speaking people not so long removed from the British Isles could sound so different. When he was coherent, he had asked Teddy Winnings about that. She had reminded him that African slaves had much influence in the language of the Carolinas.

'Perhaps you can help me, sir,' he asked. 'I came into port here some eleven years ago, when this place was the Winnings establishment. What happened?'

'Mr Winnings died of yellow fever and his widow sold the property to the current owner,' he replied.

That was a fine how-de-doo. Now what?

'Where do the widow and her family live now?' he asked.

The counter man shrugged. 'She didn't have any family. Don't know where she is.'

'No family? I distinctly remember a daughter,' Jem said. Who could ever forget Theodora Winnings and her quiet, understated loveliness? Obviously he hadn't.

'No. No daughter.' A pause. 'Where are you from, sir?'

'Nowhere, I suppose,' Jem said, surprised at himself. 'I am a ship captain.'

'From somewhere north?'

'At one time. No idea where the widow is?'

The shop's front bell tinkled and three men came in. The man at the counter gave Jem a polite nod and dismissed him. 'Sirs, may I assist you?'

Jem took the hint and left the mercantile. He stood a

brief moment on the walkway, then turned south, confident the Sisters of Charity hadn't left their convent.

There it was, much the same. He recalled ivy running over the walls, but someone had mentioned a hurricane years ago that had stripped some of it away. The Virgin smiled down at him from her pedestal perch, reminding him of his first view of the statue while lying on his back on a stretcher. With some embarrassment, he remembered shrieking like a girl because she seemed to be falling on him. Oh, those malaria fever dreams.

He rang the bell and waited for quiet footsteps on the parquet floor within. He never prayed much, if at all, but he prayed now that someone would know where Theodora Winnings lived. He squared his shoulders to face the reality that if Mercantile Man said Widow Winnings had no children, then Teddy might be dead, too.

'Don't disappoint me,' he said out loud, not sure if he was trying to exert his non-existent influence on God Almighty, or the world in general, which had been stingy with blessings, of late. He remembered himself and thought, *Please, sir*, that and no more.

Before he could ring the bell again, the door opened on a young face, probably one of the novitiates. In her calm but practical way, Teddy had told him that every yellow fever epidemic meant more young girls in the convent because they had nowhere else to go.

'Sir?' she asked.

He took off his hat. 'I am looking for Theodora

Winnings, who used to assist here. Her father owned what is now South Carolina Mercantile. Can you help me?'

She opened the door and he stepped into the familiar coolness that had soothed his fever almost as much as the mere presence of Teddy sitting by his bedside, doing nothing more than holding his hand.

'I will take you to our Abbess, sir,' she said. 'Please follow me.'

He walked beside her down the long hall, breathing in the faint odour of incense and something sharper that still smelled of disease and contagion. Underlying it all was the still-remembered rot of a warm southern climate.

The novice knocked on a carved door, listened with her ear to the panel, then opened it. She stepped inside and motioned for him to wait.

He stood in the hallway during the quiet conversation within, then entered the room when the nun sitting behind the desk gestured to him. The novice glided out quietly.

The nun behind the desk indicated a chair. She clasped her hands on the desk and wasted not a moment on preliminaries.

'I have not thought of Theodora Winnings in years,' the nun said. 'Apparently you have, sir.'

He could blush and deny, but he was long past the blushing stage of his life. 'I have, Sister… Sister…'

'Mother Abbess,' she corrected. 'And you are…'

'Captain James Grey of His Majesty's Royal Navy.'

With that announcement, she gave him a long look, one that came close to measuring the very small-clothes he sat in, down to his stockings. 'I remember you, sir. We despaired of your survival for several weeks.' She permitted herself a smile. 'Even your ship sailed away.'

'With a promise to return,' he reminded her. 'Aye, you have me. I didn't think I would live, either. At times, death sounded almost welcome.'

She chuckled, probably all the emotion her order was capable of permitting. 'Teddy held your hand when we had done all we could.'

It was his turn and he took a page from her no-nonsense book. 'I doubt you knew this, but I left her a letter the morning I walked out of here under my own power to rejoin my frigate. I proposed marriage in that letter, but I never heard from her. I want to know how she is. That's all. The man at the mercantile said Widow Winnings had no children, but that can't be right. Where is she?'

Only an idiot wouldn't have noticed that he had disturbed the serenity of a woman probably committed by oath to be calm in all matters. She stood up quickly and turned her back on him to stare out the window.

'If she's dead, I understand,' he said. 'I want to let her know I would have moved heaven and earth to respond, had I known of her letter's existence. Her letter was misplaced and I only received her reply in September. Granted, eleven years is a long time...'

He let his voice trail away. He knew enough of

people to tell, even with her back to him, how upset Mother Abbess was. 'I had good intentions,' he insisted. 'I proposed, after all.'

She turned around. 'You don't understand.'

'Understand what?' he asked, fearful and bracing himself for what, he had no idea. 'Mrs Winnings must have had children. Teddy was one of them.'

'Teddy is a slave.'

Chapter Four

'Shame on her for not telling you,' Mother Abbess said as she sat down.

Astonished, Jem couldn't speak. He took Teddy's battered letter from his inside coat pocket and spread the paltry thing on the nun's desk. He stared at the few legible words through new eyes. 'But you need to know…' suddenly made sense. So did, 'I should have…' farther down the page.

'She didn't come here of her own free will, just to be kind?' he asked, perfectly willing to ignore obvious evidence, even though he understood the shamble of a letter now. *I want to see her anyway*, kept bouncing around in his brain. 'Maybe?'

'No, sir. During fever times, and when we ask, some of the better class of ladies send their slaves here to help.' She made an offhand gesture. 'They're just slaves. If something happens to them…well, you understand.'

'No, I don't,' he said, uncertain if he were more

angry or more appalled at her words. He closed his eyes, which was the only way he could glimpse Theodora Winnings' ivory skin. True, her hair was curly and her lips full, but God above, he had curly hair, too. 'She's so fair-skinned.'

'So was her mother, but by half,' the abbess said. 'Roxie was a house slave and a great beauty. If memory serves me, Roxie was the daughter of a plantation owner and another slave. I assume Mr Winnings fancied her and bought her for his own purposes. Theodora was *their* child, with a quarter African blood, therefore not so noticeably of African descent. It happens all the time.'

Mother Abbess's callous appraisal caused the growing gulf between them to yawn wider by the second. They sat in the same small room, worlds apart. Jem did his best to control the complicated emotions beginning to pinch at his heart like demons from a painting he had seen in a Spanish monastery, thrusting pitchforks into some saint or other.

'I like sailing the oceans,' he said finally. 'The thing I hate the most is patrolling the Middle Passage where we sometimes encounter slave ships.'

He watched her eyes, in his dismay pleased to see some of the complacency in them disappear. 'They stink to high heaven. I have never seen more wretched people, thirsty, starving and chained below decks. Mothers holding their dying babies up to me, as if I could help them. God, it chafed my heart.'

Her face was still serene, but she rattled the beads

on the rosary that hung from her waist. 'Why are you telling me this?' Mother Abbess asked.

'I don't know,' he said. 'Should Teddy have said something earlier? I mean before I fell in love with her, because fall in love with her I did.'

'Certainly she should have told you,' the nun said with some vigour. 'More shame to her and good riddance.'

'If you were a slave and you saw a way out of this... this... I don't know what... Would you have said something?' He asked, irritated that his voice was rising.

Silence. The beads rattled louder.

Jem went to the door, eager to leave the suddenly stifling office. 'Can you...or will you...at least tell me where Mrs Winnings took her household, after her husband died and she sold the business?'

Perhaps Mother Abbess saw he was in complete earnest. She joined him at the door to her office. 'Some slaves were sold at auction. Others went with Mrs Winnings to Savannah, where she was from. It was years ago. I doubt any records remain. Leave it alone.'

'I have the time,' he heard himself say. 'I also have the means and the inclination. Good day. Thank you for your ministrations to me eleven years ago. I do owe you for that.'

She opened her mouth to speak, but Jem had no desire to hear another word. He outdistanced the novice who had seated herself in the hall, and had the satisfaction of slamming the front door hard.

On the other side of it, he shook his head at his own childish behaviour and took a deep breath, which brought a whiff of the harbour, and tar, and the sugary fragrance of gardenias, in bloom in December.

He stood there in front of the convent, angry at himself and wondering if he had wilfully overlooked signs of Teddy's parentage. In Italy and Greece he had seen lovely women with cream-coloured skin like hers. Had he assumed she was of Mediterranean extraction? He looked down at his feet, distressed with himself. Did it even matter? He loved Theodora Winnings.

What now, you idiot? he asked himself, as uncertain as he had ever been in his life. A man across the street was scrubbing steps leading up to a modest house, and children were jumping rope beyond the servant. Jem had the distinct feeling he was being watched so he turned around slowly, and laughed at his folly. It was the statue of the Virgin looking over him.

'Am I an idiot?' he asked her, then felt instantly stupid for talking to a statue.

He felt disgusted with himself for tossing away money and time on a long voyage to the United States, on the highly unrealistic chance that nothing would have changed from the time he sailed away. God Almighty, he had chastised midshipmen at length for that kind of illogical thinking, and now he had committed worse follies than theirs.

His breathing slowed down as he began to admire

the pretty statue's carved serenity. He had long harboured the nagging suspicion that his was not destined to be an easy life, or even a lengthy one. A realist, he knew the Treaty of Amiens would only last until First Consul Napoleon felt he was sufficiently prepared with new warships sliding down the ways into the sea around Spanish Gibraltar. The war would begin again in more earnest. When that happened, he did not think it would end anytime soon. Like other men of his class and career, he would have to fight on until the armies wore themselves out, and the seas ran with blood.

The more fool he, that on the Atlantic crossing he had begun to imagine for a tiny moment a happy life with Theodora Winnings, who was waiting for him in Charlestown with love in her heart, even after eleven years. What folly. He had no idea where she was.

He looked at the statue with the modest downcast eyes. 'Any suggestions, madam?' he asked, after looking around to make certain he was still alone on the street. 'Please consider the season. My mother used to tell me that wonderful things happen at Christmas.'

Nothing. *What now, oh, brilliant man?* he asked himself. He could go to Savannah, but for all he knew, Teddy Winnings had been sold down river and wasn't there. He could also travel north to Boston, which he wanted to see again. Admiralty had no idea where he was, and he had enough funds to chase any number of will-o'-the-wisps.

Do I go north or south? he asked himself, uncertain, perplexed, irritated and above all, sad.

As he stood there, he took a deep breath and another. Each breath brought the fragrance of gardenia, roses and other blooms to his nostrils. Cardinals flitted in the trees. He knew Savannah promised more of the same. His chances of locating Teddy Winnings were slim to none, but he could at least spend one warm Christmas, which might render his misery less excruciating. He remembered Christmas in Boston, and decided he had no wish to be cold *and* sad. Warm and sad had more appeal; it also made him smile.

He waited for the idea to sound ridiculous, but it didn't. 'Savannah, it is,' he told the statue, and gave her a little salute. 'What do I have to lose?'

He went back to the shipping office, where the agent behind the counter took his money and informed him that the next coasting vessel would sail on the tide.

'Towers,' he said, and returned some silver to Jem's palm.

'Beg pardon?'

'Towers, *Sir.*'

'I don't understand what you mean by towers,' Jem said, speaking distinctly, and wishing the agent would do the same.

Appearing remarkably put out, the agent pointed to the clock and measured down from two to four.

The mystery was solved. 'Two hours,' Jem said, trying to decide whether to laugh or bang his forehead on the counter. He did neither; a post captain in the Royal Navy has some pride.

He took his ticket and left the office, hearing laughter behind him at his expense. He mentally rehearsed blistering profanity that would make him feel better, but only briefly. He decided in the spirit of the season to be a bigger man than that.

It didn't hurt that the tavern next to the inn had crab cakes, something called okra that luckily tasted better than it looked, and excellent rum. The tavern owner's slave served him well-remembered spoon bread that went down with equal ease. He finished it all with bread pudding and whiskey sauce, staggered back to the inn to pick up his duffel, and took his way to the wharf again, and Savannah.

He knew the distance between the cities wasn't great. He secured a deck chair, propped his booted feet on the railing, and slept.

Chapter Five

A spanking wind off the mainland brought the little coasting vessel to Savannah by midnight. As slapdash as ship's discipline seemed to be, Captain Grey had to give the man at the helm all due honour. Jem knew how tricky it was to sail in the dark near a lee shore, but the captain had managed such a feat, a testament to years of practice from the grizzled look of him.

Jem woke up when he felt a difference in the direction of the wind on his face. He went to the railing and watched as the vessel turned west into the river's mouth and proceeded upstream to the city proper, past the barrier islands of Tybee, Cockspur, Long and Bird, names he remembered from poring over colonial charts when he was much younger. Amazing what a man could remember. Beacon lights burned along the route as the sea diluted itself into the Savannah River.

Now what? he asked himself as the ship docked right at the wharf, tying up handsomely. Dockside, he looked around, overcame his natural reticence and inquired of a fellow passenger where a man might find an inn.

The traveller gave him a leisurely look—Lord God, didn't anyone do *anything* in a hurry in the South?—and stated his opinion.

'You, Sir, appear to be a man of means,' the man said and pointed. 'Up a street to Bay, turn right and you'll see the Arundel.' He tipped his hat and walked slowly into the night.

Up a street and right Jem went. The Arundel was a two-story affair with the deep verandas he was growing accustomed to. The lobby was deserted at this midnight hour. Opening the door must have set off a bell ringing somewhere, because a man in a nightshirt and robe emerged, rubbing his eyes. In a few minutes, Jem had a room on the second floor. He climbed the stairs, let himself into Number Four and was asleep in minutes.

He slept late, enjoying the quiet, until a soft tap on the door and a quiet 'Sir?' admitted a child with water, towels and soap. Jem took his time washing, shaving and dressing, appreciative of the early morning warmth that signalled life in the South. Dressed and hungry, he opened the glass doors onto the balcony and stood in silent appreciation of the city below.

Coasting vessels and smaller boats carried on the watery commerce. He wondered how on earth he was going to find a woman named Theodora Winnings, who was probably married by now and with some man's name. That is, if she hadn't been sold downriver to work the cotton, or died years earlier in one of the regrettable yellow fever epidemics he knew haunted these shores.

The folly of his enterprise flapped home to roost on the railing like one of the seagulls he noticed, squawking with its feathered brethren. He knew nothing about Savannah. He hadn't a clue what to do. How did a man find a slave, or anyone for that matter, in a town where he knew no one? He had already been the recipient of wary looks because of his British accent. How would he even know if anyone would willingly help him? The war for independence wasn't that long in the past.

He frowned and regarded Bay Street, lined with shops, some of a maritime variety advertising turpentine, tar and candles. Another sign swung in the breeze and proclaimed Jephthah Morton to be proficient at tooth pulling.

Jem shuddered and turned his attention to a larger, better-kept sign next to the tooth extractor, advertising a dining room. He could eat and walk around, to what purpose he could not have said. Savannah was too large to go door to door. Had he attempted that, he could see himself run out of town as a suspicious character.

He looked beyond the sign of the bloody tooth and experienced what was probably going to be his only good idea in Savannah. He squinted. The paint was faded, but he could just make out *Savannah Times and Tides*, with *Weekly Broadside* underneath in smaller letters on a building that seemed to lean with age.

He pulled on his suit coat, checked his wallet for money, and walked down the stairs. The fragrance of ham and hot bread coming from the open doors of the dining room was nearly a Siren's call, but he walked past the tooth puller, where someone inside was already screaming, and in the door beyond.

He entered cautiously, because the building seemed to list even more when seen up close. 'Hello? Hello?' he called, and tapped on the doorframe.

No one answered. He sneezed from the veritable army of dust motes that floated in the air, and sneezed again.

The sound brought a man wearing an ink-stained apron out of a closed door. He was as wide as he was tall, with a long beard that looked as though birds of prey had been poking around in it, searching for something edible. Spectacles perched on the end of his nose appeared to hang there in defiance of Newton's carefully thought out law of gravity.

'How may I help you?' Jem heard, and rejoiced that every syllable was enunciated. This was *not* a man from the South.

'You really publish a broadside?' Jem asked. 'I need to place an advertisement.'

The man bowed as far as he could, which wasn't far, considering his bulk. 'Then you will be my first advertiser in a long, long time, sir.' He held out his hand, took it back, wiped off some ink, and held it out again. 'Osgood N. Hollinsworth, publisher, editor and chief correspondent of the *Times and Tides.*'

'Captain James Grey of the Royal Navy,' Jem said as they shook hands.

Osgood N. Hollinsworth blinked his eyes. 'What? Surely we are not at war again and Savannah has already surrendered?'

Not yet, Jem thought. The question made him wonder how long that would be the truth. Already Secretary of State James Madison had warned the Sea Lords in a carefully worded document just what the United States thought about the Royal Navy stopping its ships and confiscating British crewmen.

'No, sir, no war,' Jem said. 'I simply need to place an advertisement.'

'Good thing you came this week, Captain,' Hollinsworth said with a shake of his head. 'I am laying out the final issue. No one in this Godforsaken town reads.'

'Really? It appears to be a prosperous place.'

'Perhaps I am hasty. Commerce here is conducted on the wharf, in the cotton exchange, at the slave auctions and in the taverns, without benefit of newspapers,' Hollinsworth said. 'I am not mistaken when I suspect that these…these…let's call them Southerners…don't trust anyone not from here.'

'Where *are* you from?' Jem asked.

'Somewhere a ways to the west of here. Considerably west,' Mr Hollinsworth said, with a vague gesture.

'I've heard Southerners like to duel at the drop of a hat,' Jem said, half in jest.

Hollinsworth shook a pudgy finger in Jem's face. 'You've never seen happy-triggered men so devoted to honour! Don't run afoul of them!'

'I shan't, sir,' Jem said, still amused. 'About an ad…'

'I can arrange it,' the printer or editor or whatever he was said. 'Soon enough, I will blow the dust of Savannah off my shoes. Do have a seat. I am so overcome by the idea that someone wants to place an ad that I must sit down, too.'

'You mentioned slave auctions,' Jem said, and felt his stomach lurch. Amazing that he could live through years of war and typhoons with nary a flinch in his gut. He knew his sailors referred to him as Iron Belly. Good thing they didn't know how he felt right now, thinking of slaves and high bidders, and Teddy somewhere in between.

'A travesty, those auctions,' Hollinsworth said with a shake of his head. 'Imagine it—a Yankee named Eli Whitney, invented a machine to take the seeds from cotton bolls. Now everyone is rushing to plant more, increasing the need for slaves.' He gave a bleak look. 'But you didn't come here on slave business, did you?'

'No,' Jem lied. 'Years ago, I spent a few months in Charleston, nearly dead of malaria. A young lady nursed me back to health. I hear she lives in Savannah now, and I want to find her.'

That was enough information for a fat little printer with inky hands, Jem decided. Besides, it was mostly true. He had no trouble looking Hollinsworth in the eyes.

What he saw smiling back at him was difficult to comprehend. If he hadn't known better, he would have suspected that this man he had just met saw right through his careful words and into his heart, that organ many a midshipman would have sworn he did not possess. *What in the world?* Jem thought, then dismissed his sudden feeling of vulnerability as the drivel it was. He folded his arms and stared back. 'I will pay you well.'

'Enough for passage to Boston, like you?' Hollinsworth said with a wink.

Do you know something about me? Jem thought, startled again. 'That seems a little high. If you are reasonable, I will be generous.'

Hollinsworth slapped the table between them and the dust rose in clouds. Jem sneezed again. 'Oops! I can be reasonable.'

He named a small sum, which confirmed Jem's suspicions that Osgood N. Hollinsworth was a right jolly fellow, and liked to tease even potential clients. 'That will be fine,' he said, and took the few coins from the change purse in his coat.

A sheet of paper and pencil stub seemed to materialize from thin air while Jem was blinking his eyes from the dust.

'What do you wish me to write?' the publisher said. 'Maybe something like, 'Where are you…insert name? Captain James Grey wants to know. Inquire at the *Times and Tides* on Bay Street.' Insert name?'

'Theodora Winnings,' Jem said and tucked away his handkerchief. 'Could you run it in big letters?'

'I can and will,' Hollinsworth said promptly. 'There isn't much news this week, beyond a warning from the mayor about hogs running loose, and a notice about two escaped slaves.'

'That will do,' Jem said as he rose, eager to leave this dusty shop before he sneezed again. 'Now to breakfast.'

'And I to work,' Hollinsworth said. 'The broadside will be distributed tomorrow. You might wish to walk around Savannah and admire what happens when a town is laid out in an orderly fashion. It's quite unlike your port of Plymouth.'

'How do you know where I...'

Hollinsworth shrugged, and looked at Jem with that same piercing but kind glance. 'A lucky guess, Captain Grey. The ham, biscuits and gravy next door are superb, and you might discover an affinity for hominy grits. Good day to you.'

Chapter Six

Osgood N. Hollinsworth had been correct about the ham, biscuits and gravy. Nearly in pain from over-indulgence, Jem pushed himself away from the table and paid his bill of fare.

Over the next few days, he realised Hollinsworth had also been right about Savannah, a pretty river town laid out in leafy squares. He came to admire the deep porches and understood their necessity. Summers here were probably blistering hot and drenched with humidity. In the deep shadows of the verandas he saw overhead fans, probably set in motion by the children of slaves doing what they were ordered to do. He couldn't help wondering if Teddy had ever been ordered to fan folks too.

But it was almost Christmas, so the fans remained motionless. He walked, admired the buildings, and breathed deep of magnolia wreaths on many a door of home and business alike. It was far cry from his memories of Boston at Christmas, with wreaths of holly and bayberry, hardy enough to withstand the aching cold. The heady fragrance of magnolia blossoms seemed to reach out to the boardwalk and grab him unaware.

He watched the faces of the city's workers, wondering if he would recognise Teddy Winnings if he saw her. Would she recognise him? A man who stares day after day into a shaving mirror can probably be forgiven if he thinks he has not changed much. For one thing, Jem knew he looked healthier than the pale, shaking malaria-ridden specimen Teddy had tended. He had put on sufficient weight and heft to give himself more of an air of command. Eleven years had done that, too.

His own curly hair was scarcely visible under his hat, mainly because his habits kept it short. He was a man grown, tested and experienced, not a lieutenant just beginning to understand mortality, and think about dangers ahead. Age could do that; so did war.

When the broadside came out the day after he bought his ad, Jem had been suitably impressed with Hollinsworth's effort. The twenty-word plea ran across the bottom of the single page in bold letters impossible to miss. Would anyone read it was the question.

In his anxiety to *find* Teddy without knowing how to do so, he began a little daily commentary to the Almighty, that unknown personage he had been addressing as *Sir* for years. He acknowledged the absurdity of it, but found himself comforted.

Several days passed. In the print shop where no one ever came, Mr Hollinsworth displayed in the window what he insisted was still the last broadside he intended to publish in Savannah. Jem watched for the small stack to diminish as readers put down their pennies, but it remained the same height, to his discomfort. This was no way to find Theodora Winnings, and so he told Mr Hollinsworth, who took his sharp comments in stride.

'I've distributed my broadsides in the squares, too,' the little man said serenely. 'Be patient.'

Jem honestly tried to be patient, going so far as to sit in the back of Christ Church in Johnson Square, the oldest of the squares, according to a shoeshine boy who gave his boots a lick and a promise each day. A choir rehearsed in Christ Church in the evenings, preparing for Christmas services, or so he gathered from their repertory. After supper in the Marlborough Dining Room, he walked the short distance to Johnson Square to listen.

He sat there long enough each night to be greeted eventually by the singers, then asked to join them. He demurred at first, well-acquainted with his own voice. In their polite Southern way, which was beginning to nestle comfortably under his skin, they asked each night until he agreed. By the middle of the second week in Savannah, he attended choir practice three nights a week.

By the end of that week, he also knew his feeble and puny enterprise had failed. How much longer could he stay in this beguiling place remained open to doubt. He had the means to stay for months, but not the inclination. A strange homing instinct was drawing him north toward Massachusetts. He wanted nothing more than to walk those familiar streets and think about his life's direction, something he hadn't questioned in years, but which now loomed large in his agile brain.

He owned to traitorous feelings, if such they were. Why was a respected post captain in the Royal Navy even for the tiniest moment considering a more permanent connection with the United States? He should know better, but he liked it here and America was compelling him to stay. *It's complicated*, he thought, as he listened to Christmas music, walked the streets and squares of a beguiling little city, and wondered about himself as much as he wondered about Teddy Winnings.

The day came when he knew it was pointless to remain any longer in Savannah. He sat on the side of his bed and silently informed *'Sir'* in his now-daily commentary that it was time to move on.

I certainly bear you no ill will, sir, he thought or prayed. He never could decide which it was. *It was a long-odds chance. I know how busy you are at this season, when I suspect many people who pray more than I do want things. I wish it had worked out. Thanks for listening...if you did.*

The day was warm and sunny, much as the day before, and probably as the day after would be. He took his time sauntering to the wharf, breathing in the familiar odour of tarred rope and maritime paint. He waited his turn at the coastal shipping office, aware of his difference among these soft-spoken, slow-moving, congenial folk.

He inquired about a passage north and was informed that he could leave this afternoon on the Charleston coaster, or hang around until the end of the week for a larger vessel being loaded now with cotton and contracted for a Baltimore destination. He decided upon Baltimore. He could take a coach or private conveyance north from there to Boston.

Dissatisfied, unhappy, he walked around that day, stayed awake at night staring at the ceiling.

Tired of his own company and wishing he had cared enough to bathe and shave, he stood on the veranda of the Arundel in the morning, looked toward the print shop and saw her.

Certain he was mistaken, Jem squinted his eyes shut and rubbed the lids. Almost afraid to look, he opened them, and knew the woman across the street, standing there with a broadside in her hand, was Theodora Winnings.

He remained where he was, rooted to the spot, certain she would disappear if he took one step closer. She wore a drab dress, unlike the pretty muslins he remembered. Her hair was invisible under a blue bandanna wrapped around and knotted high on her forehead. He had seen this head covering on slaves in Charleston and Savannah. She was slimmer than he remembered, which told him all he needed to know about her hard life. Holding his breath, he looked down and saw bare feet.

'Good God, Teddy,' he whispered, then addressed his silent partner. '*Sir*, why didn't anyone take care of her?'

It was my job, he told himself. He walked toward the woman he knew he still loved, no matter her circumstances, her race, her current matrimonial status, her anything.

'Theodora,' he said, when he was halfway across the street.

The woman had been staring down at the broadside, and then looking at the dilapidated print shop, as if wondering what she was doing there.

Maybe he was wrong. Maybe it wasn't Teddy. He cleared his throat and spoke louder. 'Theodora Winnings.'

Honest to God, if he didn't feel his heart pound like a drum when she looked at him. He stood still in the middle of the street, barely mindful of a carter cursing at him to move. He gave a don't-bother-me wave of his hand to the driver but consciously willed himself to move.

She stared at him, holding the broadside in front of her as if to shield her body. Slowly she raised it to cover her face, which broke his heart.

He stood right in front of her now. Silently he took the broadside and pulled it away from her face. 'Teddy,' he said. 'Teddy. I owe you such an apology.'

Now that he looked at her, really looked at her honestly, without any of his malaria fever dreams, he could see the smallest trace of Africa. His recent weeks in Savannah had accustomed him to the beautiful shades of dark brown, barely brown, and Teddy's own creamy complexion found on the kindly, patient people who waited on his table, changed his sheets, and ironed his shirts.

'Lieutenant Grey?' she asked, her voice as musical as ever.

He smiled. 'Captain Grey, actually, Miss Winnings, like it says in the broadside,' he told her. 'I grew a little smarter and achieved some rank.'

He wanted her to smile because she looked so serious, with sorrow writ large that he knew was his fault, because he had failed her.

To his dismay, she did not smile. Her shoulders drooped. 'I should have told you,' she said simply, and turned to go.

He reached for her, but she was quicker. 'You don't want to make a scene here,' she said in a low voice. 'Believe me, you do not.'

He lowered his hand. 'Why did you come then?'

'I had to see you, Captain Grey,' she said and took a deep breath. 'Now I've seen you.'

'But I…' He saw the tears on her face as she kept backing away.

'No,' she said. 'No.'

'*Sir*, this is not fair,' he said out loud. 'Not at all.'

She looked around, as if wondering to whom he spoke, when the door to the print shop banged open and Osgood N. Hollinsworth stood there glowering.

'Get in here right now, Teddy! Your mistress promised me a day's work!'

Chapter Seven

She ran inside the shop as Hollinsworth glowered at her as though she were a disobedient servant. Jem stood in front of the open door, astonished, wondering what power the man had to command someone he probably had never seen. Jem could have staggered under the weight of the whole awful business when he realised that in the eleven years since they had met, Teddy had become subservient and knew when to obey a white man. Either that, or she knew a ruse when she saw one. Jem already knew how intelligent she was.

'*Sir*,' he whispered under his breath to the Lord above. 'Help me know what to do.'

Once Teddy was inside, Hollinsworth's expression changed to his usual cheery demeanour. Jem understood. 'Captain Grey, we're going to let every flying insect into this print shop. Hurry up and come in!'

He hurried, closing the door after him. Teddy stood behind the drafting table, as if afraid of them both. Her eyes were huge in her face until Hollinsworth bowed from the waist and introduced himself. To Jem's relief, she smiled.

'Miss Winnings, I had to do *something* to get this slow-moving captain out of the street. He doesn't understand Savannah the way we do, does he? Do have a seat, please. No one here is going to harm you.' The printer gestured toward the stool in front of the drafting table. He propped a broom against it. 'If anyone sets the doorbell tinkling, start sweeping.'

Teddy nodded and sat. With a pang, Jem watched her smooth down the rough fabric of the shapeless dress she wore, recognising the graceful gesture from many a time when she sat beside his bed in the hospital in much better clothing. His heart eased, as he realised Teddy was still Teddy.

Jem had to admit that Osgood N. Hollinsworth had a certain charm, something he had not noticed before in their various exchanges. Teddy appeared to relax as the tension left her face. 'Yes, Sir,' she said. 'I can sweep.' Jem saw the dimple in her cheek and relaxed further. 'No one will know I don't belong in here.'

The capable, assured, confident post captain that James Grey knew himself to be had vanished. He stood there like a lump, awkward as though his feet and hands were five times larger than usual. At least so he felt, until Hollinsworth took his arm in a surprisingly gentle grip and motioned him toward the other chair beside the drafting table.

Hollinsworth regarded them with something nearly

resembling beatific goodwill toward men. 'Talk,' he said. 'I am going to the Marlborough for some food. Captain, do you have any money? You know what a poverty-stricken editor I am. Why is it writers cannot make an honest dime?'

Wordless, Jem reached inside his coat and took out several bills. 'What do you like to eat, Teddy? I remember macaroons and something with pecans.'

She smiled for the first time, and Jem felt his heart cuddle down into a little pile. 'You remember well... Jem?'

'That's still my name,' he said, even though all he had heard in years was Captain Grey, or something more informal. 'My men call me Iron Belly, but only out of my hearing.'

Her smile grew larger. 'I recall a time when all you did was puke.'

Hollinsworth rolled his eyes. 'My land! Eleven years and this is the best you two can do? I'm going, before I smack you both!'

Jem laughed, and Teddy put her hand over her mouth, a gesture he remembered as though the hospital was mere days ago, when she was a lady and too polite to laugh out loud.

'Fried chicken and greens? Corn bread?' Hollinsworth asked. 'Crab sandwiches?'

'It all sounds wonderful, sir,' Teddy said. 'I haven't had chicken in a long time.'

The door closed, and Jem absorbed the sight of Theodora Winnings, still the loveliest woman he had ever seen, and he had been in many a foreign port since his proposal by letter. He wished he could tell her he had been a chaste, celibate man, but that would have been a lie. He wished he had received her letter years sooner.

He could have said all that; instead, he held out his hand to her. He could have died with delight when she held out her hand and grasped his in a firm hold. Her hands were rough and her grip strong, much like his own. He remembered her delicate touch and the softness of her hands, but much time and many tides had rolled over them both since he wrote that letter and she answered it.

She opened her mouth to speak. He held up his free hand, ready to break a social rule.

'A gentleman would let you speak first, Teddy, but I have to start. I won't have you apologise for anything when I owe *you* the apology.'

It didn't work. 'Jem, I'm a slave. I always was. I never told you.' Her voice was low and earnest. 'It was wrong and I've regretted it for years. May I please apologise first?'

'No, you may not.' He felt like he floundered, but he was still a man used to command. 'Teddy, I didn't get your letter until September.' He reached in his pocket and pulled out the fragile thing, setting it carefully on the drafting table. 'You see what I could read. Mrs Fillion had set a box on top of it, and there it remained for years.'

'You told me to send a letter care of the Drake,' she said. 'Her hotel?'

'We officers of the fleet based in Plymouth have long used the Drake as an informal place to store our personal effects. Everyone passes through there sooner or later,' he explained. 'What happened in this case is that the owner of the box on top of your letter died.'

'So there it sat,' she said with a sigh.

'Every so often, Mrs Fillion advertises in the newspaper, listing the names and property, hoping next of kin will claim the items,' he said. 'Someone finally did. I happened to be in port when she found the letter underneath.'

'And you dropped everything and ran away to the United States? Captain Grey, I don't remember you as an impulsive person. Aren't you at war? Did you bring your frigate with you?'

The way her eyes twinkled made him laugh. Funny how they had picked up where they left off. When his malaria fevers had begun to subside and he lay there in the convent, stupefied and even unsure where he was, Theodora Winnings had jollied him out of the doldrums by reading a book of wise remarks and tomfoolery by Benjamin Franklin. He knew she liked to laugh, and by God, he could have used a few laughs in the past decade.

'There *is* no war right now. First Consul Bonaparte has foisted the Peace of Amiens on us.'

'That's a good thing, I would imagine, Jem.'

He smiled to hear her affectionate name for him. Amazing how eleven years could nearly vanish. With a start, he realised that since his parents' deaths years ago, no one called him that except Teddy Winnings.

'Amiens is good for me,' he assured her. 'Most of us post captains were thrown ashore on half pay, which meant I could book passage on the first ship to the United States and the Royal Navy is none the wiser.'

'You came all this way without knowing even where I was or whether I was alive or dead?' she asked.

He heard the wonder in her voice. He could assure her that was the truth, or he could be honest. Which would it be? He knew now she was a slave, a woman of Ashanti or Ibo origin two or three generations back, someone who had to bend to the will of others. He could chat with her, satisfy himself she was well, and leave for Baltimore at the end of the week, as planned.

He might have done precisely that, if he had not looked into her eyes and remembered what it was beyond her amiability and breathtaking beauty that made Theodora Winnings so memorable. Kind eyes looked into his and he recalled with delight her amazing ability to give whomever she was talking to her complete and undivided attention. He knew it was a rare gift. He would be honest, because she was paying attention to him, completely focused.

'Teddy, I wanted to assure myself that you were alive,' he said. 'I had no doubt you would be married and with a family of your own.'

'Not this slave,' she said. 'Why else are you here then?'

He couldn't help looking around to make sure British spies weren't pressed against the front window, peering in and listening. *I'm an idiot*, he thought, suddenly weary.

'You can tell me,' she said, putting her hand over his. 'I don't expect you to come to my rescue. You had no idea I even needed rescuing. What else?'

Her hand was warm. He turned his over and interlocked their fingers. 'Teddy, I wanted to go home again to Massachusetts. After I assured myself that all was well here, I was…well, I am…taking ship north to Baltimore and then to Boston.'

He felt her fingers tremble and tightened his grip. 'You told me eleven years ago how a howling mob burned your house when you were a boy, killed your dog, and sent you all fleeing north to Halifax,' she said. 'Why would you ever want to return there?'

'I liked Massachusetts,' he said simply. 'I wish I had a better explanation. Have you ever just *liked* something?'

She nodded. 'Since we are truth telling and it sounds to me like you've already booked passage…' Her voice trailed off and he heard the regret. It might have been wistfulness, or even envy that he could travel about on a whim.

'Have you?' he asked.

'I liked *you*,' she said, her brown eyes claiming his total attention. 'You sailed away at Christmas, Jem.

Every year I wondered how you were doing. I lit a candle every year at Congregation de St Jean-Baptiste, hoping you were still alive.' She broke off her glance. 'I wasn't going to this year. I was done with it.' She looked up and he felt his heart start to beat again. 'But here you are, at least for now. I know you are alive and I suppose that must suffice.'

'Then why are you crying?' he asked, his voice soft.

Chapter Eight

The shadow of a man passed the door and Teddy gasped, tears forgotten. She grabbed the broom and began to sweep a floor that looked as though it had not been touched in a generation. Dust flew and Jem sneezed.

When the footsteps receded, Jem grabbed the broom. 'Hey now, lady, he walked on by.'

He tried to pry the broom from her grasp, but Teddy was strong and hung onto it. 'You don't understand that I am a slave and this is the South,' she said and yanked on the broom. 'Let go.'

Jem released the broom, acutely aware of the terror in her eyes. He watched her edge toward the door and knew he had no incentive to keep her there, if she wanted to leave. Her fear told him chapter and verse of what could happen to a slave alone with a white man. Eleven years had changed Theodora Winnings even more than it had changed him. Better keep talking.

'When I did not hear from you, I was moderately

philosophical about the matter, I'll admit,' he told her. 'Who was I, after all? A Royal Navy first lieutenant barely alive and still shaky. I assumed you were the pampered daughter of a Charleston merchant, determined to do good in a fever hospital. I was nothing but very small fry.'

As practical as he remembered, Teddy shook her head. To his relief, she put down the broom and moved away from the door, not far, but far enough to give him reason to hope. It began to matter to him more with each passing minute that she not leave.

'Captain Grey, no one volunteers at a fever hospital,' she said, enunciating each word in a most un-Southern way. 'Mr Winnings hated it, but Mrs Winnings volunteered me all the time. I had no choice.'

'My God, what kind of woman is she?' he asked.

'A sad woman who could not produce any children of her own and could only look on as I was born and cherished by her husband,' Teddy told him. 'He even taught me to read and write, which is illegal, I assure you.'

'White folks are afraid you'll get ideas?' he asked, unable to mask his disgust.

'Most likely.' She sat down. She smiled at him, and years fell away. 'Don't get a swelled head, Captain Grey, but going to the fever hospital became the best part of my week.'

The smile left her face soon enough and she settled into that neutral expression he had seen on many a slave's face in his brief tenure in the South. 'I should never have walked through the convent grounds with you when you started feeling better.'

'Probably didn't have a choice, did you?' he asked, his understanding growing of Theodora Winnings' life spent balancing on the tightrope of keeping Mr Winnings happy and not irritating Mrs Winnings too much.

'I did, actually,' she said. 'For all that they were cloistered, religious women and unacquainted with actual life, some of the nuns could see what was happening between us. They told me I should find another patient, or at least tell you of my parentage.' Her expression softened. 'They didn't order me away, however.'

As he watched her, Jem wondered how easy it would have been to ignore that ruin of a letter Mrs Fillion gave him. He could still be in England, restless at being ashore on half pay, and thinking about nothing more interesting than what he would be having for dinner that night. All things considered, this was better. Come to think of it, any time at all in Theodora Winnings' gentle orbit was better. Maybe this was his odd little Christmas gift from St Nicholas.

She sat back on the chair, her guard down again. 'Every morning before I went to the hospital, I told myself it would be the last time. I ordered myself to tell you I was a slave, and every morning, I could not.'

In for a penny, in for a pound, he thought. 'The thing is, Teddy, it would have changed nothing,' he said and took his own deep breath. 'I remain firm in my resolve.'

'You can't be serious,' she replied.

'Never more so.'

'Even if you know any sort of…connection between us is impossible?' she asked.

He shrugged. 'Why? I assume you could not tell me the truth because you loved me.' He touched the ruined letter on the drafting table. 'Your letter confirmed it eleven years ago.'

Teddy opened her mouth to speak, then gasped as another shadow approached the door and opened it. She leaped to her feet and crouched behind the drafting table as Osgood Hollinsworth opened the door, bearing a pasteboard box of food.

Go away and let me talk to this lady, he wanted to shout as Mr Hollinsworth set the box on the desk.

'You can talk after we eat,' the printer said. 'I'm not going anywhere until we do. Chicken, greens, Johnny cake!'

How was it that this round little man seemed to know what he was thinking? *I am losing my mind*, Jem thought, exasperated.

'Captain Grey! Coax that pretty miss out from behind my drafting table. You can be as high-minded as you wish, but we need to eat. You know, as we puzzle out what to do.'

'There is nothing we can do,' Teddy Winnings said as she left her hiding place and sat where Mr Hollinsworth pointed.

Hollinsworth blinked his eyes in surprise and clucked his tongue. 'Missy, you have a lot to learn. Doesn't she, James?'

Hollinsworth looked from one to the other, smiling as though all was well in the world. 'Must I do all the thinking?' he asked the air in general. 'Eat something.'

Maybe the chance was gone. Teddy seemed almost relieved not to venture deeper into their conversation. She arranged the food, setting it just so, as if seeking order to a life suddenly out of kilter.

So be it. He was hungry. He could be superficial, too, although for how long he did not know. The chicken was tasty enough for Jem to ask her, 'Miss Winnings, can you cook like this?'

'Certainly, sir,' she said, after she chewed and swallowed. 'I can cook chicken anywhere.'

'Don't be so...so...blamed trivial!' Hollinsworth declared, and waved a chicken leg for emphasis. 'Miss Winnings, how did you find my broadside? Just curious.'

The soul of manners, she wiped her fingers delicately on a piece of newsprint. 'It was the strangest thing, sir. I was hanging up the wash today when the broadside just sailed into the yard on that high wind, and dropped in my hands.'

'There wasn't any wind this morning,' Jem said, reaching for another chicken piece.

'There was,' she insisted. 'Are you a wind expert?'

'Actually, I am. No wind,' he said firmly.

She gave him a look that would have skewered a

lesser man. 'Wind. The broadside seemed to attach itself to my hand. Don't laugh! I dropped everything and came here. You don't know everything, Captain Grey.'

I like this spirited Theodora, he thought, but decided wisely to keep his comments to himself. 'I bow to your greater knowledge,' he said, unable to resist some repartee, even as he longed to yank the conversation back to her words spoken just before the printer opened the door.

Hollinsworth, damn the man, seemed to have other ideas. 'Miss Winnings, enlighten us. What happened after your father's death?'

She glanced at Jem, apology in her eyes, but obedient in her attention to the printer. Jem decided that the intervening years must have been a harsh school for a slave who lost her only advocate with her father's passing.

'Mrs Winnings sold the business, bought a house and moved us here.' She shook her head over a thigh fried a crispy brown. 'Savannah was her childhood home.'

Jem took heart when she turned to him and touched his arm. 'Jem, Mr Winnings died not long after that Christmas when you sailed away. He died in January of ninety-one. When I was tending him at home because he could no longer go to the mercantile, Mr Winnings showed me his will, already notarized. Upon his death, I was to be freed and provided with two hundred dollars.'

Sudden tears spilled onto her cheeks. 'Jem, when the will was read, there was no mention of my freedom or any money. When I asked Mrs Winnings about it in private, she said solicitors could be easily unconvinced.' She put her hands over her ears. 'I can hear her still.'

In the silence that followed, Jem could almost hear Mrs Winnings, too. He thought of his own life in those few months since he had left Teddy the letter, hopeful she would answer, determined to return for her, despite duty and war. Time passed. He never grew any more in stature—he was tall enough—but he grew in cynicism and then a complacent sort of acceptance, where Teddy was concerned.

'I wish I had known,' he said. 'If only there was a way to know instantly what goes on in others' lives.' It was absurd, but he had to say it.

Teddy gave him a faint smile. 'You can't imagine how I prayed you would find out and save me. I prayed and prayed. Nothing.'

He bowed his head in sadness at the same time Mr Hollinsworth blew into his handkerchief, muttering something about being stretched too thin, which made no sense to Jem. At least the man felt like crying in solidarity with them. How could he be busy? Nothing seemed to happen in Savannah.

'She sold the business and moved here,' Jem said. He put down the chicken thigh, hungry no longer.

Teddy nodded. 'She bought a house near Ellis Square. It burned in the fire of ninety-six and we moved to a smaller house on the edge of Green Square.'

How many times have I walked by it in the past two weeks? Jem asked himself. He amended his thought. He had only walked there once, because it was a ramshackle area, unsafe. 'I've been here long enough to know that as a come down,' he said.

'It was,' Teddy replied. 'She started selling off her slaves.' He heard the sob in her throat. 'My friends!'

He stared into her eyes, chagrined to see that deep gaze of men who had been in combat on sea and shore. He knew he had that same stare, but he had never seen it in a woman's eyes before and it unnerved him.

'Theodora...'

'I am last,' she said quietly. 'I believe I was her hedge against ruin.'

Chapter Nine

Reticence be damned. Jem took her arm, pulled her toward him and held her while she sobbed. Between breaths that shook her, she murmured something about card games and one losing streak after another. He listened in horror and heard the dreary pattern of a desperate widow gambling at cards, trying to recoup some shred of a formerly prosperous life.

He glanced at Mr Hollinsworth, who seemed involved in sorrow of a different sort, an inward examination. Jem had not known the man a few hours before he had seen him as a jovial fellow, with ready quips. Who was this new fellow?

He held Teddy close on his lap and realised he had not been a callow fool in 1791, infatuated by a pretty face and figure. He had told his story a few times in frigate wardrooms, usually to hoots of laughter, until he had begun to think perhaps he had been a naive boy, recovering from illness, who mistook kindness for attachment of a more permanent nature.

He held her, felt her tears dampening his coat, and understood the nature of what he had felt in 1791, love so deep it shook him even now. 'Help me, *Sir*,' he whispered to that friend of his.

He glanced at Mr Hollinsworth just then to see him nod ever so slightly, his own countenance anything but trivial, or jovial, or shallow or any of those weary adjectives describing someone lightweight.

'Aye, laddie,' Mr Hollinsworth said.

He let Teddy's tears run their course, pressing his handkerchief into her palm. 'Blow your nose and dry your eyes,' he said. 'I will return with you to Green Square and I will buy you. I didn't come here penniless.'

She didn't bother with his instruction, beyond wiping her nose, her face stained with tears. 'You're too late. She sold me yesterday to William Tullidge. I am only hers until after Christmas. She insisted.'

Mr Hollinsworth gasped. 'He's one of the richest men in Savannah. Cotton, land, slaves.' He shook his head. 'Influence.'

'Then I will buy you from him,' Jem said, undeterred. 'What did he pay?'

'Two thousand dollars,' she said, then looked away, unable to meet what he knew was his own horrified gaze. 'Do you have that much money?'

He shook his head. He had more, clearly outlined in a legal letter of transfer from Carter and Brustein to any counting house in North America, but such a transfer took months. 'Not on hand.'

'Then I am ruined,' Teddy said. Dignified even in her despair, she got off his lap, straightened her dress and started for the door. She turned back to give him the level gaze that told him he commanded her total attention.

'Captain Grey, I came here for one reason only. I know there is nothing you can do to save me, at this point.'

'But I can tr—'

She help up her hand. 'Stop. Let me speak. I came here solely to see you. I came here to assure my eyes—no my heart—that you are well and whole now. I came here to apologise…' She gave him a fierce look that closed his mouth again. 'Deny that you came here for the same reasons only. I dare you.'

She had him. 'I came here for those precise reasons,' he admitted, because it was true.

Her hand was on the doorknob now. He knew he had lost, but he had to try once more. He knew what he had to say would brand him forever in her eyes as a fool, but he had to try. He glanced at Mr Hollinsworth for… For what, he had no idea. Support? Compassion? Empathy? And he saw an amazing sight.

Somehow, the little round man seemed to grow a foot taller. His eyes bored into Jem's eyes, telling him without words that he had a potent ally in this odd quest that had turned into a mission so important that he felt it in his entire being.

'Listen to him, Theodora,' Mr Hollinsworth said, and it was no suggestion.

'Something happened in Charleston,' Jem began.

Maybe Teddy felt something unusual in the dusty room, same as Jem did. Whatever it was, she walked back and sat on the stool.

'I learned who you were in Charleston, and it didn't send me rushing to take ship back to England,' he said. 'I stood outside the convent and I must have prayed. Me! I never pray.'

He looked for scepticism in those lovely eyes and saw something else. Eyes still cast modestly toward her bare feet, she smiled.

He couldn't help his sudden intake of breath. 'Teddy, that statue,' he said, and couldn't think of words, he who had commanded, and fought, and blistered his frigate's air with admonition.

Total silence filled the room. He watched dust motes dance. Theodora didn't raise her gaze. She placed her hand near her heart. He waited, barely breathing.

'You sailed in December of 1790,' she said. He leaned forward to hear her soft words. 'In September of ninety-one, a hurricane struck the city.' Her breath came quicker. 'The statue outside the convent literally blew away. The winds stripped all the ivy from the buildings. Such a storm.'

As she raised her eyes to his, Jem remembered to breathe. 'My father commissioned another statue, one in stone this time. I was the model. It was the last thing he did before he died.' She hesitated.

Now what, he thought. *Now what?*

'I think you should challenge William Tullidge to a duel,' Mr Hollinsworth said, and rubbed his hands with something close to glee.

'He'll shoot me dead,' Jem said immediately. 'I am a terrible shot.'

The room grew silent again, as the others seemed to expect Jem to say more. 'A duel is nonsense. I can offer the man a down payment and see if he will wait three or four months for my money to arrive.'

'Tullidge is impatient and used to matters falling out in his favour,' Mr Hollinsworth said. 'I doubt he ever waited a week for a dime owed him.'

'We have until the day after Christmas,' Teddy said, dignified as he remembered, but with something else. He could nearly feel her excitement, as though the wheel was suddenly turning in her direction.

'What about Mrs Winnings?' Jem asked. He felt sweat dripping down his back as he contemplated staring down the muzzle of a pistol aimed at him. 'Could she stave him off? What was the nature of this devil's bargain the two of them made?'

'Mrs Winnings has finally lost all the money she received for Papa's store. Her house burned in the fire six years ago,' Teddy told them both. 'She gambles at cards…'

'Badly, I would say,' Mr Hollinsworth said.

Teddy sighed. 'She is always certain the next turn of the card will recoup her fortune. I fear gamblers are like that. She staked her house, a poor ruin of a place, mind you, on the turn of the card and lost it.'

'He played her deliberately, didn't he?' Jem asked.

'Emphatically yes,' she replied. 'He's been eyeing me this past year and more, and it unnerves me. He promised she could keep her house and he would give her two thousand dollars for me.' She paled visibly at her own words and covered her face with her hands. 'She was saving me for an emergency, Jem.'

'That is an unheard-of sum,' Mr Hollinsworth said, his face pale.

It's not a penny too high for someone as beautiful as Theodora Winnings, Jem thought, shocked, too, but not as surprised as the printer.

'I was her insurance against total ruin,' Teddy said, and bowed her head.

That was all she needed to say. Jem thought about the barrel of that pistol, then dismissed it. He had been on lee shores before, when nothing good was going to happen unless he and his crew exerted supreme effort. His crew had never failed him. He looked around at his crew—Teddy, and a fat printer from somewhere— and grinned at them.

'Teddy my dear, I can't explain this, but when I looked at your statue in Charleston I felt some odd assurance that things would work out in my…in our favour. I didn't even know where you were, but something told me to go to Savannah. I know it's nonsense, but what is that, measured against a duel to the death with a Southern gentleman?'

His crew laughed, indicating they were as certifiable as he was. Emboldened by their reaction and amazed by his own words, James Grey, usually a thoughtful man who never performed a hasty act, remembered Mrs Fillion's admonition in Plymouth and decided to have faith.

Further emboldened, he kissed Theodora Winnings' cheek and told her to go home before she got into trouble with the silly gambler who had controlled a good woman far too long.

'Heaven knows you are probably in trouble with Mrs Winnings right now,' he said, as he opened the door for her. 'What will she do?'

'She has a silver-backed hairbrush,' Teddy said with touching dignity. 'It hurts.'

He stared at her in shocked silence, realising how naïve he was.

'Too bad I cannot duel with her, too,' he said, pleased with himself that he controlled the anger threatening him. 'Do you dare leave her house in the evening?'

'She goes to her room by nine of the clock,' Teddy said.

'I'll be at Christ Church then.' He couldn't help a chuckle, even as he wondered why in God's name he had any right to be cheerful, not with death by duel on his menu this week. No doubt about it: In the past few months, he had gone through more emotions than Edmund Keene on the Drury Lane stage. 'The choir has asked me to join them in Christmas carols.'

'I didn't know you sang,' she said.

'I didn't either, Teddy,' he told her, and kissed her

lips this time, something he had wanted to do for the past eleven years. 'There's a lot I didn't know, before I ran away to the United States.'

She smiled at that, touched his cheek for a too brief moment with the palm of her hand, and left the printing shop. He watched her hurry away, looking right and left, maybe hoping no one had seen her. Usually a bustling, busy thoroughfare, Bay Street was surprisingly empty. He chalked it up to an unexpected blessing.

'Well, now, Mr Osgood N. Hollinsworth,' he began, turning back to face the printer, 'since you seem confidently sanguine that I should challenge a poor specimen of manhood to a duel, do you have any idea how I can survive it and live happily ever after with the woman I love?'

'Not one single idea,' Hollinsworth assured him cheerfully. 'I have found in life that it's often best to make up things as I go along.'

'I wish I found that reassuring,' Jem replied. 'Where away?'

'The residence of Mr William Tullidge, Esquire,' Hollinsworth replied. 'You have a date with destiny.'

'I wish you wouldn't look so cheerful,' Jem groused.

'Have faith, Captain. Didn't you just say that?'

'I did,' Jem replied, his mind resolved. 'Lead on, sir. What could possibly go wrong?'

Chapter Ten

To call William Tullidge's residence in Ellis Square a mansion without equal would be to denigrate it. Even in his occasional hurried visits to London, Jem had never seen a house so well suited to its surroundings and beggaring any description except magnificent. He stared in open-mouthed wonder, his terror at the approaching encounter momentarily forgotten.

'Pardon me, Mr Hollinsworth, but what pays this well in Savannah, a town that we will agree is pleasant, but not a metropolis?'

'Slavery, Captain, pure and simple,' his companion said. 'He has built an empire with a lash on the backs of souls bought with blood money. He raises some cotton, but deals more in slaves.'

Startled by the intensity in the generally congenial voice of the printer, Jem stared at Hollinsworth. 'Sir, with your vehement views, I am astounded you didn't shake the dust of the South off your shoes years ago.'

'I had my reasons for staying, Captain,' he replied,

and there was no mistaking the grim cast to his countenance. 'I have almost satisfied them and will leave soon.'

'He's not going to see things our way, is he?' Jem asked calmly enough, considering how his heart started to bang against his ribs.

'Unlikely,' Hollinsworth said, but he seemed to have inexplicably regained his good humour. 'I should warn you that he bears no love for the Royal Navy that burned his plantation on Tybee Island, among others, during our late unpleasantness.'

Jem took a good, long look at Mr Osgood N. Hollinsworth. 'Why do I have the nagging suspicion that you are *enjoying* this whole business?'

Trust the old rip to drag out a flippant response. 'Captain, at times it seems as though centuries pass in my life where nothing much happens. Oh, there is always the usual, but you and Miss Theodora Winnings have piqued my interest.'

'I am not reassured,' Jem said dryly. 'Ah, well. I'm in too deep to back out.'

'I hoped you would say that.'

Jem gave him a withering look and walked up the steps to the imposing front doors. He noticed the pineapple carved into the woodwork over the door.

'I remember this from Massachusetts,' he told the fat man puffing along behind him. 'Hospitality's symbol?'

'I wouldn't hold my breath, Captain,' Hollinsworth said, as Jem knocked on the door.

A butler ushered them in and suggested they wait in the hall, once Jem stated he was Captain James Grey, Royal Navy.

'If what you say is true, that should at least get the man's attention,' Jem said. 'My mere mention of the Royal Navy kept us out of the sitting room, eh?'

It did. Jem stood in a foyer of stunning beauty, with a parquet floor of some intricacy and what looked like leather wall coverings with an embossed design. *Built on the backs of slaves, eh?* Jem thought, as he admired and deplored at the same time.

'Here he is,' Hollinsworth said under his breath, as a man older than Jem came down the central staircase, looking not a bit pleased.

'What business can I possibly have with the Royal Navy?' he asked with no preamble, no bow and certainly no hand extended, either.

'Theodora Winnings,' Jem said, determined to be as brief as the man with rancour in his eyes who stood before him. 'Mr Tullidge, I am Captain Grey, and I wish to acquaint you with my interest in that lady.'

'Lady? You've been misinformed.'

'Lady,' Jem repeated firmly. 'I met her years ago in Charleston and proposed matrimony by way of a letter. Her reply in the affirmative went astray for eleven years. I am here now, and I intend to claim her.'

'You intend to claim her?' Tullidge asked. He laughed. 'You intend to *claim* her? I won her in a game of piquet. Mrs Winnings belies her name. She *never* wins, and we all know it.'

How distasteful, Jem thought. 'Apparently you and friends of yours play cards with her, knowing you will win.'

'We do. Should be ashamed of ourselves, shouldn't we?' he asked, unrepentant.

James saw no point in dignifying such meanness with a comment. He remained silent.

'Poor, poor Mrs Winnings never could figure out what to discard.' Tullidge shrugged. 'A little loss here, a little loss there. She finally gambled away her house, and then she gambled away her last slave.' He made a sad face at Jem that was utterly overruled by the triumph in his eyes. 'Poor, poor you.'

'I love her,' Jem said. It was the first time he had said the words out loud, and they felt so good. 'Do you?'

'Love? She's a slave and I fancy her.' Tullidge laughed again. 'Too bad your letter went astray, Captain. It fairly breaks my heart.'

'Miss Winnings told me you have guaranteed her mistress her house again, plus two thousand dollars,' Jem said. He felt like the last cricket of summer, chirping on a hearth, with winter coming. 'I will offer you five hundred dollars now against another two thousand, once my letter of credit and remittance is approved in a Savannah counting house of your choice.'

'How long will that take?' Tullidge asked. 'Three months? Four months? Longer?'

'It will come,' Jem said.

He knew disappointment was the only outcome of this conversation. He knew that before he knocked on the door, but a man has to try. 'Does she mean anything to you?'

'Certainly not,' Tullidge said, 'but Lord, she is a beauty, even if she is too old for my tastes, really. A year or two and I will sell her.'

Jem heard a great roaring in his ears and felt an ache in his jaw unlike anything he had experienced before. This was worse than combat, worse than bringing his frigate alongside the enemy and pounding away at close range. The tender woman he loved was at stake. He felt a great helplessness, he who was renowned in both fleets for his capability under fire and his innate sense of what to do when there was nothing to do.

'I want to buy her, free her, and marry her in a northern state,' he said, pressing on doggedly because he had to, even when there was no hope. 'My intentions are honourable.'

'You are a member of a hated nation to me, Captain Grey,' Tullidge declared. 'You damned British burned my plantation on Tybee Island and scattered my slaves and I could do nothing. Nothing!'

His voice rose to great heights. Out of the corner of his eye, Jem saw heads pop out of doors, and withdraw just as quickly.

I'm not even British, Jem thought, taking a tiny moment to marvel that in the space of one awful interview, he had admitted two things to himself—he loved a lady and he wasn't an Englishman. Amazing how a fraught situation had sharpened his senses.

'I take it your answer is no?' he asked calmly, and smiled because it sounded humorous to him. Might as well go down with the ship. Standing there in the foyer of a mansion built with blood and belonging to one of Savannah's most influential citizens, Jem felt strangely calm.

Tullidge laughed at him, and Jem joined in, which made the slaver stop and stare. 'By God, you're a cheeky fellow.'

'And you, sir, are a bona fide, certified, dyed-in-the-wool bastard,' Jem said, crossing a barrier and committing himself to death. 'I challenge you to a duel.'

Tullidge stared at him, his expression incredulous. He turned around and shook his head at nothing, then whirled around so fast his coattails flared out.

'Why not? I doubt you are much of a shot, and it will be duelling pistols. You challenged so the weapon is my choice. When do you plan to be shot?'

'Tomorrow at eight in the morning. I don't want to waste my time in Savannah,' Jem replied. 'A freighter jobbing to Baltimore will pass down the channel around that time, and I don't want to miss it.'

Tullidge's eyes widened in surprise, but he did not laugh. The colour left his face. 'Eight of the clock at my *burnt-out mansion!'* He shouted the words but Jem did not flinch.

'Do you have a second?' Tullidge demanded. 'A

surgeon? Do you even have a clue what the rules are in Code Duello?'

'Not one,' Jem said, getting into the mood of this. 'I'm a dreadful shot.' He turned to Osgood Hollinsworth. 'Will you second me?'

'Absolutely,' the printer said. 'Wouldn't miss it. I even know a good surgeon. What say you two go back to back, march fifteen steps, turn and fire?'

'Sounds fine,' Jem said. 'Tomorrow morning then, Mr Tullidge? If you change your mind, I'm staying at the Arundel. Good day, sir. Looks a bit like rain.'

Jem turned on his heel and marched out of the foyer, Hollinsworth right behind. He stopped long enough to knock some street dust off his shoes, then made his way deeper into Ellis Square with all deliberation, feeling Tullidge's eyes boring into his back from the still open door. Silent, he walked through the square until he found a secluded spot by a hedge, where he promptly threw up.

From somewhere, Mr Hollinsworth must have found a damp cloth. He wiped Jem's face.

'Well done, Captain. I am impressed.'

'You realise I'm going to die tomorrow morning and Teddy will be in that man's hands after Christmas day,' he said, sucking on a clean corner of the cloth.

'Pish-posh, ye of little faith,' Hollinsworth said. 'I'm not named Osgood N. Hollinsworth for nothing.'

'What, pray tell, is *that* supposed to mean?' Jem asked, as equal measures of terror and exasperation seemed to roll down his back in waves like sweat.

'In good time, lad, in good time,' Hollinsworth said, and patted Jem's shoulder. 'I am certain I can talk my dentist friend Jephthah Morton into being your surgeon. His life has been a little slow, of late.'

'You're enjoying this,' Jem accused.

'Guilty as charged,' the printer said, looking not even slightly repentant. 'I will arrange for a small sailing vessel to take us to Tybee.' He ticked off his fingers. 'I'll need a table for the pistols, the dentist, and perhaps another observer.'

'An undertaker?' Jem asked.

'Oh, mercy no!' Hollinsworth said with a laugh. 'We need an impartial fellow to examine the pistols, once they're loaded. Go on now. Have a good dinner. I'll make all the arrangements. Aren't you going to meet Miss Winnings at Christ Church tonight for a little cuddle in one of the pews?'

How did Hollinsworth know *that*? 'Aye, that is my plan,' he admitted. 'Then I suppose I am to go back to the Arundel, pay my bill, get a good night's rest, and prepare to die at eight of the clock.'

'Have faith, laddie,' Hollinsworth said, his eyes calm.

Why do I keep hearing that? Jem asked himself. *I must be going mad.*

'You're quite sane,' the printer replied, as if he could read Jem's thoughts. 'Love does that to people, I hear. Toodle-loo until tomorrow.'

'Seven o'clock dockside?'

'You took the words from my mouth, laddie,' Hollinsworth replied, all good cheer. 'Get a good night's sleep.'

You, sir, are certifiable, he thought, but smiled at the old fool anyway.

'Takes one to know one,' Hollinsworth teased.

They parted in the square, Hollinsworth waddling off and humming, and Jem sitting on a bench, grateful none of his brother captains could see him now, with bats in his belfry, ready to duel to the death for a woman.

'I was a reasonable man once,' he said in amazement.

A cat slinking through the underbrush hissed at him. 'Let's see you do any better,' he said, as the stray arched his back, darted sideways in that way of felines, and disappeared. 'At least it isn't raining yet.'

He sighed as large drops began to pelt down, coming faster and faster until he was drenched.

Really, Sir, he thought. *Can this get any worse?*

It was a good question. He did something he had never done before when addressing *Sir*, his silent partner through most of his life, even though he had only recently acknowledged it. He listened. He watched.

He didn't hear any words, but he wasn't expecting words. He waited in silence and then appreciation as the rain stopped, and a rainbow arched through the sky. It stretched from a great height right down to the Savannah River.

In all his years at sea, the only thing remotely resembling this splendour had been Northern Lights, seen in breathtaking majesty in the far north latitudes. Rapt, he had watched glowing pulses of light, and on another occasion, the somehow sinister ripple of a green curtain. And there was the sprightly dance of St Elmo's Fire from mast to yardarm to the very sheets themselves. Even the most hardened sailor had stared in wonder.

The welcome sight of the Southern Cross in the Antipodes made him pause and reflect, but nothing made his heart as happy as this lovely display. He watched in delight as a smaller rainbow appeared below the larger one, almost as if seeking protection.

He swallowed and thought of Theodora Winnings, who needed him as she had never needed anyone. He was a captain, used to the awful burden of stewardship over every soul in each ship he commanded. He took his duty as a matter of course. He knew he was looking at duty right now, the sort of duty requiring courage above and beyond the simple working of a ship, or even sailing into battle.

This duty was for him alone, special, intimate and feeling less onerous by the second. He was Theodora Winnings' protector. Years may have passed, but his letter offering protection remained valid and in force, even though he had not known when he wrote his letter just what that meant. Did any man?

'I don't know how I am going to win, *Sir*,' he spoke to the sky. He knew he wasn't whining; he really *didn't* know.

Or did he? He watched the rainbows hang there

and gradually fade as the light shifted and dusk approached. Hadn't every one and every thing since Mrs Fillion's dining room been telling him? This was faithful service he would give gladly, no matter the outcome, because it was the honourable thing to do. All it required was faith.

Faith. He waited for it to seem corny and foolish and the stuff of boring sermons, but it did not. *Fair enough, Sir*, he thought. *Fair enough.*

Chapter Eleven

Eating was out of the question. Even after his peculiar epiphany, Jem knew nothing would stay down. He spent a few quiet moments at the front desk, paying for his stay, and assuring the clerk he would be gone by morning.

He tried to breathe deep, slow his heartbeat and remind himself what he had just learned in Ellis Square. Why did such a prosaic phrase as 'gone by morning' set his heart racing, and his pulse pounding?

When the clerk had expressed polite dismay at his leaving, and wished him all the best in his journey, why had Jem's thoughts turned to that journey from which no traveller returns? 'Good Lord, the man is only making conversation' vied with 'Repent and prepare to meet your Maker.'

He had faith, but he knew there was something he still lacked, the one ingredient that would get him through this ordeal, however it turned out. No matter; he had enough faith to buoy him into believing he would know what it was before the moment he aimed and fired tomorrow.

Maybe it was also enough to know the identity of that Sir he had been addressing for years, perhaps forgot, and then been so forcefully reminded in Charleston. He relaxed in the chair, smiling to remember sunny days in the South Pacific under full sail, feeling the very pulse of his ship and remembering to thank his silent partner.

'I trust I didn't make a fool of myself too many times, Sir,' he said out loud as he watched the winter sun sink in the west. 'Thank you again for keeping the heart in me when we sailed into battle, Sir. Thank you for the rainbows. I'll do my best tomorrow. Or should I say 'Thank Thee'?'

He closed his eyes and plopped his cares in someone else's generous lap, knowing he had done it many times, but without this new-found awareness. *Call me a late bloomer, Sir*, he thought, satisfied to nap. *I should have known it was Thee all along.*

His natural pragmatism resurfaced. Quite possibly his great good friend the Lord Almighty was far too busy with day-to-day events to concern himself exclusively with one of his sons. It may even have been abominably prideful of him to think Sir was that interested in one puny individual. Besides, Jem knew this was a busy season. Possibly Sir had helpers.

As he lay there half-awake, mostly dozing, he searched his brain to recall if there was a guardian angel for sailors. Whoever he was, Jem was fairly certain that personage or spirit—call him what you will—had been his steady companion through the years. All he could think of right now was St Nicholas, since this was the saint's season of merrymaking and good tidings of great joy. It was enough; he slept.

Jem woke in time to wash his face, comb his hair, put on a new neckcloth and walked to Christ Church, where the choir was straggling in. He singled out the choir master and asked for a moment of his time. Sitting in a pew with him, he told the master he was leaving in the morning for Baltimore.

'Mr Grey, it will be Christmas Eve. You couldn't stay another day or two?' the master asked.

'Times and tides, sir,' Jem said, and the man nodded. Anyone who lived on a waterfront knew what that meant.

'Would you at least sing with us this one last time?' he asked.

There it was again—*one last time*, spoken casually, but words that had weight and heft to them for James Grey, soon-to-be duellist who had courage to spare now, but little skill to fight.

'Alas, no. I will be listening from a back pew, however,' he said, and felt his face grow warm. 'There's a young lady… She's a good friend I knew in another place.'

'Would we know her?' the choirmaster asked. Why did Southerners have to be so politely interested?

'Unlikely,' he said, and quickly changed the subject, because the rector of Christ Church was approaching. 'Excuse me, sir, but I have a question for this good man.'

More pleasantries, and then the question: 'Father, is there a saint or guardian angel for mariners?' Jem asked.

The rector permitted himself a laugh in the church, maybe because Christmas was nearly upon them and he was a tolerant man. 'Mr Grey, I've learned enough about you to know you are a man of the sea, and quite possibly not too observant as a Christian?'

'That might be changing,' Jem said. No need for even a rector to know just how dependent Captain Grey was on his omnipresent Sir, and whatever guardian angel helped out, too. He knew he could never explain the significance of the two rainbows to anyone but Teddy.

Another realisation hit him—was *he* the smaller rainbow, under the protection of a greater one? *Humility*, he thought, relieved, as the last puzzle fell into place. *I can be humble, no matter my circumstances.*

'Mr Grey?'

'Pardon me. I was…uh… I was wool-gathering.'

'To answer your question, it's St Nicholas, the same as blesses our hearts at this season,' the rector said. 'I believe he is also called the wonder-worker, the saint who helps those in trouble. Which would be sailors, you would agree.'

'I would, sir. Wonder-worker. I like that.' Nodding

to both men, he walked to the back of the church to wait for Teddy Winnings. *Wonder-worker is it, St Nicholas?* he asked silently. *Work some wonder for me.*

He didn't wait long. Teddy quietly lifted the latch on the gate-like door to the pew and sat down beside him. His heart turned over when she sighed as though she had been holding her breath, or maybe because she suddenly felt safe.

Gone was the slave's bandanna; she wore a bonnet on her curly hair. Her dress was dark blue muslin, worn with a shawl of some Scottish plaid. She wore shoes. She was the loveliest woman he had even seen. He wanted to tell her that, but his natural reticence stopped his tongue, at least until he decided that *Sir* and St Nicholas expected a bit more.

'Teddy, you are lovely,' he whispered. 'I like the bonnet.'

She leaned closer and he breathed in the faintest lavender. 'I was coming here bareheaded, and who should appear but Mr Hollinsworth with this very bonnet. He wished me Happy Christmas and insisted I keep it.'

He reminded himself to laugh quietly; the choirmaster had his hands raised for a downbeat. 'He amazes me.'

She looked ahead at the choir, smiling.

'I hope you didn't get in too much trouble today,' he whispered. 'You were gone so long.' He sighed. 'You said Mrs Winnings keeps that hairbrush handy.'

'No trouble at all,' she whispered back, moving

closer because the choir had started to sing. He didn't mind. Her breath was soft on his ear. 'So strange. It was as though I had been gone mere minutes, and not hours. She never missed me.'

'A wonder,' he said.

He took her hand and kissed it, then set her hand on his leg, where she patted him. There was so much he wanted to tell her, and he knew time was his enemy. 'Teddy, like most of the captains, I complained about the Peace of Amiens. Mark you, it will end soon enough and we will be at war again with France. No one likes to be cast ashore on half pay, although most of us post captains have amassed enough prize money to not feel quite the pain that a young lieutenant feels.'

'As you were once,' she said. 'My goodness, I fell in love with a pasty-faced, trembling lieutenant with nothing to recommend him, didn't I?'

'And I fell in love with a beautiful lady who was kind enough to tend me.'

'So you thought,' she teased. 'I had no choice.' Her expression changed to kindness itself. 'And then I couldn't leave. Didn't want to.'

'I am grateful for that Treaty now,' he told her, pausing for a few minutes while the choirmaster gave instructions, then nodded to the pianist to continue. 'It gave me a chance to leave the country, spend seven weeks on a sailing vessel, and think.'

'What did you learn?' she asked.

'That in all those years, I have never been out of

love with you.' He turned slightly and took both her hands in his. 'If I survive tomorrow, marry me.'

She flinched at his words and he saw tears gather in her eyes. He watched her master them, as she had probably mastered tears all her life. A slave hadn't the luxury of emotion.

'I accepted your proposal eleven years ago,' she reminded him. 'Nothing's changed.' She took a deep breath and another. 'You will survive.'

'But if I don't…' He reached in his pocket for a ticket and handed it to her. 'Don't come to the island with me tomorrow, Teddy. Gather all your possessions, take this and get on the *Molly Bright*, bound for Baltimore. Wear what you are wearing now, and maybe a cloak, if you have one. It's a Baltimore freighter. They won't know your connections here in Savannah. I visited the wharf and the captain told me you should be aboard the *Molly* by eight o'clock.'

'I would rather come with you to Tybee Island,' she told him.

'You might not like what you see, and there would be no escaping after that,' he said bluntly. He took a packet from his coat. 'Here is seven hundred and fifty dollars.'

She put her hand to her mouth and her eyes grew wide. 'No, no.'

'Seven hundred and fifty dollars,' he repeated, showing her two letters in the packet. 'This one is from Carter and Brustein in Plymouth, where I bank. It is permission to transfer all funds from there to a bank or counting house of my choosing in the United States. In this letter, I've notarized everything over to Theodora Winnings. I want you to go to Massachusetts and settle there. Do what you wish once you are there, and remember me. Take it. You must.'

Lips tight together, her eyebrows drawn down into a deep frown, she took the packet. She closed her eyes and bowed her forehead against the pew in front of them. Without a word, she dropped to her knees onto the prayer bench.

He knelt beside her, no thought in his head except the word *Sir* over and over. It calmed him.

A hush fell over the church as the choir finished 'Come, Thou Long-Expected Jesus.' The notes hung on the incense-fragrant air. The peace of the season settled on James Grey, reminding him of a warm blanket placed around his body by a surgeon after the battle of Camperdown, once the man stitched a sabre wound on Jem's thigh. He felt the same drowsy somnolence, and thought he might even sleep tonight.

He walked Teddy Winnings home through magnolia-scented air. There was enough breeze to set the Spanish moss swaying in the oak trees near Green Square. They had started with his arm properly crooked out and hers threaded through it. As they approached the little house and Teddy slowed down, his arm went around her waist, and hers around his.

He kissed her at the back door of the darkened house, holding her close and kissing her several times more. With an ache, he noted how well they fit together. He knew she would not object if he came inside with her and stayed the night in her bed. She was tugging gently on his hand right now, the door open. He also knew what folly that could become, if he got her with child as his last act in mortality.

He told her that as she tugged on him. She nodded and released his hand, but not before kissing it, placing it against her face, and kissing his palm.

'I hope to see you on the deck of the *Molly Bright*, when I climb up the chains from a little boat. After I'm done with Tybee Island,' he said as he backed away.

'You'll see me, dearest sir,' she said, went inside and quietly closed the door.

Chapter Twelve

He did sleep, waking to a quiet knock he had requested from the desk clerk. He lay there a moment, thinking how inexorably time was going to rule for the next few hours. The emotion reminded him of sailing into battle, knowing nothing was going to change the forward movement. Once engaged, whatever puny skills he possessed, or those of his crew, would be put to the test until the issue was decided.

He knew how paltry his talent for this contest, when it came to firearms. He had never been a good shot, choosing wisely to let his Marines aboard his frigates exhibit their marksmanship from the yardarms and ratlines while he stayed out of their way. Too bad he could not post sharpshooters in the trees at Tullidge's plantation.

He washed and dressed with care, not wishing whoever had the task of embalming him to look askance at soiled smallclothes or an untidy neckcloth. He frowned at his nearly full bottle of bay rum, then wondered if he should dump it over his head. It seemed a shame to waste such good fragrance. Perhaps Osgood N. Hollinsworth would use it.

Dressed and with his duffel packed, he shouldered it and went across the street, stopping to eat a bowl of hominy grits, for which he had discovered a fondness during his Southern sojourn. He ate a few bites of shirred eggs, just to placate the cook one last time. The woman was a bit of a martinet.

One block, and he stood on the dock, spending a moment to admire the early-morning bustle, something he was long familiar with, and which never failed to lift his heart, even this last morning in Savannah, possibly his last morning on the planet. Another rainbow would have been reassuring, but the sky was bright with dawn.

Hollinsworth had said there would be a sailboat tied up and ready at the wharf, and he was right. Jem felt his heart sink to see Teddy already seated amidships, a small satchel in her arms.

'You are supposed to take the *Molly Bright*,' he commented as he sat beside her.

'And leave you alone?' she asked. 'I could no more do that than fly.' She twined her arm through his, content to rest her head on his shoulder.

'When we get to Tybee Island, at least stay in the boat,' he insisted, well aware he had lost this round to a determined woman, and thank goodness for that. Argue with himself all he wanted, he knew he did not care to face this dreadful ordeal alone. 'Stay in the boat at Tybee! That way, Mr Hollinsworth can still see you to the *Molly* in the channel…after.'

'Perhaps,' she replied.

He heard no compliance. Obviously he needed to take another tack. 'See here, Teddy, if by some mysterious, highly unlikely miracle I survive this ordeal, am I to gather that you will oppose me whenever it feels right and just to you?' A potential husband ought to know these things, after all.

'You could gather that,' she agreed. 'I have opinions.' She folded her hands in her lap and stared straight ahead. The sides of the bonnet hide her profile, but Jem hoped she was smiling.

In short order Jephthah Morton joined them, carrying his black leather bag and wearing a shiny black suit with a funereal cast to it. Next came Mr Hollinsworth lugging a wooden folding table, which he stowed aboard. He held out his hand to steady a gentleman unknown to James.

He was dressed in black, as Jem suddenly realised they all were, with the exception of Teddy in her blue muslin and brown cloak. Jem swallowed, wishing he could scare up some saliva. Nothing.

'James, may I present Constantine Larkin, Esquire, of Charleston. Max, this is Captain James Grey, late of the Royal Navy,' Hollinsworth said.

Jem couldn't help wincing at 'late.'

'Not late yet, sir,' he said, as he bowed but did not rise in the bobbing craft. Or perhaps he was precisely that. A glance at the lovely woman seated so calmly beside him told him that if he survived, he was staying in the United States, whether the nation wanted him or not. Maybe he *was* late of the Royal Navy.

'Do the honours, Jem?' Hollinsworth asked and indicated the tiller.

Jem moved aft and took the tiller. A few unnecessary words to the deckhand, who knew his business, sent them into the river and quickly past the *Molly Bright*, with its crew aboard and making ready to begin her voyage up the coast, then into Chesapeake Bay to Baltimore.

'You were supposed to be aboard the *Molly* by now, Teddy,' he reminded his dearest darling, who had cautiously moved back to sit closer to him.

'I had other ideas, Captain Grey,' she said.

'Am I to gather further that if I survive, you will call me Captain Grey when you are perhaps slightly irritated with me?' he asked, enjoying himself as he not thought possible, this close to death. He gave all the credit to his patron saint.

'You could gather that, too,' she said, then made no more comment as she turned her attention toward the receding shore.

He wasn't sure which of the barrier islands was Tybee, but the deckhand kept him on target. By the time they docked at what appeared to be a little-used wharf, fog had begun to roll in from the nearby ocean.

The hand leaped from the boat and caught the line that Mr Hollinsworth threw with surprising skill. Another line aft secured the boat. The printer helped Teddy from the sailboat.

'I want her to stay in the boat,' Jem said. 'Mr Hollinsworth, I want you and your crew to get her to the *Molly* when this is done.'

Why did he feel like no one was listening to him? Perhaps because no one was. 'Please, Teddy,' he tried again. 'You don't want to see this.'

'I'll stay out of sight.' She made no objection when he put his arm around her and pulled her close to his side. 'This fog…'

Mr Hollinsworth seemed to know right where to go. He led out with Mr Larkin from Charleston, followed by the deckhand with the table. Looking like a black-coated heron, the dentist brought up the rear as he stalked along on thin legs.

'This is a strange assembly,' Jem said. 'Pray for me, Teddy.'

'What have I been doing for eleven years?' she asked. 'I'll pray more. Jem, I love you. If things…' She stopped and took several deep breaths. 'I'll follow your instructions to the letter.'

'That's all I ask, dear heart.' He kissed her cheek and pointed her toward a smallish boulder by a tree. 'There's a good place to wait. I don't want Tullidge to spot you.'

She shivered. 'I don't, either. Good luck, Jem. Go with God.'

She didn't make their farewell hard, kissing his cheek and hurrying toward the boulder, where she was soon nearly invisible in the enveloping fog. He followed the muffled sound of two men laughing, and wondered what on earth Mr Hollinsworth and Mr Larkin found amusing about this situation.

He squinted, and soon noticed other figures. Here it came again, that feeling of time moving too fast now, every moment bringing him closer to standing and firing, all for the honour of a woman he adored, and who his enemy saw as chattel to be used and tossed.

I am a long way from England, he thought. *Maybe I always was.*

William Tullidge stood beside a younger man who looked much like him, possibly his son.

'I thought perhaps you had shown the white feather,' was Tullidge's greeting.

'Not I, sir,' Jem said. 'And this is…?'

'My son, Geoffrey, serving as my second,' Tullidge said. 'I've already told him that when I tire of Theodora, I will hand her down to him. He'll be tired of his wife by then.'

Only by supreme effort did Jem tamp down a howl of rage. His eyes bored into Tullidge's smiling, self-satisfied, confident face but he kept his counsel, acutely aware that the slave owner sought to unbalance him even further.

Nice try, you bastard, he thought. *I have fought sea battles that would cause you to make water.*

The roaring in his ears stopped. 'Sir,' was all he said. Tullidge looked his way, but Jem was not addressing him. Mr Hollinsworth came closer to touch his arm. 'Good choice, laddie.'

'Mr Hollinsworth, who *are* you?' he asked.

'A simple printer, and not a very good one,' he replied with a shrug. 'Don't worry about that now.'

Mr Larkin cleared his throat. He stood behind the table that held a highly polished wooden box with brass corners. He indicated the box.

'Mr Tullidge, these are your pistols?'

'They are, and lovely ones, I might add.'

Mr Larkin said nothing to that, but merely stared at the slaver, which made Tullidge shift his feet and mutter something. Mr Larkin held up his hand.

'My old friend Mr Hollinsworth summoned me from Charleston, since I know the rules of Code Duello, and he does not. Sir, you say you loaded these pistols while you waited for us to arrive? You say this on your word as a gentleman, and your honour that all is proper?'

'I do.'

Mr Larkin turned to Jem. 'Have you any objections?'

Jem had many but what could he say? 'None, sir,' he said, pleased at how firm his voice sounded, even as his insides writhed. 'He says he is an honourable man.'

'Very well then, let us be about our business this morning,' Mr Larkin said. He looked at both of them. 'Back to back, if you please. Ah, yes.'

'I have never stood this close to a reeking, cursed captain in the Royal Navy,' Tullidge murmured.

'How odd of you to say that,' Jem whispered back. 'I bathed and doused myself in bay rum this morning, just for you.'

Hollinsworth chuckled, then coughed and look away. Mr Larkin glowered at them both. 'Gentlemen! Kindly pace off fifteen steps, then turn, but do not raise your pistols.'

Sir, keep me brave, Jem thought as he walked away from Tullidge. *It's for Teddy.*

He stopped and turned, then squinted. Good Lord, the fog was thicker.

'This will never do,' Mr Larkin said. 'Take five steps closer, if you will.'

Five steps brought them in sight of each other, as the teasing fog made them visible and dangerously close, then barely visible once more.

'Could you not postpone this duel until later in the day, when the fog burns off?' Mr Larkin asked.

'No, sir.'

'No! I have business in town today.'

'Very well, you idiots. Heed me. You may raise your pistols. I will ask each of you if you are ready to fire. You will reply, but you will not fire until I give the word. Do you understand?'

They did.

'Raise your pistols.'

Jem did as commanded, gratified to see his aim was steady.

Teddy, you will be my last and final thought, he told himself. *Sorry, Sir, but that is the way I feel. Wish I had time to gather more faith.*

He waited. And waited, then jumped in surprise to hear Mr Larkin's voice much closer.

'Gentlemen, put down your pistols.'

Jem lowered his weapon. 'Sir?' he asked Mr Larkin.

'I cannot account for it, but I have the most profound impression that I should look at your pistol. Hand it over, Mr Grey, if you please. Both of you approach the table.'

Mystified, Jem walked toward the table. He glanced at Tullidge and saw a man as puzzled as *he* felt. He watched in curiosity as Mr Larkin pulled back the hammer, then peered closer.

'Stand away, gentlemen,' he said. He pointed the pistol out and down in the direction of the burned-out mansion. He squeezed the trigger. Nothing. He squeezed again. Nothing beyond an audible click.

'Your pistol, Mr Tullidge,' Mr Larkin said, his voice distinctly frosty now.

Wordless, his mouth open in what Jem thought was genuine astonishment, Tullidge complied. Mr Larkin pointed his pistol out and down and fired. The weapon went off with a louder report than Jem expected and he jumped. So did Tullidge.

'Sir, I...'

'Mr Tullidge, for shame,' Mr Larkin said. 'On your honour as a gentleman? What foul business is this?'

'I loaded them both,' Tullidge insisted. 'I am a gentleman.'

His words hung on the foggy air. Jem stared at him, certain he saw nothing in the dueller's eyes but confusion and amazement. *I believe you*, he thought. *I truly do.*

'I declare this duel null and void,' Mr Larkin said. He stepped close to Tullidge until the man backed up. 'Mr Tullidge, do you know who I am?'

'Uh…well…a man from Charleston? I know the n-name Larkin is prominent there.'

'Indeed it is, sir. I own and edit the new *Charleston Post.*'

'He does,' Mr Hollinsworth said, speaking up for the first time. 'I should dislike the man, because I know his influential paper quite overshadowed my little Savannah *Times and Tides*. I wanted him here because I know he is a fair man. If you cannot trust a journalist, who can you trust?' He clucked his tongue. 'Mr Tullidge, you disappoint me.'

'But…'

Jem looked from one angry face to the other. Mr Larkin seemed to be just getting warmed up. 'I write a column, sir. *You* will be my subject next week,' Mr Larkin snapped.

'Please no. There is some mistake,' Tullidge said. 'I loaded both of those weapons, upon my honour.'

'Honour? Honour?' Mr Larkin glared at him. 'I can see the headline now—"No honour in Savannah."' He laughed, and the sound held no amusement. 'Just as we suspected in Charleston.'

Silence ruled. Jem looked on Mr Tullidge's face, all colour drained away.

Mr Hollinsworth spoke, his words more conciliatory this time. 'This is harsh indeed, Mr Larkin. You could ruin him.'

'I can and I will, because he is no gentleman,' Mr Larkin said.

'Please no, sir!' Tullidge begged again. He went down on one knee and rested his forehead on that knee.

Jem watched Mr Hollinsworth, and saw something close to unholy glee in his eyes. *What business is this?* he thought. He glanced at Mr Larkin, saw a similar expression, and waited.

Mr Hollinsworth cleared his throat. 'Mr Larkin, what say you do not print that column, although this poor specimen richly deserves to be driven out of Savannah. I am through printing newspapers here, so I will write nothing. I suggest the following conditions.'

'They had better be good, Mr Hollinsworth,' Mr Larkin snapped. 'I am a hard man to convince.'

'Tullidge here allows Mrs Winnings to keep her home that he won at the turn of a card, and gives her five hundred dollars besides,' Mr Hollinsworth said.

'And the slave?' Mr Larkin asked.

'She should be freed. Tullidge here has not an iota of good intentions regarding her.'

Jem glanced toward the boulder where he could

plainly see Teddy now. She leaned forward as if straining to hear.

'Well, Tullidge?' Mr Larkin asked, then made what looked like a great show of reluctance to Jem. 'I suppose since this is Christmas Eve, we can be merciful. Do you agree to these terms? You allow Mrs Winnings to keep her house, you pay the widow five hundred dollars, and Teddy goes free.'

Tullidge nodded. 'I agree,' he said in a small voice. 'No gentleman here will ever speak of this morning's work? No one will know?'

'Not one of us will say a word,' Mr Larkin assured him. 'Go on now. Take your duelling pistols and chuck them in the river. Only gentlemen duel and you are no gentleman.'

Jem watched as a broken man picked up the box with the pistols nestled again in their velveteen frame. He sighed when Tullidge's son shook off his father's hand and walked far away from him. *Can anyone repair that?* he thought, surprised to feel pity.

The man from Charleston, the dentist, the editor and the Royal Navy captain stood close together. 'No gentleman will ever mention this again,' Osgood N. Hollinsworth said, his voice crackling with rare authority. 'Is that understood?'

They all agreed. Jem glanced at the deckhand, who had begun to fold up the wooden table, their business done. The man was silently laughing to himself, his face lively, his shoulders shaking. No gentleman would speak of it again, but as sure as Jem was about to grab up Teddy , running toward him now, he knew without a doubt that the deckhand was under no constraint to remain silent.

What's more, he knew the gentlemen in this strange cabal on foggy Tybee Island knew it, too. Before nightfall, the story of William Tullidge's moral lapse and lack of honour in a duel, in a place where such things mattered, would have circulated far beyond River Street. The story would be whispered from dock slaves to house slaves, to genteel ladies in their boudoirs to their honourable husbands. By the time Christmas Day tomorrow was a gentle memory of too much ham and turkey consumed, and too many drinks downed, Tullidge would be ruined anyway. He almost felt sorry for the man. Almost.

Chapter Thirteen

The timing could not have been more impeccable; Jem felt justified to dub it miraculous. The *Molly Bright* swung into the channel in the calm place right before the river met the Atlantic Ocean. Jem assured a terrified Theodora Winnings that she wasn't going to drop into the channel on her way to *Molly*'s deck.

'Look you there, my love,' he said. 'The deckhands have already rigged a bowline slide. Here it comes. Stand up and hold still.'

In tears, she did as he said, raising her arms as he widened the knot and pulled it over her head. When it was snug against her waist and she held the rope in a death grip, he gave the worldwide signal for them to pull. She shrieked, the deckhands chuckled, and Teddy Winnings went up the side in a flash of skirt, petticoats, and handsome legs that he only peeked at, because he was a gentleman.

He turned to Mr Hollinsworth. 'I think I am on to you,' he said, which brought a smile to the editor, and a modest ducking of his head. 'One question. Who are man from Charleston and the dentist *really*?'

'People who have owed me favours through the centuries,' he said.

'Will I owe you a favour now?' Jem asked. 'Just curious.'

'That's more than one question, laddie. I'll ask one small favour in a few months. Hug me and get aboard that ship. Times and tides are out of my control.'

After he embraced Mr Hollinsworth, Jem followed Teddy to the deck by climbing the chains.

The grinning deckhand in the sailboat sent their luggage topside when the rope came down again. Jem gave him a small salute. 'If you ever want a job in Massachusetts, I have a suspicion that Mr Hollinsworth will know my address.' The slave saluted back.

Teddy had retreated as far from the railing as she could, but Jem stayed there, his mind and heart on Mr Hollinsworth in the craft bobbing below. He didn't know what to say. What he *wanted* to say would have branded him as a crazy man and a crackpot. *Sir?* he asked, then immediately knew the right words.

'Thank you, Mr Hollinsworth,' he shouted down, as the sails billowed and *Molly Bright* picked up speed. 'Satisfy my curiosity, once and for all. I know it is another question, but humour me on Christmas Eve. What does your middle initial stand for?'

'Nicholas, of course, laddie. Fair winds,' the little man shouted back.

No one will ever believe this, Jem thought, his eyes on the man in the boat. A sudden rush of fog obscured the smaller boat from his sight. When it cleared, the boat appeared to be one person lighter. He watched the others, who carried on as though nothing had happened.

Molly Bright was a seagoing freighter and soon left the coastal shipping lane. Jem quickly discovered that his intended wife was no mariner. He loved her anyway, but not right then, as she spent the few days of the voyage sitting on the deck of the cabin they shared, a bucket in her lap.

Baltimore couldn't have come soon enough for Theodora. Pale and hungry, she let him help her to a quayside tavern for a hearty luncheon of dry toast and consommé. She recovered enough to glower at him for polishing off crab cakes, more hominy grits and eggs and bacon, washed down with ale.

He knew she was on the mend from monumental *mal de mer* when she filched a strip of bacon from his plate and asked for her own bowl of grits. Satisfied and not a little relieved, he watched her eat.

He knew how great her courage was when he suggested they spend the night in Baltimore to allow her to recover. She shook her head, even though he could nearly feel her exhaustion. 'No, sir. We will take the next stage to Philadelphia. I will not spend another moment in the South,' she said quietly, but with fervour.

They were married two days later in the City of

Brotherly Love. One of their fellow travellers on the stage from Baltimore to Philadelphia was a lawyer well acquainted with the new nation's matrimonial rules. In fact, he walked them to the courthouse, where he located a magistrate and explained the situation, even though it was closing time and everyone was headed home. New Year's Eve was nearly upon them.

The magistrate asked a few gentle questions, which they answered honestly. He didn't hesitate over Teddy's quiet admission of slavery, and Jem's own declaration of his status as a captain in the Royal Navy, but a native-born son of Massachusetts.

He shook his head when both of them offered documents. 'I don't need to see them,' he said. 'Your honour and right intentions are obvious to anyone looking at you both.'

He married them, stamped the document and took the liberty of kissing Theodora Grey's cheek, after a glance at Jem for permission.

His new wife was silent as they walked down the steps and stood on the sidewalk full of lawyers, office workers and passers-by heading for homes and dinner and a quiet evening before the fire. Theodora shivered in her light Georgia cloak. He generously whisked his cape around both of them as they stood to the side of people passing, and stared at their marriage license from the state of Pennsylvania.

For what turned out to be the final time, his jaw ceased aching. 'Theodora Grey,' he whispered in her ear as her shaking finger traced the words. 'You're safe now. You're my wife and under my protection.'

Trust Teddy to know him already. 'And you're safe, too, dearest,' she told him. 'You're home.'

She was too exhausted for any sort of wedding night beyond cuddling close to him in the first bed they shared as husband and wife. By morning, she agreed to bare her shoulders and show him where Mrs Winnings had laid on that hairbrush. By the time he finished kissing each mark, Jem was willing—no, eager to show Teddy Grey that wicked sabre cut on his thigh.

Events moved along swiftly after that. Her tender touch and the serious comment, belied by her laughing eyes, how relieved she was that the sabre hadn't cut any higher made him gather her close, and prove that everything had healed well and he was in no way impaired.

'Perhaps I should mail your surgeon some special something from the United States to express my gratitude,' his wife said a half hour later after matters had taken their logical course and the room had stopped spinning.

''Some special something'?' he teased. 'Teddy, I know you are generally more articulate than that.'

'Give me time,' she replied with some dignity, then ruined it by kissing his whole scar, giggling the entire length and width of it.

If he had spent a more wonderful week in his life, James Grey couldn't remember it. Room service most obligingly kept them fed. The weather cooperated divinely—oh, that word—by rain turning to snow until only idiots would venture out of doors. And the Greys were anything but stupid.

By the end of the week, though, Teddy insisted on leaving the hotel to stand in the lightly falling snow. His heart tender, he watched as she stared like a child at the tiny, individual snowflakes highlighted against her cloak.

'She's from Georgia. Hasn't seen snow before,' he commented to one of the passers-by who smiled at them, and tipped his hat.

One afternoon when they were contemplating each other's bare toes, Jem admitted to some uncertainty about their next move. 'I want to go to Massachusetts— well, you remember the letter I gave you...'

'Oh, my, I forgot,' Teddy said and got out of bed, wrapping the sheet around her that had come loose from its moorings.

He smiled at the sight of her innate modesty, still covering up when the matter was entirely unnecessary. He rose on one elbow as she picked through her satchel until she found a letter. She handed it to him, and abandoned modesty by dropping the sheet and sitting cross legged beside him.

An hour later, they got around to the letter, crumpled now and underneath her. 'Mr Hollinsworth told me to give it to you when we reached Philadelphia.' She blushed. 'I forgot.'

He laughed, straightened it out, and pulled her close

so they could read it together. 'That man,' he said when he finished. 'He gave this to you *when*?'

'I was eating chicken and you had gone out back to the necessary, I think,' she said. 'You know, that first day we met again.'

'That was before anything had happened. Days before the duel.' Why he thought to argue the matter escaped him. Osgood Nicholas Hollinsworth had proved himself capable of anything, as any good wonder-worker might.

'Where's New Bedford?' she asked, pointing to the words.

'It's a seaport due south of Boston,' he told her. 'Frankly, I would have thought he might recommend Nantucket, which is more up and coming, in my opinion,' he said. 'But no, he says we should go to New Bedford.' He thought about both places and had a quiet laugh inside. Teddy would have to cross open water to get to Nantucket Island, and he didn't relish *that* scene. He had been a husband a mere few days, and he already knew where not to venture.

She took the letter from his chest and nudged him over so she could share his pillow. '"There is a man there, name of Benjamin Russell, who is looking for a partner in a shipbuilding enterprise. Tailor-made for you, laddie,"' she read. She returned the letter to his chest. 'We had better start economizing right now, husband, if that money of yours is our future. How much have we spent?'

'You mean the seven hundred and fifty dollars?' he

asked. 'Barely fifty.' He started to laugh then, stopping when she gave him a less than genteel poke in his ribs.

'You are up to something, husband,' she accused.

'Not really, wife,' he joked. 'Did you look at that letter from Carter and Brustein?'

Her eyes troubled, Teddy shook her head. 'I couldn't. I didn't want to bring you bad luck in the duel.'

What a tender woman she was. 'You have no idea what I am worth, in navy salvage and prize money.' He whispered the figure in her ear and she gasped.

After she caught her breath, she told him they were getting dressed and she was going to find a modiste for new clothes. 'You can afford me.'

He couldn't have agreed more. By the time they left Philadelphia ten days later, Mrs Grey looked like the stylish wife of a seafaring man about to change careers.

He wrote a letter to Osgood N. Hollinsworth the night before they left Philadelphia in a private chaise, thanking him for everything and assuring him he had made Theodora his bride at the first opportunity. He invited the little round fellow to visit them in New Bedford.

He had no idea where to mail the letter. On one of their admittedly few jaunts about Philadelphia he had asked a priest about St Nicholas. The priest had informed him of St Nicholas's birth in Patara, in Asia Minor. On a whim, he addressed the letter to *Patara*,

Asia Minor, and put it just outside their door, next to his shoes to be shined. To his delight, but not his surprise, the letter was gone in the morning.

He wrote another letter to Michael Cameron, the proprietor of the Marlborough Dining Room, where he had taken many a meal during his Savannah visit, and where they had struck up slightly more than a nodding acquaintance. He had some questions.

After a spine-jostling ride over awful winter roads, they arrived in New Bedford in mid-February, both of them resolved never to travel again. Teddy was pale and nauseous, and well-acquainted with the basin in each of the inns where they stopped. By the last night on the road, she suggested with a blush that maybe it wasn't merely travel sickness. He had a silly grin on his face when he folded her in his arms.

Events moved much as Mr Hollinsworth had predicted in his letter. Benjamin Russell, a man about his own age, was easy to locate in the seaport. He was well-known as an innovative builder who needed more capital to fulfil what no one on the docks doubted would be the making of both Russell and New Bedford. A few evenings together while they chatted in Benjamin's study and their wives knitted and got acquainted in the sitting room, marked the beginning of Russell and Grey Shipworks. Both men argued that the other's name should go first. The matter was settled with a coin toss.

Formal papers were drawn up, and the two cou-

ples went in search of a suitable house for the Greys.
Jem's only stipulation was that it overlook the water.
Teddy requested lots of bedchambers. Furniture and
rugs followed. Months later, a much-travelled letter
arrived from Savannah, Georgia. Her face betraying
her worry, Teddy brought the letter to Jem in his new
office. She shook her head at the untidiness of blue
prints and ship models, and handed it to him.

He kissed her forehead and massaged the frown
line between her eyes. 'No fears. We're a long way
from Georgia,' he reminded her. 'Have a seat.'

One chair had blueprints and the other a bolt of
canvas, so he held out his arms and she sat on his lap.

'My whole family came to see me,' he said, patting her rounded belly. He opened the letter and held
it in front of them both. She finished reading before
he did, and she gasped.

'You're too fast for me,' he protested, and pointed
to the paragraph where Mr Cameron noted that William Tullidge had left town one night, never to be seen
again. Rumours circulated that he had moved west
to Mississippi, seeking land not played out by cotton
yet, but no one knew for certain. His wife and son had
remained in Savannah, and they had nothing to say.

He didn't gasp when he read Mr Cameron's con-
clusion, although it gave him a jolt.

'Teddy, no one's going to believe this,' he said.

'We won't tell anyone,' she replied. 'Do you think
our children will believe us?'

'Hard to say. Not if they're as practical and sceptical as you are. Ow!'

She kissed the ear lobe she had tugged on so hard.
'Saints alive, sir,' she whispered. 'See you tonight.'

After she left, he reread the last two paragraphs of
the dining room proprietor's letter that was going to
go into his office safe immediately.

*Mr Grey, I have to wonder about you. No one
has been in that print shop since the end of
the revolution. The former editor of Savannah
Times and Tides was a Loyalist we ran out of
town in 1780. Maybe you meant someone else?*

*In fact, the city is demolishing the old eyesore
soon, along with that vacant office next door.
Rumour has it there used to be a dentist there,
but no one is certain.*

'St Nicholas, you are a sly one,' Jem said out loud.
He turned back to the letter. '"As for Osgood N. Hol-
linsworth, no one can recall anyone by that name.
Ah, well, Tullidge is gone and that is good enough.
Yrs. Sincerely…"'

He put the letter in the safe, certain it would be
gone when he returned in the morning. He was right.
The letter might never have existed, which surprised
him not a bit.

What made his heart turn tender and grateful was a
medal left in its place, similar to one of Teddy's saints
medals she kept in the drawer with her lacy things.
He closed his eyes in gratitude and thanked the Lord

Almighty, who had taken the time in a busy season to help a man searching for a woman long gone, and a country never forgotten.

Sir.

When he opened his eyes, he saw a small piece of paper. He read it with a smile.

We sometimes get the chance to work some won-
der, laddie. What's Christmas for, if not that?
Name your boy Nicholas James. That is my only
stipulation.

He slipped the scrap of paper in his pocket, along with the St Nicholas medal that would go in Teddy's drawer. He looked out the window where his partner was getting ready to lay down the keel on their first vessel, one built sturdy and solid and destined to travel the world. He had already suggested to Ben they name it the 'St. Nicholas,' that patron of sailors and children, captives, as well as friend of all in need and jovial guardian of Christmas.

'Wonder-worker, too,' he said as he went to the window and watched, his heart light, his mind at rest, his jaw relaxed. He touched the medal in his pocket, but felt no surprise that the paper had disappeared. No matter. Teddy would be happy to know she was going to have a son. She might argue that it should be James Nicholas rather than Nicholas James, but there was time to change her mind. And St Nicholas was right: It *was* a small favour, one gladly accepted.

'Mr Hollinsworth, there should probably be a Nicholas in each generation from here on out,' he said to the window. 'What say you?'

He felt sudden warmth in the pocket with the medal. 'Aye, then? Aye.'

* * * * *

HER CHRISTMAS TEMPTATION

Christine Merrill

To Nicola Caws. Merry Christmas.

Dear Reader,

I'm sure you're all familiar with the song "The Twelve Days of Christmas". It originated at a time when the Christmas season really was celebrated as a twelve-day holiday, lasting from Christmas to Epiphany—the coming of the Three Kings.

My story this year centres on Twelfth Night, the grand finale of the season, and some of the special games and festivities attached to it. Though no one sings about a partridge in a pear tree, my characters probably knew the song, which was old even in the Regency. The first publication of the lyrics we know of was in the 1790s children's book *Mirth Without Mischief*.

Happy reading and Merry Christmas!

Christine

Chapter One

As he trudged through the cold, wet streets of London on Boxing Day, James Leggett slipped a hand into his pocket to check for the hundredth time that it still contained the leather box that held the family betrothal ring. It felt odd to be giving Beatrice such a familiar thing. Two years ago, she'd seen it on her brother's fiancée. The next season, it had gone from her to his brother to give to the woman he intended to marry. Now, James had retrieved it from his sister-in-law. Leggett brides all wore the ring, until it could be passed along for the next engagement. As a member of the family, she would know that tradition was important.

A distant member of the family, he reminded himself. Marrying a cousin was not so very unusual. Marrying a second cousin was even less so. It would not really come as a surprise to anyone in London when they read the announcement. He'd made no secret of his fondness for Bea, nor had she hid her liking for him. Bonds of friendship that had been forged in childhood had deepened as they'd grown. He could honestly say that no other woman understood him so completely.

If he was to marry anyone, it should probably be her.

He sighed. If he was to do this correctly, he must raise more enthusiasm for proposing. When she saw him today, she must not realise what an effort it had taken to come to this decision and the even greater effort was taking to follow through. They had seen the tumultuous marriages of both their parents and vowed together that they would settle for nothing less than a true union of hearts. To his relief, he'd found that, if a man did not need an heir, then he had no reason to trouble himself about matrimony. There were infinite pleasures to be had without it and many that would be denied him, should he burden himself with a wife.

But, for a gently bred woman it was quite different. They needed the protection, both physical and financial, that only a husband could provide. He had promised Bea that, if her Season was not successful, they would formalise an arrangement they had talked about for years. He felt bad for her, of course. She'd had hopes. As had he. When he had made his half-hearted offer, he'd assumed it was to give her the confidence of knowing that she need not take the first man who showed interest, whether she liked him or not. If no one suited, he would still be there for her, as single as ever.

But it had been the last straw when he'd heard a friend at his club jokingly refer to her as a sad spinster. Damn it all, he could not stand by and watch her become a source of humour for men who, had they taken the time to know her, would have realised what a gem she was and fallen over each other for the chance to offer. Parliament had ended in June, and most of the eligible bachelors had scattered to the country. But there had been no news of a betrothal. Something had to be done.

When he'd written to suggest that they get on with the plan, her reply had hinted at a union in the offing and requested a few weeks more. Her next letter had wanted a month. And then another. Then she had stopped answering him at all when questioned on the subject, writing of nothing but the weather.

Now, it was December, and time to end the nonsense. His knock on the door of her father's town house was greeted by the butler, who directed him to her worried mother. There was much hand wringing and a few tears, but James put it all to rights by displaying the ring box and asking for the location of the fair Beatrice.

He stopped only briefly at the door to the salon where she was hiding with her needlework, glancing into a nearby mirror to smooth his hair and check the knot in his cravat. No matter what disappointment she was feeling, he would not allow her to think that this was in some way an inferior proposal. Since he had to do it, he would do it right and treat her as if she was his first and only choice.

He stepped through the door with the announcement of the servant, smiling and holding out his hands to her. 'My darling Bea.'

'You.' Her tone was a sullen as her gaze.

'No smile for me?' He clutched his heart. 'I am wounded. Daggers from the eyes of a lovely woman are twice as deadly as steel.'

She responded with an exasperated huff. 'Do not think to charm me into humour with flattery, James. It will not work.'

He dropped on to the couch beside her, not waiting for an invitation. 'I must charm you with something. You are in a frightfully bad mood and I have done nothing to deserve it.'

'Not yet,' she said ominously. 'But you are about to.'

He clutched his heart again. 'When have I ever? Have you not always said I was your favourite person in the world?'

'I have,' she agreed, reluctantly.

'And you are mine,' he prompted. 'We have known each other almost since birth and spent many fine summers in each other's company.'

'They were delightful,' she said with a small sigh at the remembered pleasure of the lazy days they'd spent tramping the grounds of the ancestral manse together.

'After all this time, we are still as close as two people can be,' he said.

'Like brother and sister,' she replied, looking directly into his eyes with no trace of affection, romantic or otherwise.

She was trying to put him off. And almost succeeding, for it made it difficult to speak of romance when she spun their kinship into something closer than it was. 'Not exactly as siblings,' he reminded her. 'Legally and morally, there is no such impossible closeness between us.'

'Perhaps not,' she said.

It was clear from the pause that followed those two words that the next sentence was going to begin with 'But…' so he hurried on. 'And you have always said you loved me.'

Her mouth opened to object, so he continued even faster, before he lost his nerve to tell the colossal lie that this situation required. 'And I love you, more than any other woman in England. That is why I wish to marry you.' Then, before the next objection, he lunged forward to kiss her.

A kiss would settle the matter in a way words could not. Though he knew himself to be a persuasive speaker, he was far more confident in his abilities as a lover. His kisses had charmed any number of women into bed when compliments had failed. Afterwards, they'd assured him that the time had been pleasantly spent and they'd gone their separate ways, content.

If there was a genuine, mutual affection, things would go even better. A single kiss might turn the proposal from an act of desperation into the logical progression of their lifelong friendship to something deeper and more precious.

That was why the clout on the ear that followed the current kiss came as such a shock to him, as did the accompanying words. 'Do not be an idiot, James.'

'Ow,' he said. For a moment, it was the only thing that came to mind. The pain should not have surprised him. He had learned during those many happy summers with her that she had an exceedingly strong right arm for such a delicate creature.

'And do not give me that injured look.' She wiped her mouth with the back of her hand. 'If you do that again, I shall hit you twice as hard and give you a real reason to complain.'

'Why?' he said, trying not to feel relieved that his seductive talents had chosen this moment to fail him.

'Because the fact that you love me more than any other woman in England is not enough. Perhaps I would marry you if I thought you loved me more than you love yourself,' she added.

'But that would be rather foolish of me,' he said, relieved to know that the problem was not with him at all but with the inherent madness of the female sex.

'That is what women expect in marriage, none the less,' she said. 'We want a man who would put our happiness before all else.'

'Then you have a far too whimsical view of the institution,' he said.

She gave another exasperated huff. 'Let me explain.

I assume you see our future thus,' she said. 'We will marry, just as we'd always joked of doing.'

'Of course,' he said, wondering where she'd got the idea that those offers had been in jest.

'Then, the lands of our parents will be combined again, just as they were before your father and my uncle reached majority and split the property.'

'It would be most convenient,' he agreed.

'After marriage, your life shall continue much as it always has, with time in London at the club, opera dancers, Cyprians, ladybirds, wayward wives…' She gave an airy wave of her hand.

'Such things are not usually discussed between a husband and a wife,' he reminded her, wondering if she expected him to flaunt his infidelities in her face. 'But if you are concerned, I do not intend to behave in such a way that will cause you embarrassment.'

'Of course you won't,' she agreed. 'Because you cannot embarrass a woman who does not give a fig who you bed, as long as it is not me.'

'Now see here…' The conversation was growing far too personal.

Now, she laid a hand on his in a way that was almost motherly and not the least what he had been hoping for in a prospective wife. 'Once we are married, you will return to the pleasures of your old life and pat yourself on the back that you have done a good deed by saving me from spinsterhood.'

'I do not pity you, if that is what you are thinking.'

She shook her head sadly. 'If it is not pity you feel,

then why do you offer so little? You will lose nothing by our marriage, not even the freedom to bed who you choose. But my life will be upended. I will be forced to run your household—'

'Forced? Now see here…'

She held up a hand, ignoring his interruption. 'I will raise your children and ignore your infidelities. In exchange, you will offer me the love and affection you always have: that of a friend. A cousin. A brother. It will never be more than that. I would rather live and die alone than settle for such cold comfort. And I could not bear it after…'

She stopped, suddenly close to tears. Then she gained control again and forced a bright smile. 'Let us just say we do not suit and pretend that this interview never happened.'

'The devil we will,' he said, leaning forward in his seat. 'Tell me who made you cry and I will see to it that he pays for each tear you've shed over him.'

'It was nothing,' she said hurriedly. But the blush on her cheek proved him right. The nothing involved a man.

'Did this *nothing* take advantage of you? Because it he did…'

'Certainly not,' she said, eager to calm him. 'It was my fault for misunderstanding the situation. It is obvious that I was more deeply engaged than he. I had no right to expect…' And there was the glint of a tear again.

'Who is it?' he said, rising up out of his chair. 'Tell

me his name and you will have an offer out of him by week's end.'

'That would be quite impossible,' she said, her smile turning brittle. 'He is marrying another, just after the holidays.'

He searched his memory for the smattering of engagements announced in *The Times.* 'You do not mean that little weasel, Cyril Fosberry.' James dropped back into his chair in surprise.

'Do not say such things about the man I love.' There was no hesitation now, no doubt at all. She had rushed to his defence without another thought.

'You love him.' He could not decide whether his words should be a statement, or an incredulous question. Of all the people he had imagined his cousin choosing, he'd never have thought of Cyril Fosberry. Though he had a decent fortune, Fosberry was by all other measures a disappointment. He was barely taller than Beatrice herself, with watery eyes and hair that had already begun to thin. In temperament, he was the sort of man a woman described as 'sensitive' and a man called weak. 'Cyril Fosberry,' he repeated, shaking his head again.

'What I feel for him is neither here nor there,' Bea said with a glare. 'And what you feel about him is even less important.' Then she sighed. 'He offered for someone else. She accepted. He is lost to me.'

In his opinion, it was not so much a loss as a narrow escape. But the truth made it no easier on his broken-hearted cousin. 'If he preferred someone else, there is nothing to be done,' he said, as gently as possible.

'But that is the trouble,' she said, furrowing her brow. 'I do not think he preferred her at all. I think he was tricked into making a proposal.' She reached into her pocket and produced a letter.

James read the brief note, which was embarrassingly tear stained and limp from rereading. 'He says that honour requires he marry another, but that his heart is yours for ever.' He frowned, trying and failing to remember the name in the announcement. 'And who is this Jezebel that has taken him from you?'

'Faith Strickland.'

The letter made perfect sense if the eldest Miss Strickland was the reason it had been written. If James had had to choose the sort of girl most likely to trick an unsuspecting fellow into an engagement, her name would have been top of his list. There was something about her that put him instantly on his guard. When they'd first spied each other across a crowded ballroom, she'd smiled and blushed like any other young maiden. Then, she'd looked to the very core of him like a general assessing strengths and weaknesses of the enemy before an attack.

If Fosberry was too foolish to protect himself from such a predatory female, he deserved to be trapped. Now that she had him, she would run roughshod, organising his life to suit herself while convincing him that it was all for the best.

But the divine justice of such a match did nothing to lessen his cousin's pain. 'Tell me what you know of this sudden engagement,' James said.

'There were rumours that he was caught alone with her in a compromising position,' she said and frowned. 'If anyone was going to be compromised by Cyril, it should have been me. Instead, I let him treat me with complete respect.'

'The bounder,' James agreed.

'You cannot imagine what a nuisance virtue is, until it comes between you and happiness.'

'You are right. I cannot.' He had never wasted a moment allowing virtue to come between him and what he wanted, and took the moment to thank God that he had been born male and above such problems. He tapped the folded letter against his leg. 'It was most unfair of her to take advantage of his innocence. In fact, it would serve Miss Strickland right if she got what she deserved for her tricks and was abandoned at the altar.'

'He would never do such a thing,' Bea assured him. 'He is too good. Too kind.'

And in James's opinion, far too stupid to do the thing that would make him happy. He sighed. 'If he will not, then I shall have to do it for him.'

Her eyes grew wide with surprise, then narrowed again with speculation. 'And how would you do that?'

'I do not know, as yet. But if the lover's knot was hurriedly tied, I suspect it can be undone just as quickly.'

'Perhaps, if he is free…' She gave another deep sigh, but this one was full of romantic longing.

'There is no perhaps about it,' James said, with a determined nod. 'If you really want Cyril Fosberry, you shall have him, wrapped in paper and tied with a bow.'

'You would do that for me?' Unable to contain herself, she threw her arms about his neck and kissed his cheek.

He carefully disentangled himself, still aghast at her choice, but resigned. 'It is Christmastide, Beatrice. And you, my most favourite of cousins, will have your heart's desire as a gift from me.'

Chapter Two

'This has been the best Christmas in years. Holly and ivy from the attic to the cellar, kissing boughs in all the rooms.' The Dowager Countess of Comstock smiled at her three granddaughters in childlike glee. 'And the Yule log is big enough to last the whole season.'

Judging by the sleet hitting the front windows, the log in the fireplace was less a holiday tradition than a sensible way to bring some much needed warmth to the ageing pile of stone that had been their home. Despite the fact, Faith Strickland replied with a dutiful, 'Yes, Grandmother.'

'I have never seen the house looking so grand,' the old woman continued.

'I am glad you are enjoying it,' Faith said, adding a forced smile. It had been the best Christmas in years, because it was the first since Grandfather had died that she'd felt confident in risking the money on frivolity. God bless Cyril Fosberry, the founder of the feast.

'All the guests have complimented me on the food. They were amazed that a goose so large could be so tender. And the pudding?' The Dowager made a faint kissing noise, as if she could still taste it, over a week later. 'For tomorrow, Cook has made a Twelfth Night cake. We will choose a king and queen, and we shall all put on fancy dress and playact their subjects.'

'I am sure it will be delightful,' the youngest sister, Charity, said in a tone that implied the last thing on earth she wanted to do was play parlour games.

'It shall be so much fun,' Faith said with more enthusiasm and followed her words with a sharp elbow to her youngest sister's ribs.

'I am looking forward to it,' Charity said with forced cheer, glaring at her as she rubbed her side.

'This will end in tears,' the middle sister, Hope, whispered in a tone that would not carry to their grandmother.

'I do not see why it should,' Faith muttered through clenched teeth, keeping the bright smile pasted over her doubts. It was hardly fair that her pessimistic sister could not manage to show appreciation for the sacrifice that was being made, since it was done primarily for her benefit.

'Cyril really is the most generous of men,' Faith added. 'When I explain our situation, I am sure he will pay for the repairs on the dower house and arrange for a Season in London for you as well.'

From her other side, Charity cleared her throat.

'Seasons for both of you,' Faith corrected. On her

list of priorities, a come out for Charity ranked well below retrieving the silver candlesticks and family jewels from the Lombard merchants. No amount of money could turn her too-smart little sister into the sort of biddable miss that men wished to marry.

'But if you are forced to accept Cyril Fosberry to accomplish it…' Hope gave a doubtful shake of her head.

'No one is forcing me to take Cyril,' Faith assured her. 'In fact, you should have expected this. You knew it was my plan to marry by year's end.'

'The wedding is in January,' Charity pointed out. 'So, technically…'

'Do not quibble over a few weeks,' Faith interrupted.

'And Cyril only offered for you because you tricked him into it,' Hope added.

'I did nothing of the kind,' Faith whispered, looking around to be sure that Grandmother could not hear them conversing.

Hope raised an eyebrow. 'After ignoring you for the whole of the year, Cyril's interest came out of nowhere.'

'Not nowhere,' Charity announced. 'It came out of the drawing room at Lady Gransby's winter ball. And how you managed to find a corner empty enough to compromise your virtue was beyond me. The place was a rout.'

'He agreed to help me search for the two of you. I cannot help what happened after,' Faith said, hoping that their parents in Heaven were not listening, for they would be disappointed with her for lying.

'You cannot help that you just happened to stumble into his arms at the precise moment that Lady Gransby opened the door,' Charity finished.

'I could not help it,' Faith repeated, thinking of the letter that was hidden in her bedside table. It had been wrong of her to open Grandmother's mail. But it had been even worse that the old woman had been concealing that lawyers and men of business for the new Earl would be arriving in a few weeks to review the accounts and inventory the house. They needed money and quickly. Since the Season had ended without an offer got by conventional means, she'd had no choice but to take matters into her own hands.

Hope glanced in the direction of Faith's erstwhile fiancé. 'Look at the poor man. It is clear he has regrets.'

She was right. Cyril was staring out the window of the sitting room like a dog waiting for his master to return. She glared at him, wishing he could at least pretend to enjoy the party, since it was thrown in his honour. 'If he did not want to marry me, then he should not have made the offer. He had but to announce that it was all an innocent mistake and I'd have agreed with him.'

'Perhaps he'd have had a chance, if you had not begun to cry,' Charity said.

'I was overwrought,' she replied. That, at least, was true. It was only natural to be upset when one learned that a distant relative was about to arrive who might turn them all into the street and send Grandmother to prison for pawning the entail.

Hope responded with an unladylike snort of contempt.

'We all have regrets at one time or other,' Faith said, staring at Cyril. 'But that does not mean our marriage will not be satisfactory.' She raised her chin in defiance. 'I mean to be a good wife for him. The best wife that he could hope for. I will organise his household, put rein to his scattershot method of living and see that he lacks for no comfort. I will be affectionate and giving, and he shall have nearly as much freedom as he had before marriage. He shall have no right to complain.'

'In other words, you mean to have him out from under foot. You do not crave his company any more than he wants yours.' Charity assessed too accurately the way Faith suspected it would be.

'My future is not your concern,' she said. 'One of us had to get married and see to the welfare of the others.'

'Or two,' reminded Hope.

'Or three,' Charity finished. 'I wish the pair of you would not look at me as if I am not just hopeless, but too ignorant to understand what you are thinking. I have no desire to be anyone's beloved spinster aunt.'

'Of course not, dear,' Faith corrected. 'We all will get married. But one of us must be first, and after two Seasons without an offer, it is high time that it be me.'

You are the oldest. Look after them.

It had been almost ten years, but her mother's final words still echoed in Faith's head. It was Faith's job to care for her sisters. If that meant marrying Cyril, it was a small price to pay.

Their conversation was interrupted by a sudden blast of frigid air, cut short by the slam of the front door.

'Who can that be?' Hope muttered. 'I thought all the guests had arrived before Christmas.'

'All of them that I invited,' Faith said and turned to see the excited expression on her grandmother's face.

'He has come after all,' the old woman said, rushing to the entrance hall.

'Hell's teeth, but it is cold out there!' The exclamation was loud enough to be heard halfway down the hall. Faith turned to follow her grandmother, trying to pretend that the chill running down her spine had anything to do with the winter weather.

She arrived at the front door to see a tall man shaking snowflakes from the capes of his great coat and stomping his booted feet to remove the slush. None of the gentlemen she'd invited would favour such a dashing Garrick. Nor would any of them have entered the house on a curse.

Then the fellow handed his hat to a servant, pulled his muffler aside with a flourish and bowed to her grandmother, smiling. 'Pardon the language, my dear, dear woman. The cold has quite frozen the manners out of me.'

'James Leggett,' Faith whispered, unable to contain her shocked announcement.

'A cup of lambswool will put you to rights again,' the Dowager replied with a blush and a titter as if there was nothing the least bit ironic in offering such an innocently named drink to the biggest wolf in London.

'Is the cider pressed from your own orchard?' Even when greeting an old woman, he had a smile that could warm a January night. 'How could I refuse?'

What was he doing here? There was no reason for him to celebrate her engagement. Faith had made certain, for the sake of all their reputations, that neither she, nor her sisters, had ever made his acquaintance. If nice girls wished to remain nice, they did not spend time in the company of Mr Leggett.

But Grandmother was long past such qualms. She was fussing over the man, offering him drinks and brushing his lapels as if she could not resist the chance to touch him.

Some rebellious part of Faith could not blame her. He might be a rake, but he had the face of an angel. Though he seemed to be at the centre of half the scandals in London, there was no hint of dissipation about him. His dress was immaculate, always the first stare of fashion, but stopping just short of dandification. He wore his blond hair a trifle too long to be proper. It was not really unkempt, but had a tendency to fall into his eyes in a way that made one want to reach out to straighten it for him, perhaps trailing a finger along a cheek that was soft as a lover's kiss. His eyes were the blue of a cloudless night sky and twinkled with forbidden knowledge instead of stars.

And his lips...

When she had first noticed them, months ago, she had been transfixed, near to staring at the beauty of him as one might admire a sculpture. But she had given extra attention to those perfect lips. She was not the first young lady who lost her train of thought at the sight of that too-mobile mouth with its almost feminine fullness.

Then, as if he truly was the dangerous animal he seemed, he had sensed her staring and turned to look at her, curling them into a seductive smile.

As if she had no will of her own, she'd taken a step toward him. Only one. But then, every path to sin began with a single step. Before she could take another, she'd locked her knees to keep them from quaking, turned her face from his and held her fan high to hide the blush on her cheek. For the rest of the evening, she made sure to keep the width of the ballroom between them. Then, she had informed her sisters that they were to refuse any offered introductions.

Though she wanted to believe it was to protect them, there was some small amount of jealousy in it as well. Suppose he met them and preferred one of them to her? Not that it mattered. The sort of offer made by a man like James Leggett would never involve marriage and she could not afford to settle for less.

Then, she had met the honourable, trustworthy and

utterly boring Mr Fosberry. He was the sort of man who would care for her and her family, and never go back on his promise to her once it was made, no matter how much he might want to. It was the only choice she could have made.

And now, her perfectly sensible plans were in jeopardy. Though she had done her best to resist him, the devil had appeared in her home, summoned by her own grandmother, who was treating him as an old family friend. 'I have saved the Tudor suite for you. It is said that Henry the Eighth himself stayed there.' Grandmother giggled again. 'Although he brought none of his wives, I doubt he slept alone.'

Mr Leggett gave a bark of laughter. 'A man after my own heart, my dear Countess.'

Faith had tried to put a guest there, just last night, but Grandmother had said the room needed airing. Which meant she had invited this scoundrel and said no more of it than she had their impending financial ruin. Now, he was proceeding up the stairs to the grandest of the manor's bedrooms as if he was a king himself.

Once he was out of earshot she rushed to her grandmother's side and grabbed the poor woman by the shoulders, resisting the unfair desire to shake her until an answer fell out. 'What is he doing here?'

'He expressed an interest,' the Dowager said with a proud smile. 'In his letter of congratulation on your engagement, he was positively angling for an invitation. So, of course...'

'You invited him,' she said with a sigh.

'Can you imagine that? Mr James Leggett, expressing an interest in us.'

'He does not know me,' Faith insisted. 'Why should he offer congratulations?

Grandmother continued as if she had not heard. 'He is every bit as fashionable as Beau Brummell and as dangerous as Byron.'

'That is nothing to brag about. You are the widow of the Earl of Comstock. He should be the one honoured by your invitation.'

'You are far too staid for one so young,' her grandmother replied. 'When I was your age, I would have been all agog to spend time at a house party with such a handsome man.'

'Not if the house party was held to celebrate your engagement.'

'Perhaps you are engaged, but your two sisters are still unencumbered,' she replied, her eyes twinkling. 'And Mr Leggett is very well off.'

Dear God, no.

Mother had charged her to care of her sisters because, even near death, Mother had known that Grandmother was too flighty to guide the three of them to a safe future. Now, it seemed she would risk their honour rather than admit the trouble she had caused and the money that would be needed to fix it. 'Mr Leggett is not suitable for any of us,' Faith whispered urgently.

'Why ever not?'

'He is a rake.'

'I know from experience that rakes make the best husbands,' her grandmother said with a knowing grin. 'Your grandfather was quite the rogue, in his day.'

If the conversation was not turned immediately, Faith would likely be rewarded with another unwelcome story on the looser morals in the early reign of good King George. She was far more interested in the answer to a question Grandmother was too awestruck to ask.

'That explains why you invited him. But why did he want to be here?' She could see no benefit for him in attending an out-of-the-way house party full of virtual strangers.

'If it is not to wish you well, then I have no idea,' she replied. 'Why don't you ask him?'

Chapter Three

As James followed a footman up the stairs to the bed-room assigned to him, he heard the patter of a woman's slippers on the marble stairs behind him. Was it possible for a lady to walk angrily? Even knowing nothing about her, he was sure it was Faith Strickland, upset by his sudden appearance and ready to tell him off. Such irrational anger made him all the more certain that she had gained her engagement by trickery. Someone who was secure and happy in her choice had no reason to be upset by one surprise visitor.

'Cuthbert!' Had he ever heard her voice before? It was deep for a woman, and surprisingly sweet, even when issuing a command to the footman beside him.

The boy turned. 'Miss?'

'You may return to the main floor. I will show Mr Leggett to his bedroom.'

There was an awkward pause as all three of them questioned the propriety of the statement before she hastily corrected it. 'To his *room*.'

'Of course, miss.' The servant evaporated from his side and he turned to face the angry woman who had remained.

'Miss Strickland.' He had seen her flustered by his smile before. Tonight, he used it on her to full effect.

She reacted with a slight intake of breath and a tiny shudder before she could regain control and offer a cool nod and a distant smile. 'Mr Leggett.'

'May I take the opportunity to offer my congratulations on your impending marriage?'

'I see no way to avoid accepting them, since you have already spoken,' she replied. 'But it surprises me that you would come all the way to Staffordshire to do so. We have not, as yet, been introduced.'

'But I am a friend of your grandmother and a guest in your home,' he said. 'At this point, the lack of formality can be forgiven, can it not?'

'Grandmother has never mentioned your acquaintance before,' she said, her voice still sweet, but her eyes narrowing.

'There are those who would say the same of your acquaintance with Cyril Fosberry,' he responded and saw her flinch. 'But that proves that none of us know all the details of another's life,' he added with another innocent smile.

She relaxed, but not completely. Now her eyes were not so much narrowed as hooded. The half-closed lids gave them a sleepily seductive quality that was quite pleasant to look upon. 'While it is true that you know nothing of my engagement beyond its existence, the details of your life are common knowledge. The many duels you have fought, for example.'

'Three is not so many,' he said with a shrug.

'It is more than is seemly,' she replied in a prim tone. 'Ladies were involved, I think.'

'They often are,' he said.

Now, her smile was spoiled by the mocking quality he had always assumed he would find beneath her outwardly sweet nature. 'And in each of them, you were the one to give offence.'

'Some people are easily offended,' he agreed. 'But my insults could not have been too great. I am still alive.'

'And unmarried,' she said.

'Not all of us are as fortunate in the marriage mart as Mr Fosberry.' He leaned against the wall beside the door to his room and admired her. Perhaps, in some ways, Cyril was lucky. She was almost too pretty, with sleek, dark hair that a man longed to touch and large, almond eyes that were the green of an Irish meadow. But, as usual, their focus was a little too intuitive. But then, she'd always struck him as a little too...everything. She certainly seemed more intelligent than a pretty, young girl ought to be.

'Have you come here, hoping to change your fortune?' At the sound of her words, something in him vibrated like a chord struck on a harp.

Yes.

'My fortune?' He touched his own breast, surprised to feel the irregular thumping of his heart.

'Why are you really here?' she asked, watching him carefully for a sign of the truth. Had the breathy quality of her question been meant to arouse him? Or was she really unaware of how easy it was to turn a man's head with the right word or two?

'I have come to celebrate your engagement, of course.'

She gave him the sort of nod that said yes, but meant no. 'If your reputation is to be believed, I think it is far more likely that you are here to cause trouble.'

'My reputation? So much idle gossip.' He tutted. 'It disappoints me that you would listen to it.'

'Until I have your word of honour that you mean no harm, gossip is all I have to rely on.'

And there was that almost unattractive good sense, hiding like steel under the velvet of her voice. Since he'd suspected it was there all along, he had no right to be disappointed when it appeared. In response, he shrugged. 'Very well. You do not trust me. I must use the opportunity of this visit to prove you wrong.'

She gave a sigh of relief, as if they were finally on solid ground and speaking plainly. 'You may do so by staying away from my sisters.'

'Of course,' he replied. 'They are lovely girls, of course. But I can honestly say that I have no designs on them.'

Her contentment dissipated as quickly as it had come. 'And the other ladies of the party,' she added, 'will you leave them alone as well?'

He touched a finger to his chin, considering. 'How can I decide, until I know who is here?'

She crossed her arms, tired of playing nice. 'It should not matter who is here. I do not want you sneaking through the halls after decent people have retired, looking for a lady's bedroom.' She gave him another pointed look. 'Married or unmarried.'

So she thought he might be carrying on an affair? Clever. But wrong. 'Looking for guest rooms? No, I shan't be doing that,' he said, surprised that it was so easy to be truthful about his intentions.

'Not even, God save us, if a woman requests your company?'

'I shall not allow myself to be seduced by any of your guests.' He laid a hand on his heart, which still beat like a trip hammer. 'I give you my word.'

'Well, that is good to know.' Clearly, she was not satisfied, but she had run out of questions to ask him.

'It is my pleasure to set your mind at ease,' he said. She was gnawing her lip now, trying to decide what it was she had forgotten. Worrying at it made her mouth plump, kissable. The sight of those lips made his true plan all the more pleasant to contemplate.

But as he watched her, so she watched him. Slowly, she became aware of his interest and aware of *him* in the pure, animalistic way that women and men knew each other when they put aside the constraints of society and followed their true desires.

Her confusion changed suddenly to realisation and she gasped in alarm. 'I... I am glad we understand each other.' She was struggling for composure. But he watched as the blush on her cheeks crept down her throat to the lush swell of her breasts at the neckline of her gown. He smiled as he imagined it travelling all the way to her toes and over all the delightful places along the way.

She clapped a hand over her bosom as if that would be enough to stop his imagination and said, in a tone too husky to be proper. 'Good evening, Mr Leggett.'

Then she turned and ran for the stairs.

He is here for you.

Faith slowed her pace as she came down the last few steps. If she did not want to incite gossip, then the other guests must not see her running in panic from the bedroom of a rake. There was nothing to escape from, after all. They'd had a brief conversation in the hallway. Nothing more than that.

He is here for you.

If he was not, then why did it feel as if, with each hurried step, her heart dropped to the floor, bounced and returned to its proper place? Just as it had been on the first night she'd seen him, something had passed between them that was beyond words.

She could find no reason for it. Other than that one glance, months ago, they'd had no interaction. It had lasted only a moment, but to her it had seemed to last for ever. He must have sensed it as well. She was meant for him. And now, he had come to claim what was due him.

But that could not be true. If he had felt anything, why had he waited? More importantly, why had he waited until now, when it was too late?

Because his intentions were not honourable.

She cursed her own pragmatism for not allowing even a few minutes of fantasy. He was not here to rescue her from her mistake. He was here to take advantage of her, simply because he knew he could.

More importantly, she was not making a mistake. She was marrying a good, kind, stolid…

She paused, trying to decide if that word was a compliment or an insult. It made Cyril sound dull. And he was not. Or if he was, the flaw was not in his character, but in her unreasonable expectations.

At the moment, he was the only person who could protect her from the dangerously exciting man who had appeared on her doorstep.

'Cyril.' She stepped forward into the small salon, where he was still staring pensively out the window. She went to his side and linked her arm in his, smiling up at him with all the adoration she could muster.

'Yes, dear?' He did not smile in return, but neither did he frown.

'Are you enjoying the party?'

'Your grandmother's hospitality is beyond measure,' he replied. 'My Aunt Hortensia was particularly taken with the sugar plums last night and vows she must get the recipe to take back to her cook.'

'It is the mace that makes them special,' she agreed. 'And just a touch of good, French brandy.' What did it mean that they were reduced to sharing recipes to evade the truth? He had avoided answering the question that had been put to him.

He nodded, as if the information truly interested him, but she was sure it did not. Like the good man he was, he was willing to stand by his decision to marry her, even though it was clear that he did not want to.

It made her feel all the worse for having trapped him into it. She owed him so much for his sacrifice that she must find some way to make it better. She tugged on his arm again, until he could not help but turn and look into her eyes. 'It is good that your aunt is enjoying herself here. But you will tell me if there is anything that you would particularly enjoy, won't you? I want nothing more in the world than to make you happy.'

'That is most kind of you,' he said, managing a faint smile.

It would almost be better if he were angry. If he raged at her, she might be able to placate him with tears. Or perhaps she could offer what it was that she suspected Mr Leggett had wanted from her, just a few minutes ago. It would not be so very wrong to succumb if they were to be married in two weeks. And once they had shared the marital act, there would surely be an unbreakable bond of affection between them that would exceed anything that James Leggett might offer.

She glanced behind them to be sure that they were alone in the room. Then, she took a deep breath and leaned into him until her breast brushed against the sleeve of his coat. 'I am looking forward to our wedding.' She changed the timbre of her voice to blatant invitation. 'And our wedding night.'

In response, he withdrew to a respectful distance and gave her a gentle pat on the arm. 'That day is still a fortnight off. Let us not spoil things by rash behaviour.' Then he turned towards the door, listening for voices. 'Shall we go and join the others? I think they are having games in the sitting room. We do not want to miss the fun.'

'Yes, Cyril.' She followed after, amazed that it could be so lonely to be one half of a couple.

Chapter Four

After a change of linen, James returned to the ground floor to join the other guests for sherry and parlour games. There was an apple bob in the entrance hall, kept well away from the dark corner where the braver souls played snap dragon, snatching raisins from a burning bowl of brandy. He had enjoyed both, many times in the past. But the absence of Miss Strickland rendered those entertainments counterproductive.

He found her, along with the morose Mr Fosberry, in the sitting room leading a game of blind man's buff. It was an ideal pastime, if one sought uncensored physical contact with young ladies. One had but to allow oneself to be caught and then see to it that the blindfold slipped enough to provide a glimpse of the right girl.

But perhaps Cyril did not understand the point of it. When it was his turn to be blind, he fumbled about the room, arms held stiffly in front of him, finding no one despite numerous hints.

When it was clear that he could not find her amongst the laughing crowd that surrounded him, his fiancée stepped directly into his path and announced, 'Well done, Cyril. You are getting warmer all the time. Continue forward.'

Perhaps he was deaf as well as blind. Or perhaps it was not possible for such a cold fish to get warmer. Though he was almost upon her, he veered suddenly to the left and walked into James with enough force to take the wind from him.

'Sorry, Leggett,' he said, yanking the handkerchief from his face and looking not so much sorry as relieved. 'Your turn, old man.'

Before he could even catch his breath, Cyril was behind him, making a great show of tying a tight knot. But in actuality he left the scarf loose enough that James might clear a sliver of vision with a simple shake of the head.

'Thanks, my good fellow,' he muttered in return.

'My pleasure,' Cyril whispered back, spinning him with force, three times around.

When the confusion was done, James stood for a moment, trying to get his bearings and gain some understanding of what had just happened. The other man clearly knew the purpose of the game. He simply hadn't wanted to catch the one woman in the room who was his proper partner. Though James had not thought much of Bea's choice, he felt a certain sympathy for the poor fellow tonight. He was not so stupid that he did not know he was being tricked into marriage. And though he was doing his best, he could not manage much affection for the trickster. To set the man free would be doing him a service. James gave a cough and a nod to adjust the blindfold, then proclaimed, 'Ready or not, here I come.'

The group around him shifted, trying to make a capture difficult.

He stared down his own nose at boots and skirts, sorting men from women, and gave a few experimental swipes at empty air to make the threat credible. This was rewarded with a smattering of female giggles, most of them silvery soprano and nothing like the throaty alto of his true quarry.

There was a breath of wind as someone rushed from one side of the circle to the other. By the hint of lilac cologne she left in her wake, he assumed it was Miss Hope. She was nearly as pretty as her sister, with chestnut hair and sherry-coloured eyes. In other circumstances, he'd have been happy to make an apprehension. But tonight, he had other plans.

Faith Strickland was easy to find in the crowd, even without peeking past the handkerchief. In a swarm of female laughter and masculine shouts of encouragement, there was an island of silence. She stood as still as a rabbit hiding from a fox, afraid that a single breath might be enough to alert him to her presence.

He made a few more feints toward the other players before making the final lunge that would catch her. But when his hands were within inches of their goal, there was a sudden flurry of activity and an annoyed cry of 'Faith!' The party laughed as his hands closed on the shoulders of a woman and a strange hard object that came between them as he hugged her close.

He released her and pulled the blindfold off to see an annoyed Miss Charity, clutching the book she had been reading when her sister had forced her into the game.

How desperate was she to avoid him that Faith would offer the girl in her stead, after forbidding contact with her just an hour ago? It did not matter. Now, he would make her regret it. 'Miss Charity? What a pleasant surprise.' Then he gave her the sort of smile that would set any young girl to blushing.

'A surprise to us both,' she said in a dry tone, unmoved by his flirting.

Out of the corner of his eye, he could see it was having an effect on someone. Miss Strickland was livid at the attention he was paying to her little sister.

He smiled back at her and gave an innocent shrug to remind her that he had been abiding by her rules until she had forced this interaction upon him.

Miss Charity was backing away from him, ready to return to her reading. But he took her hand again and prised it from her arms. 'Come, Miss Charity, do not be so shy.' He set the book on the mantel. 'It is your turn to be Blind Man.'

In his experience, the youngest daughters in families were often neglected by both their sisters and the gentlemen courting them. These girls were the ones most in need of a little gentle flattery to break them from their shells. But by the irritated look she was giving him, it was Charity who had been neglecting the party and not the other way around. She sighed. 'If I must. Let us get this over with.'

She turned her back to him so he could tie the blindfold. Then he spun her three times around and gave her a gentle push in the direction of a young man on the opposite side of the room.

His encouragement resulted in none of the giggling he was accustomed to from other young women her age. Instead, Charity was facing the game with the sort of deadly focus he expected from a man picking his way through a bog who feared that one wrong step would result in disaster. She paused, like a hound scenting the air. Then she walked in a steady pace towards her oldest sister, tapped the girl once on the shoulder and removed the blindfold.

Faith looked at her with unconstrained frustration. 'You could have found someone more appropriate.'

'I could,' Charity agreed. 'But I found you, since I know that you enjoy this game far more than I.' She handed the blindfold to her sister, took her book down from the mantel and retreated to a chair in the corner that was well out of the way of the festivities.

James resisted the urge to shake his head in amazement. Perhaps the whole family was peculiar. But at least Miss Charity seemed aware of the fact, though not particularly bothered by it.

Her departure left Miss Strickland standing alone, holding the handkerchief in her hand as if unsure of what to do next. After a moment's pause it became clear that her fiancé had no intention of helping her with it, so James stepped forward, pulling it from her hand. 'Allow me.'

'I really don't...' But her denial was half-hearted, for she must have realised that Fosberry was about to snub her for the second time in an hour.

It served her right. She deserved to suffer for the pain she had caused Beatrice and the lifetime of misery she was inflicting on Fosberry. But James could not help but feel a little sorry for her. He put a gentle hand on her shoulder to turn her away, then tied the handkerchief in place and turned her until she was dizzy.

She swayed on her feet for a moment. Then, without thinking, she reached out to him for support.

A single step forward, and she would stumble into his embrace. What sane man would refuse such a delectable armful? More importantly, allowing it would further his plans. Any intimacy between them might drive a wedge into the cracks already forming in her engagement. Her intended husband might not want to hold her, but he could not be so foolish as to allow her to cling to so disreputable a fellow as James, in plain sight of his family and friends. James had only to do nothing and let the inevitable occur.

Then, against all logic, he planted a hand firmly between her shoulders and shoved her into Fosberry's arms, to the laughter and cheers of the other guests.

And then he went off to find a drink.

Chapter Five

'The thing you are looking for is in the cabinet to your left.'

The sound of the voice, just behind him in in the empty study, caused James to drop the candle he was holding, plunging the room into darkness again. 'Miss Charity?'

He heard soft steps as the girl crossed the rug to open the door to the hall and find another lit candle. He watched as she shut it again, circumnavigating the room to light the sconces. In some families, he might proclaim each daughter prettier than the last. The Stricklands had not been so blessed. Charity's hair was not mahogany or chestnut. It was simply brown. And her eyes were not meadow green or brown as sherry, but that green-brown shade that could not quite decide to be one or the other.

'The cabinet to your left holds the brandy,' she said, paying no attention to his scrutiny. 'The glasses are on the right.'

'How did you know…?'

'Where to find you? Or what you were looking for?' She did not wait for an answer. 'After what happened in the parlour, I suspected you would want a drink and privacy. What could be more private, or more likely to hold the best brandy, than the study of the late Earl of Comstock?'

Impressed, he nodded and helped himself to the liquor, which was just where she said it would be. Then he turned back to her, holding out an empty glass.

'No, thank you,' she said primly. 'It is bad enough that I am alone in a secluded room with you. Should someone discover us, it would be better if you were not plying me with brandy.'

'Men have been forced to offer over less scandalous behaviour than that,' he said and wondered if trapping unsuspecting men into marriage was a family habit.

She smiled as if well aware of what he was hinting at. 'Do not worry. I have no intention of taking advantage of you in the way Faith did Cyril. It was terribly rude of her.' She frowned. 'Of course, so is inviting yourself to other people's parties in an attempt to break their engagements.'

He coughed on his brandy.

She ignored it. 'And good luck to you, Mr Leggett. None of us has been able to dissuade Faith from this foolish union and we had quite given up hope that it could be avoided.'

'What makes you so sure that is my intent?' he asked cautiously, still not sure if he was being tricked.

'Logic,' she replied in a cold, unwavering tone. 'I have not seen you take an interest in either of my sisters for the whole of the Season. If they were your quarry, surely you would not have waited until now to pursue them. Your goal must be Cyril.' She paused to give him a probing look that he found more than a little unnerving. 'I saw no signs of homosexual attraction between the two of you during the game tonight—'

'Good God, woman.'

She ignored his interruption. 'So you must mean to win him for someone else. And though Faith did not notice it, I remember the look on Beatrice Leggett's face when the engagement was announced. Her hopes were clearly dashed, though she has made an effort to pretend they weren't.' She gave him another look. 'She is your cousin, is she not?'

'My favourite cousin,' he corrected. 'Your perspicacity amazes me.'

'Thank you,' she replied without a blush.

'Since you are being so candid, explain to me why your family objects to the match and why your sister is so set upon it. I see no real signs of affection between the two of them.'

She gave him a look that said she could not fathom the level of his foolishness. 'You do understand that, as women, we have no say in politics or finance and exist on the foresight of the men that lead our families?'

He nodded.

'And you must have noticed that my family has no patriarch. I cannot blame my grandparents for not being sensible in the matter. They had three children, all boys. An heir and two spares should have been more than enough. They distributed them in the most traditional manner, as well. Uncle Arthur was trained to take the earldom, Uncle Geoffrey was given a commission, and my own father read for the church.' At this, she rolled her eyes.

'You did not approve of your father's calling?'

She frowned. 'One might be named after a virtue, but it does not magically imbue character. Personally, having seen both parents die while nursing the village through a typhus epidemic, I am quite put off by charity.'

'I can see why you might be,' he agreed.

'Then Geoffrey took a ball at Talavera and Grandpapa and Arthur were lost to age and apoplexy.'

'Leaving you alone,' he finished.

'The Crown is searching for an heir to take the title. There have been rumours of a distant cousin and Hope's plan is to marry the fellow immediately upon his appearance. But that is rather optimistic of her, I think, since there is no guarantee that he will be single. He might be old and miserly and put us out of the house without a care to our future.'

'So Faith decided to marry,' he said.

Charity nodded. 'Grandmama's settlement is not enough to provide for all of us.' She frowned, puzzled.

'In fact, it is rather surprising that she has managed to stretch it as far as she has.'

'Cyril Fosberry has a very nice income,' James agreed.

'He also proved to be exceptionally gullible,' Charity added. 'Although I am sure he prefers to think of himself as honourable. When they were discovered in what appeared to be an embrace, Faith wept.' Charity smiled. 'She really does cry most prettily. It would take a heart of stone to resist her.'

'I will remember that,' James said. More than one woman had accused him of hard-heartedness. While he had been weak this evening, with Charity's help he might steel himself against further mistakes.

'When she got no offers, we all encouraged her to wait one more year to try to find someone better suited to her character.' Charity sighed. 'She would not listen. Of late, she has been in a panic to settle the matter as soon as possible and refuses to listen to reason.'

'What sort of man would suit her?' he asked, surprised to find himself actually curious. But if he wished to mould himself into her undoing, he had best know what it was.

Charity was observing him again, as if she saw something he did not. 'Intelligent. Determined. Ruthless. And wealthy, of course.'

'Ruthless?' he echoed in surprise.

The responding smile was cold. 'After the death of our parents, we all learned that it did not do to be too soft, but she is the worst of the three of us. As the oldest, she tries to be both mother and father to us.'

'That is most admirable,' he said.

Charity sighed. 'In an elder sister? Perhaps. But when it comes to choosing a wife, men do not want women who are too plain spoken, too sensible, or too able to stand on their own two feet. They want girls to flutter and simper, and hang upon their every foolish word.'

'But she is willing to do so for Cyril Fosberry,' he reminded her. 'At least until the knot is tied.'

'I suppose you think her a heartless adventurer,' she said. 'She is merely practical, as all women are forced to be, given the rules of the society in which we live. This is not some shallow disguise to be cast off after the wedding. In exchange for the protection of his name and his income, she fully intends to give up all that is uniquely her and be the woman he wants her to be for the rest of her life.'

He frowned, trying to understand. Ruthlessness did not begin to describe Faith Strickland. While she was willing to trick an innocent man into a marriage that would destroy his happiness, she was also capable of erasing her own nature to appease the fellow that she'd caught, if it had to be done for the good of the other two. 'And this is why your family opposes the marriage?'

'If she would listen, I could give her several solutions to our troubles that would be better than a union of two martyrs,' Charity replied. 'I cannot decide if their marriage will be more tiresome to them, or the people around them. But she will not hear me out. Despite what her name might imply, she has faith in no one but herself.'

'But if someone were to destroy this engagement...'

'Someone like yourself, you mean,' she said, smiling.

'It will quite possibly destroy your sister's good name and leave her unmarriageable,' he warned. 'The scandal might taint your reputation and Hope's as well.' He had not even considered the prospect when setting out on this adventure. What had seemed like the simplest of schemes was growing more complicated by the second.

Charity gave him another enigmatic smile. 'Do not concern yourself over our futures. I have a plan that will provide for us with or without the advent of husbands. Rescue my sister from her bad decision and let me take care of the rest.'

In Faith's opinion, there were two types of homes. In the first, the library was by far the most inviting room in the house, with comfortable chairs and a warm fire. Even if the books were not desirable, one gravitated to such a room, content to read a dog-eared novel. The other type had libraries that were designed more for the comfort of the books than the readers.

The Comstock manor library was the latter: a dark, unpleasant room with hard chairs but a truly excellent selection of books. Efforts had been made to improve it with brighter lamps and better furniture, but there was something about the space that seemed to leech all the joy from the additions as soon as they were made. Though she'd seen to it that the room had been as well decorated for the holidays as the rest of the house, the greens on the mantel were already wilting and the kissing bough was showering the rug with mistletoe berries before a single kiss had been stolen.

Since guests rarely made it past the threshold, it was the perfect place to go when one needed to think in privacy. And after the debacle that had played out in the sitting room, Faith was ready to hide in the darkest corner of it and mourn her lost dignity.

Cyril had spurned her when they were alone and been just as standoffish when in company. The whole point of the game they were playing was to end in the arms of a sweetheart. But he'd chosen Mr Leggett instead of her as a punishment for what had happened the night he'd been forced to offer.

James Leggett's interest in her was just as distressing as Cyril's lack of it. Even though she'd sacrificed her sister to avoid him, he'd still managed to find an excuse to touch her. When he had, she'd enjoyed it far too much. She'd closed her eyes as he'd tied the blindfold and imagined his fingers stroking her hair. His hand had lingered on her shoulder for a moment, before he'd turned her, leaving her confused and breathless and wondering if his kiss would do the same. Then, traitor that she was, she'd reached for him. She had pretended to be unsteady, but it was a lie. She'd wanted him to touch her again, if only for a moment.

Instead, he'd pushed her at Cyril who had been as responsive as a block of wood. By the time she'd been able to remove the blindfold, Mr Leggett had disappeared, leaving her to the man who would share the rest of her life.

Her eyelids prickled and she blinked back the tears. Self-pity was a weakness that she could not afford. Even if he did not want her, Cyril was a decent man who would stand by his offer. There were far worse things than an apathetic husband. Newgate prison, for one.

She was likely being melodramatic. Her grandfather's mysterious heir might be kind and merciful when he discovered that Grandmother had replaced the Comstock diamonds with paste. But kind, merciful gentlemen did not usually order audits and inspections before introducing themselves to their predecessor's widow.

If she could not persuade Cyril to forestall disaster, then seeing at least one of her sisters properly launched and married before it hit would make up for the lack of marital passion in her life.

Since she'd had no experience with romantic love thus far, how did she even know it existed? It was possible that the overwrought emotions described in Minerva novels were just another fiction.

The hall door creaked on its hinges and she slouched in her chair. Perhaps whoever had found the room would get a book and leave without noticing her presence.

'Miss Strickland. What a surprise to find you here, and not at your fiancé's side.'

'We are not married as yet, Mr Leggett.' She straightened. 'My time is still my own.'

'And you choose to spend it alone in a darkened room?'

'I am reading,' she said, hoping that he did not remark on the absence of a book in her lap.

'It is a wonder that you can see the print,' he replied, allowing her the lie.

'There is enough light for one,' she said, hoping he would take the hint and leave her.

'You could at least use a proper candle. Tallow rush lights are no good to read by.'

But they were cheaper than beeswax and she intended to save what few pennies they still had left. 'I am not bothered by them. If you are, there are other, brighter rooms.'

'But none with such good company,' he said, smiling in the dimness. 'Why don't I throw on another log and it will be brighter and more pleasant for both of us.'

'It was quite pleasant enough, before you arrived,' she lied.

He ignored the insult and walked past her to feed the fire, prodding life into the dying embers with the poker. 'So, Miss Strickland, tell me about your intended.'

She was glad that he faced the fireplace, so he could not see her shock at the impertinent request. 'If you were actually here to celebrate our impending marriage, you would already know him.'

'I do know him,' Mr Leggett replied. 'But I do not know the details of your courtship. That is the sort of story that young ladies normally tell, *ad nauseum*, when they finally manage to capture the attention of a man.'

'I did not capture him,' she snapped, then cursed herself for reacting so strongly to what was probably nothing more than a harmless euphemism. 'Nor was there anything about the offer that would make for a good story.'

'You make an unusual couple,' he said, still staring into the fire.

'And just what do you mean by that?'

'Nothing in particular,' he replied without turning. 'Merely making an observation.'

'Well, please stop studying me,' she said, feeling worse than ever.

'Do not worry. I am not,' he said, offering a brief glance in her direction and looking away again.

'But if you insist on conversing with me, you could at least turn around.'

'Which is it to be?' he said, finally turning to give her another innocuous smile. 'Do you wish my attention, or not?'

'I do not…' She stopped. She was not sure what she wanted any more and speaking to James Leggett only made it worse. 'I do not want you to judge me for my engagement to Cyril.'

'How can I help it? You do not love him and he does not love you.' He was leaning back against the mantel, his long legs stretched toward her, a picture of louche indolence. But there was something in his voice that sounded sincerely concerned.

'Love rarely has anything to do with marriage,' she said.

'I am well aware of the fact.' His face was still in shadow, but she could swear she saw a trace of sadness in it.

'There comes a time when one must stop chasing fantasies and see things as they are. We have no money and no other prospects.' It was more honest than she had meant to be, especially with this particular man. 'I am the oldest,' she added.

'Not so very old,' he reminded her.

Perhaps not. But time had run out for her. 'Cyril is a good man. I am content with my choice.'

He snorted. 'Content. When you dreamed of marriage, was that what you hoped for? To be content?'

'It is all I have been able to manage,' she said, rising from the chair because she could no longer stand to see him looking down on her, diminishing her choices. 'Perhaps you cannot imagine it, Mr Leggett, since no one can resist your charms. But there are some of us who are not so lucky. We must seize what opportunity comes and make the best of the results.'

He pushed away from the wall and suddenly he

was both taller and much closer to her. 'If by settling for an opportunity, you mean trapping a near stranger into an engagement with pretend compromise and false tears, then you have succeeded. But do not lie to yourself that it was the only choice you had. If you had been brave enough to speak to him, there was one who might have had you without tricks, or even in spite of them.'

The silence stretched between them as she tried to understand his words. He could not mean what she thought. Even if he did, it had to be a lie. It was nothing more than a trick, as bad or worse than the one he accused her of playing on Cyril. Even if he truly felt something for her, he had no right to raise hopes now that it was too late to act on them.

But when she looked into his eyes, there was some part of him that was as surprised as she was by his admission. She turned away, afraid to look too long, lest she be trapped into believing in him.

He reached out to her, taking her hand and turning her back to face him again. Before she could stop herself, her fingers twined with his, squeezing tight to keep the fragile connection from slipping away.

He sighed and squeezed back, pulling her close as his other hand came up to touch her face. Then, he shook his head, clearly regretting the action even as he leaned forward and kissed her. It was a gentle meeting of mouths, over almost as quickly as it had begun. It was not exactly her first kiss. Who had not been bussed under the mistletoe? But it had never happened, alone in a darkened room, nor had it ever been done with such tenderness.

And it was not enough. It was like taking but a single bite, when the table was set with a feast. She closed her eyes, imagining what might happen next, and felt her lips pucker in invitation.

Then he groaned, as if trying to resist a temptation she should never have offered. She had not really meant to ask for his kiss, had she? But before she could open her eyes and rescind the invitation, he was kissing her again.

He was right. She did not want to settle for a man who could barely stand to touch her. Not if this was what she would be losing. His lips moved easily over hers, coaxing until she parted them. And then, to her surprise, his tongue slipped into her mouth. She had never heard of such a thing, but it must be terribly wicked to feel so good. And it felt even better to kiss him back, teasing his tongue with hers and tasting his mouth.

Best of all, he did not shrink from her as Cyril did. He wanted to touch her. His hands moved on her back as if he wanted to feel every inch of it. Then they reached her waist, then her sides, then travelled up her stomach, not stopping until he was cupping her breasts.

What was she doing? Her fingers were tugging at the tie that held the bodice tight to her body, inviting him to touch her.

He accepted the offer, closing his fingers on her

exposed nipples. The shudders passing through her body were like nothing she'd felt before. But they did not compare to the feeling of his lips as he broke from the kiss and dropped his head to suckle them.

It was wrong. So very wrong. And though she did not know what it was, she was sure there was more to come. Her whole body hummed with anticipation, wanting him. When he offered it to her, she could not accept. Cyril...

Cyril had refused her and would do so again. Even if he claimed the rights of a husband, she doubted he would care for her happiness.

And now, as if he had sensed her realisation, James Leggett pulled away from her, panting, and ran a clawed hand through his hair. When he looked up, his eyes were dark, more black than blue, and bottomless.

She clutched at her gaping dress, if only to keep her hands from reaching out and dragging him back to her.

'I trust that now you understand the folly of your plan,' he said in a voice still rough with lust. 'Fosberry might give you his money. But he will never give you what you truly want.'

'Damn you,' she said, surprised at how easily a curse had come, when she'd never spoken one before. But he deserved it. Her only hope for future happiness had been ignorance of her own desires and he'd taken that away.

'I am likely damned, without your help,' he said

with a smile. 'Save yourself a similar fate. Cry off this farce of an engagement and find a man who will treat you as you should be treated.' Then he pushed past her and left the room without looking back.

Chapter Six

It was probably a good thing that he'd begun this trip on Boxing Day, when his valet was having a well-earned rest. It would have been terribly unfair to put the fellow through the chaos that James was causing on Twelfth Night morning. He'd slept hardly a wink all night, thinking of the incident in the library.

There was one who might have had you without tricks...

He could only hope that she had misconstrued the words, or forgotten them. But as he remembered them, it had sounded very much like he'd been about to make an offer. Over the years, he'd said many things to many different women. But he had never promised even a hint of permanence.

Then Beatrice had proclaimed him too selfish to marry. Perhaps he was. But caring for one's self before others was not such a bad thing. He had only to look at his parents and know that it was better to be alone.

Or at Miss Strickland. She was miserable in her

engagement and would be even more so in marriage. And all because she put devotion to family over common sense. Ruining her would be an act of mercy, much like shooting an injured horse to end its suffering. Better not to marry at all than to spend a lifetime divorced from her own desires.

After kissing her, he had confirmed what he'd always suspected. Faith Strickland had fire in her and was in no need of a wet blanket like Cyril Fosberry to douse the flames. What she needed was James.

The first time he'd seen her, he'd wondered what it would be like to hold her in his arms. Their eyes had met in a fleeting glance across the ballroom and locked for what had felt like an eternity. In that moment, they'd understood each other as if they'd been lovers for a lifetime. He had always assumed that when mating, people were supposed to seek their missing half. Two people who were too much alike were the last two people on the planet who belonged together. But there was something in those emerald-green eyes that was far too familiar.

She must have sensed it as well. She'd made no effort to meet him and they'd studiously avoided each other from that point forward.

Last night's pleasure proved it had been foolish to shun her. If he'd succumbed to temptation and stolen a kiss on their first meeting, the passion for her might have passed out of his system by now.

Or he might have lost his head and married her.

Just the thought of marriage had him packing his

bags, ready to escape into the darkness rather than face the girl again at breakfast. Then he'd remembered the reason for his visit and unpacked again. He could not return to London without Fosberry in tow.

He'd promised an end to tears for Beatrice. Though James did not think much of the fellow, he might be quite all right for Bea. They had similar, gentle natures. And his willingness to stand beside a scheming temptress proved he put a lady's honour ahead of his own happiness. Cyril might be an idiot, but he was Beatrice's idiot.

James had pulled his shirts back out of his valise and refilled the wardrobe. Then he'd sat on the end of the bed, waiting for morning. There would be some awkwardness, when he came down to the table. There almost always was after a romantic interlude. The smouldering glances that passed between lovers or near to lovers were unavoidable. Especially when the woman was as innocent as Faith Strickland. If she had looked close to smitten when they'd met in a ballroom, what would he see in her eyes now that he'd kissed her breasts?

He smiled as the answer to his problem presented itself. If she made a fool of herself over him, Fosberry would notice. It was one thing to repair a lady's reputation when one had damaged it and quite another to allow oneself to be cuckolded by that woman's continual indiscretions with others. Cyril would cry off and James might never have to risk his peace of mind on another liaison.

* * *

When he arrived at the breakfast room, the table was set not just for eggs and kippers, but for the exact scenario that he had wanted. He took a place on the opposite side from Miss Strickland, and let Fosberry occupy a place that was the third point of a lover's triangle down the table from both of them. The fellow had but to look up and get a plain view of anything that passed between them.

After a few moments watching him eat, James was certain that success was assured. Cyril was not one of those gluttons whose eyes never left the plate. He was fully engaged with the diners around him, looking from face to face and following conversation. He would see every blush and stammer.

James filled his plate and beamed across the table at Faith Strickland, then waited for her embarrassed reaction.

It did not come. She was not precisely ignoring him, but she showed no sign of giving his presence any more importance than the other guests.

He would have to help matters along. 'Miss Strickland, may I trouble you for the toast rack?' He added the sort of smile that would make everyone in the room think he was asking for something much more intimate than a piece of dry bread.

'Certainly, Mr Leggett.' She gave him a pleasant smile and passed it across to him. Just a smile. Nothing more. No indication that they meant anything to each other above the level of hostess and guest.

'You are most welcome, Miss Strickland.' He grabbed for it so he might brush her fingertips on the exchange, but she gave no indication of noticing, other than to carefully wipe the hand on her napkin afterwards.

'Did you sleep well, Miss Strickland?' This time he gazed at her as if he'd loved her to exhaustion and wanted the whole room to know it.

Still she did not blush. Her eyes slid slowly from side to side, catching the attention of her neighbours at the table, offering them puzzled smiles as if to ask if they thought Mr Leggett's behaviour was as odd and inappropriate as she did. 'I slept very well. Thank you, Mr Leggett.' She rolled her eyes again and returned to her breakfast.

Cyril glanced between the two of them, not with the jealousy he'd expected, but with a faintly disappointed expression, as if he was actually hoping for a sign of infidelity that did not come.

'Did you sleep well, Mr Leggett?' Miss Hope asked, resting her head on her fists and eagerly awaiting his answer.

'Remove your elbows from the table, Hope,' Faith said, barely looking up.

'Not a wink,' James answered, adding a lovelorn sigh.

'Was it because of a woman?' she whispered.

'Do not ask impertinent questions of the guests,' Faith said, hardly looking up from her plate. But there was still nothing in her face to hint that the conversation was anything other than the common lecturing of an elder to her charge.

'When is it not a woman?' he replied, frustrated by his failure. Perhaps if he tried a more obvious appeal he might be more successful. 'Alas, she does not know what I feel for her.' Then he stared directly at Miss Strickland, devouring each feature with his eyes as though his nourishment depended on the sight of her.

'You must write and tell her, before it is too late,' Hope said, glancing in her sister's direction, silently begging her to look up.

'You must write a *billet doux*,' the Dowager agreed, impervious to the undercurrents. 'Every lady should have at least one of those before she is married.'

Everyone at the table looked sharply at her, unable to believe what they had just heard. Everyone except Faith Strickland, who continued to eat as if nothing had been said.

'Actions speak louder than words,' Charity said, her eyes returning to the book sitting beside her plate.

'But it might be better to not speak all.' Faith's complexion was still the same creamy white it had been when he'd entered the room, and though her tone was censorious, it seemed directed at her sisters and not at him. 'You know it is not appropriate to gossip at table, Hope. I am very disappointed in you.' She glanced down at her empty plate, considering it for a moment before declaring the meal finished. Then she set her napkin to the side and rose to leave.

James rose as well, as did all the men at the table.

He made one last attempt to catch her eye, only to see her turn to Fosberry and smile at him as though they were the only two people in the room.

Her instincts to avoid him had been correct. James Leggett was the most odious person she'd ever met.

Faith walked into the hall, the smile still frozen on her face. Were last night's kisses not torture enough? She would remember them until her dying day and mourn their absence. It grew clearer every minute that Cyril had no such desire for her. After they married, her bed would be as empty as her heart.

But what was James Leggett's purpose in coming to down to breakfast and attempting to embarrass her in front of her family?

'Faith. Wait for me.' Hope was hurrying after her, tugging her arm and glancing toward the morning room, clearly wanting a private conversation.

Faith sighed and followed her, closing the door behind them.

Before she could ask the reason for it, her sister blurted, 'Mr Leggett was flirting with you this morning. And last night as well. While we were playing, I think he was trying to catch you.'

It had been as obvious as she'd thought. If so, there was no point denying it. 'I am well aware of it,' Faith said at last.

'What do you suppose it means?'

'I suppose it means he is an evil man who cannot stand to see people happy,' she said.

'But you are not happy,' Hope said. 'You are miserable.'

'And I will be even more so if I allow him to seduce me.'

Hope laughed triumphantly. 'At last, you admit that you are unhappy.'

Once again, she'd revealed more than she intended. 'Only because everyone is badgering me about a decision that has already been made.'

'But what about Mr Leggett's feelings towards you?'

'He has no feeling, other than lust. If he achieves his goal, he will disappear,' Faith said, wishing it were not the truth.

'But how do you know that?' Hope prodded, gently. 'Suppose he is sincere in his courting of you?'

If he had even a spark of genuine feeling for her, there might be another way. But a man who did as he pleased no matter who was hurt, and would rather duel than apologise, was not likely to display a faithful heart like some sort of Christmas miracle. 'It does not matter,' Faith said, pushing the regret from her mind. 'I am to be married in two weeks.'

'To Cyril,' Hope said, with a disappointed sigh.

'If you are so enamoured of Mr Leggett, then perhaps you…' What was she thinking? She did not want to share him with her sister any more than she had on the first day she'd seen him. 'You should stay away from him. He will play you just as false as he did, I mean, will…'

Hope raised her eyebrows in surprise. 'You admit that the flirtation is mutual?'

'I admit nothing,' Faith said.

'But if you did,' Hope said, 'would you not want to follow your heart?'

'My heart is not what is involved,' Faith said, frowning. When she'd awakened this morning, her limbs were still trembling from the night before. It was as if some part of her had been awakened and would never sleep again.

Hope's eyes widened in interest. 'Tell me more.'

'Certainly not. You are not old enough to think of such things.'

'You are not my mother, you are my sister,' Hope said. 'And only older by a year, at that. If there are things you have learned about what goes on between men and women, then I wish you would tell me what they are, or I am sure to find it for myself in a most inappropriate way.'

'Do not even tease about such a thing,' Faith said sharply. 'I am not sacrificing my future just so you can ruin yourself on the first rake who smiles at you.'

Hope gasped in shock.

Now that the words were out, there was no way to change them. She did not just sound unhappy, she sounded bitter and as if she blamed Hope for her misery. 'I'm so sorry,' she said, aching with the inadequacy of her apology.

'If you are, then you will do what I truly want you to do,' her sister said. 'Do not worry about Mr

Leggett or my precious feelings. We can deal with all that when the rest is settled. But you must cry off your engagement.'

'And ruin all our reputations with the scandal?' Faith said, shaking her head. 'And there are other things you do not know about...' Nor would anyone, if she could only follow through on her plans.

Hope ignored the unfinished sentence and leaned forward to embrace her, kissing her on the cheek as if Faith was the one that needed the protection of an older sister. 'Whatever it is that worries you, we will find a way to survive it. But what happiness will there be for any of us if you marry a man you do not love? You must be honest to Cyril and to yourself. Let him go, Faith. Let him go.'

Chapter Seven

James had more than enough experience with them to consider himself a fair judge of the female sex. But Faith Strickland had to be the most cold-blooded woman in England. Granted, she'd been warm enough in the library, last night. But by her behaviour at breakfast, it had not moved her in any way.

Everyone at the table had all but encouraged him· to seduce her, including her fiancé. Only she stood against it, stubbornly insistent that marriage to a man who did not want her was preferable to spending time with a man who might actually make her happy.

Like so many before her, her tune would change after the wedding. She might act as though he was not good enough for her now, but after experiencing the boredom of the marital bed she would come begging for the things she could have tonight, if she would just unbend long enough to ask for them. It would serve her right if he refused her.

He stopped in the middle of the hallway, surprised

at the nonsense he was thinking. First of all, one did not cut off one's nose to spite one's face and refuse a woman who looked like Faith Strickland, even when angry with her. If she showed any interest, now or in the future, her skirts would be over her head before she could change her mind.

Secondly, he was here to stop the marriage, not punish her for following through on her plans. If he accomplished his mission, she would have no regrets that needed consoling. Bea must have Cyril, whether he bedded Miss Strickland or not.

'Psssst!'

He glanced around for the source of the sound and saw the woman he'd been thinking about waving furiously to him from the half-open door of the library.

He pointed to his breast, feigning surprise. Perhaps she was not so unreachable after all.

She gestured again. When he did not respond, she reached out and took him by the hand, pulling him over the threshold and through before shutting the door behind them.

'You wished to speak to me?' he said, leaning his back against it to block her escape.

'I never want to speak to you again,' she said. 'But right now, contact is unavoidable.'

'You don't want to talk. Very well, then.' He held out his arms to her and waited for her embrace.

'You know it is not that, either.' For a moment, her brow furrowed and her eyes squinted shut, as if mastering her emotions. Then she opened them again and spoke in a desperate whisper. 'I want you to leave me alone.'

'It was you who lured me here, remember?' he said, folding his arms.

'I am not talking about this moment,' she said with a frustrated stamp of her foot. 'I am talking about your being here, in this house. And what happened last night.' Her volume dropped even lower as if afraid to speak of it, even in private. 'We did not know each other. You had no reason to be here. And I certainly did not intend for anything to happen between us. And then, this morning at breakfast...' She stopped and swallowed as if too overwrought to continue.

'You did not seem the least bit bothered by me, when we were at table together,' he reminded her.

'I did not dare show my true feelings. But everyone else knew who you were talking about.' There was a faint colour to her cheeks that had not been there this morning and he flattered himself that he had put it there.

'You have feelings?' he coaxed.

She swallowed again, and whispered, 'I do not want to. But I am human. Of course I feel. But that does not make those feelings wise, or good. There can be nothing more between us, surely you know that.'

She was right, of course. They might have a delightful evening or two. But, devious creature though she might be, she was still an earl's daughter who would expect a proposal to accompany any liberties he took. And he was not some Fosberry who could be tricked into staying with her once the pleasure was done.

'You are probably right,' he agreed at last and reached out a hand and stroked her cheek with his knuckles. 'But it is a shame, is it not?'

She shuddered and closed her eyes before opening them again and moving out of his reach. 'Then you agree that you must go? Because, if you stay, something will happen that we might both regret.'

He imagined her, naked and under him. If something happened, only one of them would regret it and he was not even sure of that. Then he remembered his purpose here, which had nothing to do with bringing pleasure to the lovely Miss Faith. 'Once you give me what I truly want, I promise you will never see me again.'

She frowned again, her green eyes fogging with tears. 'I do not understand.'

'I want you to end your engagement. But not for me,' he added hurriedly. 'Do it for yourself. You deserve happiness. And you will never have that if you marry a man who has no feelings for you.'

'But what will become of my sisters if I cry off?' The first tear spilled down her cheek, like a drop of perfect crystal. 'There was scandal enough when Cyril offered. It will be even worse if I refuse him. And some will think Hope and Charity are just as bad...'

Her lower lip was trembling ever so slightly. He could imagine the feel of it against his mouth, when he offered to kiss away the fear. 'It will be all right,' he said, his breath catching in his throat at the sight of a second tear.

'You know it will not. After seeing you here, the news will travel back to London that I was seduced away from a decent marriage.'

'You did nothing wrong,' he whispered back, trying to ease her doubts.

'It will not matter.' She shook her head and another tear trailed down her fresh, unpowdered cheek. 'Society will judge me and my sisters as well.'

What had he done to the poor girl? What had he done to the whole family? He would be making a family of spinsters in exchange for Bea's happiness.

'And there is so much more wrong. More than you can possibly understand.' She lowered her eyes, deep, green pools shaded by long, black lashes. A few more tears fell.

His own throat tightened at the sight and his hand rose of its own volition to wipe them away. Whatever it was that she made her cry, he would find a way to fix it for her. 'I'm sorry. I did not think…'

'But how can you?' Another tear trickled down her cheek. 'If I do not marry, and quickly, we will all be ruined. If only there had been another offer, from a man who truly wanted me…'

And suddenly, he realised that there was something he could do for her. Something that would leave Cyril free to marry Beatrice. Something that would make her as happy as she deserved to be and preserve the honour of her sisters.

Her sisters.

There was something else he was not thinking of. It clawed at the back of his mind like a trapped rat trying to dig its way free. Something to do with the sister who did not need rescuing. The one who'd told him how easy it might be to trap a man into making a mistake.

Pretty tears.

'Oh, no.' He snatched his hand away and shook the finger still wet from touching her cheek. 'You will not have me as easily as you did Fosberry, crying like a crocodile as you swallow up my freedom.'

The tears stopped just as quickly as they started and the trembling lip became a resolute frown. 'And you will not have *me*, either,' she replied. 'Not that you truly want me.'

'On the contrary,' he said. 'I want you quite desperately. Only a fool would not.'

'For an evening, perhaps. Nothing more than that.' She shook her head in disgust. 'You have been strutting about my home like a peacock with its tail spread, hoping I will forget myself and fall at your feet. But it is quite plain, from your behaviour just now, that you have not a single thought for what will happen once you are gone.'

He had given the future all the thought that was necessary. Once the engagement was broken, Cyril would trot back to Beatrice like a loyal puppy. She would forgive him and be happy again. And James would be equally happy to be free of the disturbing Miss Strickland. 'Once I am gone, things will be as they should have been, until you started meddling with their natural order and insinuating yourself into the lives of men who do not want you.'

Perhaps that had been too harsh. For a moment, she looked as if this assessment of her behaviour had pained her to the point of tears. Then he remembered how easily she could cry and how little truth there was in it. He folded his arms and gave her a dark look to show that it would not work again.

She swallowed and wiped her eyes with the back of her hand. When he looked again, the tears had been replaced with an icy stare. 'Very well, then. If we are being blunt, then I will explain it to you as you have done to me. No matter what you pretend, it is clear by your words just now that you loathe me, almost as much as I loathe you, and all the sheep's eyes in the world will not persuade me to come within ten feet of you.'

'That is fine with me,' he said, before realising that it was not fine at all. It was exactly the opposite of what he needed, if he wished to persuade her to do the sensible thing and cry off. 'But what of poor Mr Fosberry, who has even more reason to hate you?'

She swallowed again and there was a protracted, but tearless silence before she could compose herself enough to speak. 'Ending my engagement will make my life even more difficult than it is. If you honestly expect me to cry off Cyril, then I shall need someone to take his place, to preserve my reputation and assure our future.' She folded her arms, just as he had done. 'Do you have any suggestions?'

His social circle was wide enough to include every marriage-seeking man in London. But looking into those bright green eyes, he could not think of a single one.

She tapped her foot. 'No one? I am not particular. Any name will do.'

Any name would not do. She deserved as much of a chance at happiness as he did. She should not be forced to trade it for financial security.

The blazing eyes narrowed. 'Thank you for confirming what I already knew. No one wants me, Mr Leggett. That is why I was forced to, as you put it, meddle in the natural order. If you have a shred of decency, leave this house immediately and leave me in peace to marry Mr Fosberry. I have made my decision and nothing you say or do shall change my mind.'

Chapter Eight

$\backsim\!\!\backsim\!\!\backsim\!\!\backsim\!\!\backsim$

At dinner that night, Faith stared into her wine glass, trying to avoid the eye of James Leggett without too obviously ignoring him. It was clear that he'd taken nothing from the conversation in the library that morning. He had not left, as she'd requested. And he'd certainly not changed his mind and made her an honourable offer.

It had been foolish of her to hope for one. She had grown quite used to rejection by the time she'd set her cap for Cyril. And she had known in her heart, when she'd cornered him this morning and tried to make him understand the seriousness of her situation, James Leggett would sidestep clear of commitment and reveal his true feelings for her.

She had known it. But that did not mean it did not hurt.

Perhaps she'd have done better without false tears. But it was only responding in kind. When they were alone, he could not decide whether to seduce her or berate her. But now that others were watching, he had the nerve to stare up the table at her, sighing theatrically, bemoaning the heartlessness of women to anyone who would listen.

Was he still hoping to trap her into revealing the indiscretion in the library? Let him try. While she was not exactly the insincere jade he seemed to think, she was at least capable of dissembling to the likes of him. Before he'd kissed her, he'd hinted that he might have feelings for her. But no man who truly cared would speak as he had this morning.

She was doing well, until the end of the meal when the Twelfth cake was carried into the room to the oohs and ahhs of the guests. Even Hope was in awe and she was rarely impressed with anything. The currant-filled cake was frosted a delicate rose and topped with two sugar paste crowns to represent the King and Queen about to be chosen.

With great ceremony, Grandmother raised the silver cake knife and cut the first slice, then plated it to pass down the table. 'Bite carefully,' she said. 'Chew well. Be careful not to swallow the surprises hidden inside.'

Those who were most excited by the game were mashing their slices with their forks, searching for a sign that they might be the honoured guest for the evening. But Faith ate the cake like any other dessert, neither expecting nor caring if she was to be the supposedly lucky lady who would be Queen for a night. Then she felt her fork hit something hard and she scraped the crumbs away to get a look at it.

'All hail, the Queen!' The gentleman next to her

was pointing to the pea on her plate as if she had found a diamond.

She pushed it to the side, more embarrassed than pleased by the congratulations of her friends. Honours, even dubious ones like this, should fall to the guests, not the hostess.

Down the table from her, Mr Leggett bit down hard and winced theatrically. Then, with a delicately raised napkin, he spat into his hand and held out the bean between thumb and forefinger. *'Voila!'* he said and smiled at her as though fate itself had announced them to be a couple.

He raised the bean to his lips again and licked the icing from it, catching a single cake crumb on the tip of his tongue.

She watched it disappear into his mouth, momentarily fascinated with the agility of that tongue. It would do unspeakable things to her, should it touch her again. She had no idea what they were. But there was something in his steady gaze that assured her he knew. In fact, he was thinking of those things right now.

'Congratulations, Leggett,' Cyril said, reaching down the table to give the villain a hearty slap on the back that made him wince and break the connection between them. 'You are King for the evening.'

At the head of the table, Grandmother clapped her hands in childish glee and produced a pair of tinsel crowns from the covered dish at her side, then passed them along.

Faith took hers, perching it carefully on her hair.

Mr Leggett took his as well, setting it on his head at a jaunty angle.

'You will be a most excellent king, Mr Leggett,' Grandmother said, beaming. 'We all must do whatever you say for the rest of the night. Given your reputation, I expect nothing less than complete scandal.'

'I am only too happy to oblige.' He smiled back at her, looking more like a devil than a monarch. 'And my first command for the evening is that we must all kiss our neighbour to the left.'

'Really, Mr Leggett, I must protest,' Faith said, having recently realised how much trouble could start with a single kiss.

But apparently, her guests thought she was the old lady, not her grandmother. Up and down the table, there was laughter, toasting and enthusiastic obedience to the King's command. She turned to the gentleman on her left, the elderly Lord Dewhurst, preparing to explain that he did not need to be bound by such nonsense, only to receive a peck on the cheek.

'Jolly fun,' he said, grinning at her. 'And now, you must kiss me, my dear.' When she hesitated, he added, 'It would do my old heart good.'

'If it will please such an honoured guest,' she said, blushing in embarrassment, and gave him an answering kiss.

He patted her hand. 'There, you see. No harm was done. What happens on Twelfth Night does not need to be discussed again.' He shook his head. 'Young people today worry far too much about propriety. I am sure, should you ask her, your beloved grandmother could tell you stories that would render your curling papers unnecessary.'

She wanted to argue that, since he was not a young lady, he had no idea what chaos might result in flaunting propriety. Nor did her grandmother, who was looking back on a long life and marriage to a titled noble. For all their fine talk, her family had left her with nothing but a level head and a good reputation. She could not afford to lose either of them.

And there, at the end of the table, sat a perfect example of the world's unfairness. Mr Leggett had a fine fortune, a winning smile and no scruples at all.

As he stared in her direction, she felt the air crackle between them. 'And what is a king without…?' Then he turned away and drew a card from the deck of characters that would make up the rest of the game and handed it to Cyril. 'Without a fool. That is the role you will play this evening, my friend.'

It was the sort of direct insult that might have caused another duel, had Cyril been a man of action. Since it was clear he meant to do nothing in response, he would be a laughing stock. 'He is supposed to choose his own card,' Faith said, glaring at Mr Leggett.

He smiled back at her innocently and yet pure evil lay beneath. 'I am the King, remember? He must obey me. And I say, I will make the choice.'

Then Cyril stared back at her with a look every bit as cold as the one she'd given to their supposed King.

'It is all right, my dear. We all know I have played the fool before. What could one more night of it possibly matter?'

Now, all eyes turned to her, speculating over what she had done to make her future husband loathe her so. She could feel her composure beginning to crack. The hurried sip of wine she took did nothing to hide the fact that she was flushed with shame.

'What an excellent sport you are,' Mr Leggett replied to Cyril, breaking the tension in the room. 'I expect you to be my right hand for the evening. Between us, we must see that there is not a scrap of dignity left by the time the clock strikes twelve.'

'But now that we have a court, we must find our subjects.' Grandmother said, pointing to the pack of character cards. 'Hand them round, Mr Leggett, and let us see who we must play. The servants have brought chests of odds and ends to the sitting room so you may all costume yourself accordingly.'

'Sir Carrus Crookback,' Hope groaned. 'Why must I always draw the old man?'

'Because you do it so well,' Charity said. When the deck came to her, she drew a card but refused to reveal it. 'And I shall be Lady Letitia Leave-me-Alone.'

'There is no such character,' Hope replied with a frown.

'Then there should be. If I am needed, I shall be in the library, with a good book.'

'Oh, no, you will not,' Faith said, shooting her sister an icy smile. 'I am the Queen for the night and I say you shall play with the rest of us like a good girl.' She rose and went to her sister, pulling the card from her hand, to display it for all to see. 'Gertrude Gossip.'

Charity gave her a sly smile in return. 'Very well, Faith. But do not complain later if I play the part you set for me. Remember, you asked me to do it.'

The deck proceeded around the table with one guest drawing a drunkard, another a fop. Old Lord Dewhurst drew a young girl with a skipping rope. He laughed so hard at the prospect that, for a moment, Faith forgot what a mess the evening was likely to be.

The other guests were equally enchanted with their parts. They rushed to the sitting room, not wanting to lose a chance at the best costume or prop to fit their roles. Cyril's Aunt Hortensia draped herself in a Spanish shawl and paste tiara to play a comic-opera diva. Lord Dewhurst found a blond wig with long braids and the required skipping rope. Hope combed her own hair forward and tied it beneath her chin for a beard, then hobbled about the room on Grandfather's cane. And, after another arch look at Faith, Charity chose a ridiculously large fan to whisper behind.

From there, the evening degenerated into enjoyable mayhem. As Queen, she was required to do little other than perform the hostess duties she'd been doing since the guests had arrived. But Mr Leggett relished his role as lord of the feast, playfully tormenting each guest in turn. He required headstands of the younger men and made the elder gentleman play the bones and bang spoons on kettles while he danced the ladies around the room in a Polonaise.

To Faith's surprise, Cyril followed him dutifully around all night, wearing a motley cape and cap and bells. Rather than being bothered by the part he had to play, he seemed to revel in it. He juggled fruit from the sideboard and peppered the group with an endless series of riddles. Anyone who was slow to respond was thrashed soundly with a bladder on a stick. He even managed to involve her sisters in innocent fun, pulling Hope's pretend beard and starting ridiculous rumours that Charity was obliged to spread around the room.

When Charity approached her, speaking in the quavering falsetto she'd chosen for her character, Faith smiled and kissed her on the cheek. 'It is about time you made an effort to enjoy the party. You spend too much time alone. It cannot be healthy.'

Charity gave her a pitying look and said, in her normal voice, 'If you had learned to be happy alone, we would all be better off. I have not been participating in these contrived revels because I see no reason to celebrate the enormous mistake you are making.'

If her coldly analytical sister was often annoying, it was because she was so often right. But if it was too late to do anything about a mistake, what was the point of admitting it? 'You must trust me to know what is best for my future,' Faith said. 'For all our futures.'

'And what of Cyril's future?' Charity whispered.

'He may seem unhappy tonight. But he will be

fine,' Faith replied. 'Marriage is a very different thing
for men than it is for women. One wife is much like
another to them.'

'That is what you truly believe?' Charity sighed and
shook her head. 'Then you leave me no choice but to
play the part you would have me do.' She raised her
fan to shield their faces and returned to speaking with
the grating trill of an old woman telling tales. 'My
dear Miss Strickland, I have the most fascinating *on
dit* that you might not have heard. There is a lady in
London whose heart is broken because her true love
has been tricked into marrying another.'

'Wait.' Suddenly, Faith was not so sure she could
enjoy the game.

Her sister ignored her plea to stop. 'Her cousin
has come to the country with the intent of breaking
up the union. Thus far, he's had no success. But he is
making quite a scandal by flirting with the girl who
was offered for. Perhaps—' the fan stopped fluttering and Charity returned to her normal voice '—if the
woman who stole a man who does not belong to her
would release him, everyone might be happy again.'

Faith was glad that the fan was large enough to hide
them both, for she could feel the shameful blush of
the dining room was returning. And this time there
would be no helpful aside from Mr Leggett to save her
from the level gaze of her disapproving sister. 'Who
is she?' she said at last.

'Beatrice Leggett.'

It might have been easier if the wronged woman

was deserving of unhappiness. But though they were barely acquainted, Faith had never heard a bad word about Miss Leggett. She seemed to be just the sort of sweet, honest, generous young lady who deserved a man like Cyril.

And Faith had ruined their lives.

Now Charity was staring at her like a young girl who still trusted that her older sister could do no wrong and waiting for her to answer. Would she still think the same when they were asked to account for the things that Grandmother had stolen and then turned out of the house by their real owner?

Faith closed her eyes and tried to think no further than one day ahead. 'Tomorrow, after the guests have departed, I will speak to Cyril. Perhaps it will save us all some small amount of embarrassment if they read the news of our parting in the papers rather than see-ing it play out before their eyes.'

For the first time in ages, there was nothing the least bit calculating in Charity's answering smile. 'You are doing the right thing, Faith. And do not worry about our future. I have a plan that will solve all our problems.'

'Of course you do, dear. You are right. We will all be fine.' Faith said, absently patting her hand. Crying off would doom them all. But Charity was behaving normally for a change and it would be a pity to spoil it by speaking the truth.

Chapter Nine

After her discussion with Charity, Faith had drunk an unladylike amount of punch and done her best to keep the spirit of the evening. Twelfth Night marked the end of the Christmas season. Tomorrow, the guests would return to their homes and Cyril would return to Beatrice.

And Faith would be free of Mr Leggett, as well. Once the engagement had ended, there would be no reason for him to feign interest in her. As she combed her hair before bed, she tried to be relieved by that one small thing. The girl she saw in her bedroom mirror was pretty enough. But rakes did not marry pretty girls. They ruined them and then they left. The fact that she was disgraced without his help proved how ill equipped she was to tame him.

Behind her, the door to her room opened, spilling candlelight into the darkened hall. James Leggett was lounging against the jamb as though he owned the house. At any moment, another guest might wander by and see him, making things even worse than they already were. 'Come in,' she whispered, rising and turning to face him.

'How kind of you to extend the invitation,' he said, stepping into the room and closing the door behind him.

'Kindness has nothing to do with it,' she said. 'You are forcing me to do so, to avoid embarrassment, just as you forced your way into my party.'

He shrugged. 'Now that I am here, do you really regret my presence so much?'

She did not know what she felt any more. But the minute he learned that she meant to end the engagement, he would be gone from her life. She had but to tell him and he would leave right now. She need never see him again.

Yet she said nothing. She was alone and afraid of the future, and it would good to be wrapped in those strong arms and forget everything, just for a little while. 'I suspect I shall regret it very much in the morning,' she said at last.

He smiled and walked slowly toward her. 'That is a surprisingly honest answer. But I wonder, will you regret what we have done, or will you regret my departure afterwards?'

From the desperate fluttering of her soul, she knew the truth of it. James Leggett was everything she should not want. So, of course, she wanted him with a desire not born of reason. And after, the loss would devastate her. 'The former,' she said, wishing that she could sound more convincing.

He laughed. Now he was close enough to touch her. He reached out and caught a strand of her hair, twirling it around his finger and tugging gently. 'Then it is a shame that you have no choice but to submit to me.'

'I have no choice?'

'I am the King of Twelfth Night. I can think of no better way to use my power than demanding the *droit du seigneur* of the bride-to-be.'

'Twelfth Night is over,' she said. 'It is after midnight.'

'And you are far too sensible for your own good.' His hand snaked around her neck, taking her by the nape and pulling her forward, into his kiss. When his lips met hers it no longer mattered that she had every reason to refuse. She knew she would not. At the first touch, she was lost. His tongue was in her mouth, hot and possessive, stroking into her, melting away the words of refusal. She balled her fists at her side, trying to resist the urge to touch him, to stroke his neck as he was doing to her.

As if to punish her, he pulled away. 'Untie my cravat.'

'I most certainly will not,' she said, struggling for a return to sanity.

'Your lord commands it,' he said with a growl, running a single finger down the length of her spine to settle at the small of her back. Heat pooled where he touched her, sinking through the skin, into the depths of her, and she felt something inside tremble.

'Untie my cravat,' he repeated.

She reached a tentative hand to the knot and tugged. The length of linen unravelled in her hands and fell to the floor.

'Very good,' he replied and his hand cupped her hip, giving it a rewarding squeeze. 'Now kiss my throat.'

This time, she did not hesitate. She kissed eagerly, licking the salt from the hollow at the base of his neck, tracing the cords back to his jaw and nuzzling against the rough places that would be shaved smooth in the morning.

The laugh in his response was as shaky as she felt. 'I've often heard that the most innocent virgins are the most eager pupils,' he mused.

She stopped. 'You do not know?'

The hand on her hip was massaging now. 'Perhaps I have not been as bad as you think. But tonight, I promise, I will not disappoint. Now, remove my coat.' He ran a finger lower, tracing her bottom through the fabric of her nightgown.

She arched against him in surprise, unintentionally grinding her hips into his, and was even more shocked to feel the hard bulge in his trousers pressing against her belly.

'Remove my coat,' he repeated.

Her hands moved from his chest upwards, as if he could control them with a word, smoothing over his collarbones and easing the coat from his shoulders, letting it drop to the floor behind him.

Without warning his hands dropped to catch her legs, scooping her up so she had no choice but to wrap them around his waist and throw her arms around his neck. The skirt of her nightgown rode up, bunching at her waist to leave her naked body pressed to the wool of his breeches. What at first felt shockingly intimate became strangely familiar, as if she had been waiting for ever to feel the warmth of his body pressing hard between her legs.

The fabric rubbed against her with each step he took toward the bed, increasing her arousal until she wanted to beg for release. Her back was pressed against a bedpost now, but his hips continued a relentless advance and retreat that made the place they touched wet and trembling. Then their mouths sealed in another kiss and he took one of her hands and placed it against the flap of his breeches.

She shouldn't. She mustn't. But a driving curiosity wiped away her doubts and she undid buttons and laces and felt something warm and hard pressing against her thigh.

He was lifting her higher and his mouth slid down her throat, following the open neck of her gown to settle on one of her breasts, sucking hard to take the nipple into his mouth.

She struggled briefly against the pleasure, then surrendered to it with a sigh. He was as bad as she'd suspected. And she was as susceptible to him as ever. She gripped his shoulders, pushing at his shirt, eager to feel the heat of his skin against hers.

And there, under her hand, was a puckered scar where the bullet from one of the duels must have marked him. She dropped her head to kiss it, running her tongue along his skin, and heard him hiss in response. 'Did you like that?' she whispered.

'I like everything you do,' he said, sounding surprised. 'I like it when you are angry with me and even better when you are not. And I will like this best of all.' He ran a hand down the length of her leg, making her shudder. Then he reached between them, pressing his manhood to her opening.

'Now tell me and I will know if you lie. Who do you want touching you, Fosberry, or me?'

'You,' she answered, without hesitation.

'Say my name,' he insisted.

'James.' She whispered the word she had not even dared to think.

'Who do you want to belong to, Faith?' His fingers stroked himself and her as well.

'You,' she said. 'You, James,' she repeated, unable to stop the truth as she felt his fingertips pushing into her.

'Who do you want to love you?'

'You. Only you. But...' Was this love? Or was it just a word he used to get what he wanted?

'Don't be afraid,' he whispered. 'I will teach you. It will be an honour.'

The fingers that had been inside her were there

again, pushing, stretching. She did not care if he meant the words or not, as long as she could have more of this feeling.

Then he took his fingers away and she felt both pleasure and pain and sudden, complete fulfilment. As he moved inside her the pain subsided, replaced by a languid gratification. This was why men became rakes and women sold their virtue to become courtesans. To live for the pleasure of the moment, to let all their troubles melt away in heated blood. To feel nothing at all beyond the sudden, urgent rush that tightened all the muscles of her body, and oh, to grip him with arms and legs and with a part of her that she did not know she possessed, as wave after wave crashed inside her in time to his thrusts and groans, and the sudden release.

She relaxed then, feeling her legs slide off his hips to the floor. They were still standing, her back pressed to the bedpost, a pile of clothing at their feet.

She looked to him, watching in fascination when that errant lock of hair fell over his face, as he bent to kiss her neck with enough strength to mark the skin. Then he threw back his head to shake it away and smiled at her.

Hesitantly, she smiled back. It was not just the feel of her breasts pressing against his bare chest that frightened her. He was still inside her. They were still one, but she felt exposed in a way that had nothing to do with her nakedness.

As if sensing her fear, he smiled at her in a way

that was both kind and inviting. 'What did you think of that, my Queen?'

What did she think? She had no words for this feeling. But as he pulled out of her, she could not help a moan of disappointment.

He laughed in response. 'That is what I hoped you would say.' Then, instead of leaving her, he stepped away, nearly stumbling over the breeches that were still about his ankles. He sat on the bed, kicking off his boots and stripping away the last of his clothing.

She could not seem to stop staring, wanting to memorise every inch of him. He was even more beautiful now than he had been fully dressed. Her mouth and her body watered in anticipation, as if hungry to taste him again.

His answering grin was every bit as wicked as she could have hoped. He held out a hand to her. 'The night is young, my Queen. And it is my turn to obey you.'

If only for an hour, he would be her slave. How could she refuse? She left her nightgown and the last of her regrets behind, and joined him on the bed.

Chapter Ten

The sun was still below the horizon. But by the subtle changes in the darkness around them, James could tell that they did not have much longer. It was a shame. If he had ever wished for an endless night, it would be this one.

When he had set upon a plan to rescue Fosberry from imprisonment, he'd had only the vaguest idea of how to proceed. Perhaps he would get the girl to cry off with warm smiles and innuendo. A mild flirtation might be necessary. Full blown seduction of a well-bred virgin was not precisely off the table, but it was far out of the bounds he usually set for himself.

That had been before he'd met Faith Strickland. The first time he'd seen her, he'd wanted to kiss her. And once he'd kissed her?

He'd wanted to do exactly what they'd now done, repeatedly and with great enthusiasm. If he'd known that the way to silence that sharp tongue of hers was to give it something else to do, he'd have thrown her over his shoulder and carried her to bed the moment he'd passed the threshold of this house.

Thinking of that clever, clever tongue had been a mistake. His blood was flowing south again and he did not have time for what his body wanted to do. Not until tonight, at least. He would not flatter himself that he had ruined her for all other men. But it was safe to say that, after what they had done together, she would want something better than Cyril Fosberry.

He rolled on his side and propped his head on his elbow, so he might watch her sleep. In the nearly twenty years since he had discovered the delight that was the womanly body, he'd enjoyed infinite variety. But what was the point of variation if it meant that he rushed away from a woman like this in the vain hope that the next might be better?

One night was more than he deserved and yet it was not enough. Had he really thought he could deflower a lady and walk away? Or had he known from the minute he looked at her that to kiss Faith Strickland was to admit defeat? His life was no longer his own. His happiness depended on hers.

Now she was pretending to sleep so she did not have to face what they had done. Her eyes were shut too tight and she was trying so hard to appear relaxed that it made his own muscles tense just looking at her. He gathered her closer, kissing her on the forehead so she could pretend to wake that he might assure her she had nothing to fear, ever again.

She ignored him.

It did not bother him when they argued. But hopefully, marriage would break her of the habit of dissembling. She would learn soon enough that she had him wrapped about her little finger and could have whatever she wanted with honesty and a promise of pleasure.

He gave her body a gentle shake and another kiss. 'Faith. Wake up. It is almost morning and I must return to my room.'

She fluttered her eyelids, pretended to rouse and then spoke in a voice far too controlled to be fresh from sleep. 'You are right. We cannot be discovered together.'

'I understand. No one can know of this, for the sake of your reputation.' Now that the moment had arrived to talk of the future, he was surprised to feel his confidence falter. There was no reason for it. When had a woman ever refused him a request made in bed? 'What we have done...' He wet his lips. 'What I have done... It cannot go unanswered. It was improper of me.'

'Let us not speak of it,' she said, dropping her eyes from his, then glancing toward the door as if willing him to leave.

'But I mean to do the right thing...' That was the wrong way to put it. What woman wanted a proposal made out of obligation instead of love? He rolled hurriedly out of his side of the bed and walked around so he might kneel beside hers. Then he held out a hand in supplication. 'Miss Faith Strickland, would you do me the honour…'

'Wait.' Rather than reaching to accept his hand, she scrambled away from it, pulling the covers high to hide her bare skin. 'You do not have to do this.'

'I don't?' Of course he didn't have to. But that did not mean he did not want to. He had done something wrong. But since he had so little experience in proposing, he was not sure what it might be.

'You don't. Really. In fact, I would rather you didn't speak.' She gave a significant glance toward the door. 'Isn't it time that you returned to your room, before someone notices your absence?'

Or worse yet, noticed his presence here. That was what she meant. She was ashamed of being seen with him. She had been quick enough to say 'Love me, James' a few hours ago. Apparently, daylight changed everything. 'If you really want me to go,' he said, giving her another chance.

'I do.'

Two little words meant to bind a man and woman for life. But Faith Strickland, contrary beast that she was, used them to send him away. 'If that's what you want, then far be it from me to refuse.' He stood, then stooped again, grabbed his wrinkled shirt off the floor and threw it over his head. Then he scooped up the rest of his clothing and headed for the door. 'Goodnight, Miss Strickland. And thank you for a delightful evening.' He turned back to her, intending to finish with an ironically formal bow, only to drop one of his boots. He bent to get it again, only to lose his coat. With a curse, he dropped everything to the floor and bundled it properly, then tugged open the door.

Then he passed through into the hall and let it swing towards a satisfyingly final slam. But a noise like that would alert the household and bring the scandal he did not want for her. He jammed his hand forward to prevent it, bruising his knuckles but saving embarrassment, then eased it closed with a soft click.

Damn all women.

On second thought, damn just one of them. He had done all he could to stop the wedding. But if she truly preferred Fosberry to him, then she could have him. There was nothing James could do to stop her.

As he stalked down the hall to his room, he remembered that there was one thing he might do. He could behave as she probably assumed he would and announce at breakfast that he had enjoyed her carnal pleasures and assure Fosberry that he was in for a jolly good ride.

Cyril would leave her and she and her sisters would be ruined, just as feared. The indifference she felt for him this morning would harden to well-deserved hatred. Not only would she never speak to him again, the memory of their night together would be permanently tainted. It was the one thing he might still do that would keep his promise to Bea, yet he could not seem to manage it. He would not sacrifice what they'd shared, nor could he hurt her more than he already had.

Sleep was out of the question. Nor could he stay here in this house with the woman he loved and the man she preferred. If he left as soon as the sun was properly up, he might never have to see her again. And she might never see the confusion, the hurt and the weakness that were probably writ plain on his unshaved face. He threw on a change of clothes, then hauled his valise out of the wardrobe, filled it and latched it, setting in on the end of bed.

And still it was barely four o'clock. Too early to ride. Too early to breakfast. But not too late for a drink and he sorely needed one. Fortunately, he knew the location of the finest brandy in the house. He stumbled down the darkened stairs towards the study, her words still ringing in his ears.

I'd rather you didn't speak.

She had not just chosen Cyril. She had dismissed him without a hearing. He had been so incredulous at the words that he was not able to protest. He had left, was leaving, like a cur with his tail between his legs. But each time he thought of turning back and telling her what he thought of her decision, he imagined the hurt it would cause her.

He could not do it. To love meant to want what was best for another. Bea would be pleased he had learned the lesson. What capricious deity would make him waste an emotion he'd never felt before on a woman who did not reciprocate it?

And why, when he needed peace and solitude to drink away the pain, did he find Cyril Fosberry in the study, sitting in a leather armchair by the window and drinking without benefit of a glass.

''Lo, Leggett,'' he' said, offering a salute with the brandy.

'You should not be drinking your breakfast,' James said, glaring at the half-empty bottle.

'Neither should you. But I expect you will see the advantages to it, once you have started.' Without waiting for a request, Cyril fumbled on the side table for a glass, filled it and offered it.

'Thank you,' James replied, taking it and emptying it in a single gulp.

'You do not sound all that grateful,' Fosberry replied, refilling it for him.

'Because this is all your fault, Cyril,' James said, with an all-encompassing gesture that very nearly spilled his drink.

'My fault?' Fosberry drank again.

Perhaps it wasn't. But someone had to be blamed for this mess. Though it should probably have been Faith, James could not seem to manage it. There was something he admired in the way she'd used them all for her own ends. Since she'd done it to provide for her sisters, was it really so bad?

Fosberry, on the other hand, was the one stupid enough to be tricked. Did one blame the rabbit, or the trap? The rabbit, he decided, and glared at Cyril, drinking until the glass was empty. 'If you were not such an utter nincompoop, I would never have had to come here at all. And if...' If Faith was not eager to choose an upright prig who did not want her over a man with love in his heart and a somewhat colourful past...

He held out the glass to be filled again. 'Never mind. Just know, Cyril, that you are utterly useless.'

Men had drawn pistols over insults milder than that. But Fosberry gave him nothing more than a look of silent reproach as he poured the brandy.

'Never mind,' James barked back at him. 'I will just go home, shall I? That is what everyone wants. You shall have Faith and I shall marry Bea, just as we have always planned to do, without any more nonsense.'

'Bea?' The man dropped the bottle and leaned forward in his chair. 'You do not mean Beatrice Leggett.'

'She is my cousin, you lackwit,' James said, stooping to collect the brandy before the last of the contents disappeared into the rug. 'Perhaps you might have noticed the similarity in our names. And I see no reason...'

And then he did not see anything at all.

Chapter Eleven

After all they had done together in the last few hours, he'd left her. She'd sent him away, of course. He could hardly be blamed for doing what she wanted him to. But perhaps, if he had not ruined it all by trying to propose…

Though it had been almost an hour since James Leggett had left her, Faith remained in the same place she'd been when he'd gone, sitting up in the middle of her very empty bed with the covers pulled high as though they could protect her from the truth.

She was in love with James Leggett. It would be the sad little secret that would carry her through the remaining years of her life. She had shared a night of passion with the man she loved. The fact that he did not share her feelings spoilt it somewhat. He had only seduced her to make her cry off Cyril, so he might go back to Beatrice.

She had been too selfish to admit from the beginning that such drastic measures were not necessary. She had wanted to lie with him and had decided that the sin would be worth any punishment she might receive.

Then he had proposed and ruined everything. How could he be so cruel as to offer something he had no intention of doing? She had wanted to scream that there was no need for further subterfuge. The decision had been made and Cyril was as good as free.

But then, one faint, nagging question had entered her mind.

Suppose he is serious?

James had admitted that he was not in the habit of lying with virgins. He might have proposed out of a real sense of obligation. And she might have freed him from it, had she just been honest from the start. Instead, she had sacrificed her honour and trapped him into proposing.

It was even worse than the trick she had played on Cyril, for she had not even realised she'd done it. But when James found out, he would not believe her. He would hate her, just as Cyril did.

So she'd saved face with a polite refusal and maintained her composure long enough for him to make his escape. Now she might cry in private and no one need ever know.

Or perhaps not. There was a quiet knock and her maid, Nell, entered the room with her morning chocolate on a tray. Without a word, the girl retrieved the crumpled nightgown from the floor beside the bed, then glanced down and picked up another item.

It was a gentleman's stocking.

'I have no idea how that could have got there,' Faith said faintly.

Nell grinned. 'Perhaps it has something to do with this.' She pulled an envelope from her pocket and offered it to her mistress. 'Mr Fosberry give it to me.'

'Really.' Faith's hand trembled as she took it, sure of only one thing. The note had nothing to do with the stocking in Nell's hand.

'Shall I return this to him?' the maid asked, flapping the stocking in the air.

'No, thank you, Nell. Leave it.' Of all the tokens for her one true love to leave her, why did it have to be that? Couldn't he have left the cravat scented with his cologne? Didn't he have a fresh handkerchief? To spend her future sleeping with an unwashed stocking under her pillow proved what a disastrous mistake it had been to fall in love with James Leggett.

Now, Nell was waiting for her to open the letter, sure it would be a love note from the man she was about to marry, thanking her for the gift of her maidenhead. She gave the girl a stern look. 'That will be all, Nell.'

'Yes, miss.'

Faith waited until the door was shut again before breaking the seal on the folded paper. She read the note. Then she read it again. And then she got dressed and went to find James.

When she located him, asleep on the floor of her Grandfather's study, she did the first thing that came to mind and kicked him in the shin. 'What have you done?'

He did not precisely start awake. It was more of a lurch to consciousness, with a slow rise to a sitting position and much shaking of his head as if he was trying to clear his thoughts.

'What have I done?' He winced. 'I do not exactly know. After your cruel rejection of me, I meant to come here for a drink.'

She sniffed, wishing that it sounded more like disapproval than the beginning of tears. 'If you managed to drink yourself insensible in such a short time, you are a drunkard as well as a rake.'

He squinted up at her. 'Fosberry was here as well and far more drunk than I. Where has he got to?'

'You do not know?' she asked and kicked him again.

'Ow,' he replied, then touched his nose and moaned again.

'Do not be such an infant. What did you say to him to make him break off with me and go back to London?'

'I said hardly anything at all,' James said, holding up his hands in surrender. 'If he'd have allowed me to finish, I'd have favoured him with a dramatic oration on the stupidity of marrying a woman he did not love. There would have been much pacing about the room, and pounding the mantel for emphasis. I would have been very persuasive.'

As if he was in a position to lecture, after the false

proposal he'd offered. She attempted a derisive snort, but it sounded far too much like a stifled sob.

He gave her an odd look and continued. 'It all ended before I could begin. He hit me.' He touched his nose again and winced, then glanced down at the drops of blood that were dropping from it. 'And he has ruined a brand new waistcoat.'

'But what did you say to make him hit you?' She offered a hand to help him to his feet. 'Whatever it is, I am sure you deserved it. But enlighten me.'

'It had nothing to do with last night, if that's what you think. I am not the sort of cad who would kiss and tell.'

'Then why did he strike you, other than the obvious reason, of course?'

'Obvious?'

'That you are the sort of man who should be struck.' This time, she had to gulp to keep the down. 'That you are the sort of man who would lecture poor Mr Fosberry about marrying me, after what you said…' She gulped again.

'Never mind what I said to him,' he said, staring at her expectantly. 'What did I say to you?'

'You proposed. And you did not mean a word of it.' The first tears had begun falling and the effort to sniff them away turned into another snort. 'You only did it so I would accept you and cry off. But you needn't have bothered. I was going to do it this morning, without your interference.'

'You were?' he said, surprised, and offered her the handkerchief he had been using to dab his nose.

'Charity told me about Beatrice. I never would have chased after him if I'd known he was meant for another.' She searched for a clean corner of the linen, and when she could not find one, she threw it back to him and wiped her face with her cuff. 'But he is already gone.' Her sleeve was soaked through, yet the tears would not stop falling, nor would the sobs that racked her body.

'And who, precisely, are you crying over?' he asked. 'It is not Fosberry, is it? Because I will bring him back, if that is what you want.'

She waved her hand, struggling to get the words out. 'I do not want him. I...never...did.' And now, her voice was hoarse from crying. She could feel her face getting blotchy and both sleeves were sodden and limp.

'Then you are crying over me,' he said with surprise, as if he had never seen a woman do it before.

'Of course I am,' she said. 'But it is none of your concern.' She made a shooing motion with her hands. 'You got what you wanted. It is over. Now leave.' She closed her eyes and waited for the slam of the door.

When it did not come, she opened them again and saw him holding a fresh handkerchief and grinning at her. 'I told him that I had no choice but to return to London and marry Beatrice,' he said. 'Apparently, it upset him.'

'Then you needn't have bothered seducing me,'

she said, rubbing her eyes and trying to gain control. 'And you certainly did not have to tease me with false offers of marriage. All you had to do was tell him you would marry his love and he would have left immediately.'

'That is probably true,' he agreed.

It made her sob all the louder.

'But then I would never have known you.'

'Good,' she said. 'And I'd never have met you. In fact, I wish I'd never have seen you at all. Because now you are going to leave me, just as I always knew you would.'

'I do not think I can.' This statement was equally soft, like a feather dragged against her skin.

She looked up at him, disgusted. 'Of course you can. It is not as if your boots are nailed to the floor.' And now she was sobbing again. 'You think I am horrible for tricking Cyril and for trying to trick you. But you were not wanted here. You should never have come.' She raised a finger, watched it tremble for a moment and snatched it back out of the air. 'Go!'

'And where would that leave you?'

Cast off. Cast aside. Of dubious reputation made even worse by the rumours that James Leggett had taken an interest in her and ruined her engagement. 'It will leave me just as I was, which was just fine.'

'You know you are not,' he said patiently, walking forward and taking her in his arms. 'Something is wrong. Your youngest sister told me that you were most pretty when you cried. But this morning, I do not think that is the case.'

'That is a horrible thing to say.' She pressed her face into his coat and let the wool absorb the last of the tears.

His arms tightened about her. 'But it is the truth. I do not think that a man should lie, when he loves a woman as much as I love you.'

'You love me?' The words were so unexpected that her tears slowed and then stopped.

'Yes,' he said with no hesitation. 'And if you are moved to such sincerely ugly tears over the loss of me?' She felt him shrug. 'I should not flatter myself with assumptions as to your feelings. But I do have hopes.'

'Then last night, when you came to my room?' She held her breath, just as afraid to hope as he was.

'I came because I wanted to be with you,' he said and she felt his lips skimming her ear.

'And when you proposed?'

He turned his head to speak so softly that only she could hear. 'It was because I wanted every night of my life to be like that one.'

'Oh,' she said in a whisper.

'Charity said you needed a man as ruthless as you were,' he added. 'I do not know if you have used that descriptor, but you have called me many equally heinous things.'

'You deserved them,' she said, immediately regretting her honesty.

'But I am wealthy enough to make up for my bad character,' he reminded her. 'And fond of both your sisters and the Dowager as well.'

And he would help them. Because he loved her. She looked up in amazement. 'Grandmother was right.'

'About what?'

'She said that rakes make the best husbands.' She stared into his beautiful blue eyes and her fears of the future disappeared.

'They make excellent lovers as well.' He smiled and released her, then went to lock the door. 'Allow me to demonstrate.'

* * * * *

AWAKENING HIS SLEEPING BEAUTY

Janice Preston

For my family.
Because Christmas isn't Christmas without family!

Dear Reader,

When my editor first asked if I'd like to write a novella for the 2017 Christmas anthology I jumped at the chance. And the choice of what to write came to me in a flash—in the past year I had already written stories loosely based on *Beauty and the Beast* and *Cinderella*, so what better than to complete the hat-trick with another story based on a fairy tale?

Of course in choosing *Sleeping Beauty* I couldn't have my heroine literally lying asleep until the hero awakened her with a kiss, but the idea of a heroine who was *emotionally* asleep intrigued me, and I began to wonder how and why she would willingly remain shut away from the world, and therefore life.

The answer, as it so often is, was family and love. People make enormous and willing sacrifices for those they love, and Diana—growing up with a grief-stricken mother—is no exception... Until her eyes are opened by her boisterous distant cousins—particularly the brooding, unsettling Aaron—and she begins to realise what she is missing.

I hope you enjoy reading about Diana's awakening... and Merry Christmas to you all!

Janice

Chapter One

'Ah, there you are.'

Lord Lavenham sidled into his wife's boudoir and closed the door behind him with a resounding thud.

Lady Lavenham winced. 'Really, Lavenham. Must you be so very…perturbing?' She raised one fragile-boned hand to her brow, her expression one of pained endurance.

'My apologies, my dear. I did not mean… That is, the door…it was louder than I expected.'

The Viscount clutched a letter before him in both hands as he hovered by the door with every appearance of a man about to undertake a dangerous assignment, leaving his escape route clear.

Diana—the Lavenhams' only child since the death of her brother eight years before—lay down the book she had been reading aloud to her mother and folded her hands in her lap to await Papa's explanation for this rare intrusion into his wife's domain. Diana's patience wore thin as the silence stretched. If Papa did not speak up soon, Mother would launch into one of her rants and they might never discover the purpose of his visit.

At length, with one eye on her increasingly fretful mother, Diana said, 'Is that a letter, Papa?'

The Viscount's bushy brows shot up. 'What? Oh, this?' He wafted the letter, describing an arc through the air. 'Oh, yes, indeed.'

He sucked in a deep breath and Diana felt the first stirrings of unease. What could be so important that Papa not only braved Mother in her boudoir, but that he did not follow his usual custom and delegate the task of relaying bad news to Diana?

'Lavenham—' Mother's voice grew peevish '—really, this is too tiresome. I have the headache. Do please get to the point.'

'It is from Cousin Sally.' The Viscount again brandished the letter. 'She is coming to stay.'

'Cousin Sally? You did not inform me you had issued such an invitation to her, my lord.'

Diana's heart sank. This would provide Mother with fuel for complaint for weeks to come and it would fall upon Diana to listen and to soothe and to deflect whilst her father buried himself in his library with his books and forgot the very existence of his womenfolk for hour after hour and day after day.

'Yes…well…'

A slash of dull red coloured Papa's pale cheeks and Diana's disquiet grew.

What is he up to?

'But… I did not, precisely… No!' He brightened. 'No. It was not *I* who invited *them*, do you see. It was Cousin Sally's suggestion.'

'Them? Not—' Mother's voice grew faint '—*not* the entire family?'

Cousin Sally was the widowed mother of seven children ranging from twenty-five-year-old Aaron to eleven-year-old Joseph.

'Well. Yes. They arrive the day after tomorrow and they will stay for the whole of Christmastide—' Papa pulled the door ajar '—until Twelfth Night.' He shot through the opening and snapped the door shut behind him.

Aaron Fleming studied Lavenham Hall with a critical eye as he tooled his curricle up the long, straight approach that cut through the parkland surrounding the beautiful half-timbered house.

'I fail to understand why you did not put Lavenham off until after Christmas, Mama.'

He glanced sideways at his mother, who he had taken up—at her request—as soon as they turned in through the wrought-iron entrance gates to the Hall. The coach carrying his three brothers and three sisters, plus the family's luggage, lumbered in their rear.

His mother, swathed in fur against the winter chill—only her mouth, the pink tip of her nose and her eyes visible—replied, 'But I *told* you this, my dear, before we left home.'

Yes, she had told him, but he was still irritated and,

in two days of travel, this was his first opportunity to quiz his mother out of earshot of any of his brothers and sisters.

Aaron had arrived at their family home, Shepcott Place, in Somersetshire full of the joyful anticipation of spending Christmastide, as usual, with his family, only to be presented with this visit to Lavenham Hall as a *fait accompli*. The servants and some luggage had already been dispatched and the very next morning the entire family had set forth on the journey north into Herefordshire. There had been no choice but to fall in with his mother's plans.

'I could not refuse Cousin Arthur's invitation. He was most insistent we visit this Christmas. Aaron... I have begged you these past two years to visit Lavenham, but you have paid me no heed.' His mother continued, 'Arthur is getting no younger and this will all be yours one day. If you had paid greater attention to your duty and less to your life of indulgence, there would be no need for this hurry and scurry now his health has worsened. You have no one but yourself and your own stubbornness to blame.'

Aaron bit back his sharp riposte. *Duty.* He'd had enough of duty in the cavalry and he'd spent the past two years trying to push the horrific sights and sounds of war from his head. But there was nothing to gain in more complaint—they were here now and it was not Mama's fault Lavenham had insisted they spend Christmastide here. He must make the best of it, no matter how much he resented this change to their normal celebrations. He did not even have any acquaintances in south Herefordshire other than Gordon Caxton, a fellow Guards officer whose estate bordered Lavenham. And Aaron had no intention of wasting any more time on his erstwhile friend after Caxton's recent attempt to manipulate Aaron into offering for his avaricious sister, Caroline.

He wrenched his attention away from the Caxtons as his mother continued her reproach.

'Try not to be selfish, Aaron. After all, you may see your brothers and sisters at any time—your brothers are home from school at times of the year other than Christmas. It is *your* choice to spend so much time in London and visiting your friends' estates in the summer months. If you spent more of your time at home, you would not be so resentful of this change to our Christmas festivities.'

His mother might be right, but that didn't mean Aaron appreciated her scold. He thrust aside the faint guilt that nagged at him. Perhaps he could have spent more time at Shepcott Place over the past couple of years but, after the discipline of the cavalry and the horror of war—he had sold his commission following the victory over Napoleon at Waterloo two and a half years ago—a period of purposeless leisure had been tempting and Aaron had embraced the life of a carefree bachelor about town, enjoying the attractions London and society offered. His constant attendance wasn't essential at Shepcott: the estate had been capably managed by his bailiff since his father's death ten years before. Aaron's father—great-great-grandson of the Second Viscount Lavenham—had built a successful career as a banker and had left his entire family in comfortable financial circumstances.

So, for Aaron—absent from Shepcott for much of the year—Christmas had become the time he spent with his family and it was, or it should have been, sacrosanct.

'I trust you to make the best of this visit. If it eases poor Arthur's mind to have his heir stay for a few weeks so he can be sure you are familiar with the estate and its people, then surely sharing Christmas with him and his family is a small price to pay?'

Aaron bit back his caustic opinion of absent-minded Arthur, with his obsession with Ancient Greece; Venetia, his demanding wife, twenty years the Viscount's junior; and Diana, their little brown mouse of a daughter.

They had reached the end of the carriageway and he steered his horses around the turning circle before halting them in front of the house. The carriage pulled up behind.

The front door already stood open and a figure now emerged into the daylight. Shock seized Aaron at first sight of the Viscount. He had aged considerably in the years since they had last met. Still tall, despite his stoop, and even slighter in stature than Aaron remembered, grey tufts now sprouted in an unkempt crescent around his bald pate. Lord Lavenham raised one hand

in greeting, but remained by the door as footmen hurried past him ready to unload the luggage.

Aaron's two youngest brothers, Harry and Joseph, scrambled down from the bench seat, where they had been permitted to ride next to John Coachman for the last leg of the journey. Sixteen-year-old George emerged from inside the carriage, followed by Harry's twin sister, Isabel—still pouting after Mama's refusal to allow her to sit outside with her brothers—and the two oldest girls, Eliza and Frances.

Aaron handed his mother from his curricle and escorted her to Lord Lavenham, still waiting by the open front door. Only as they reached the Viscount did Aaron notice a tall, willowy figure standing in the shadows beyond. He shot a questioning glance at his mother: *Who is she?*

His mother returned his look with an enigmatic lift of her brow.

'My dear Arthur.' Mama approached Lavenham with outstretched arms and kissed him on the cheek. 'How good it is to see you again after so many years. Correspondence can never replace the joy of an actual meeting.'

Lavenham returned her embrace. 'I am delighted to welcome you to Lavenham, Sally. You are well, I hope? And the journey was not overly taxing? Now, let me see… I remember Aaron, of course…' he shook Aaron's hand '…a fine young man, indeed. You must be…what?…five-and-twenty? Time you thought about

settling down, m'boy. I hear your sister is to be wed soon.'

Aaron set his jaw as Lavenham chuckled. It was bad enough Mama constantly quizzing him about getting shackled without Lavenham joining the chorus.

I'll wed when I'm ready and not before.

He was only five-and-twenty—plenty of time yet to think about setting up his nursery. And when he did decide to enter parson's mousetrap, it would his decision and his alone. If there was one thing he could not abide it was being nagged or—worse still, after his experience with the Caxtons—manoeuvred. Fortunately he had realised their plan in time to thwart their attempt to entrap him, but he still regretted not confronting the pair of them. Instead, he had merely avoided them as much as possible and discreetly declined any further invitations.

'She is indeed, Arthur,' Aaron's mother said. 'Cousin Arthur, meet Eliza.' The eldest of Aaron's sisters, nineteen-year-old Eliza, curtsied.

'Eliza…a pretty name for a pretty young lady.'

Lavenham's forced bonhomie grated on Aaron, seeming out of character for such a scholarly type.

'You will need to remind me of the other children's names, I am afraid, Sally.'

Mama beckoned the rest of the family forward. As she did so, Aaron's gaze met that of the young woman who stood silently erect behind the Viscount. She could only be his daughter, Diana. The little brown mouse. Well, she might still legitimately be described

as brown, with hair and eyes of that hue, but she could by no stretch of the imagination be described as either little or mouse-like. Rather, she had a feline air, with her slanting eyes, her stillness and a peculiar watchfulness in her stance, as though she might at any moment spring into action.

He suppressed the guilt coiling in his gut that he, and not she, would eventually inherit her home. It was the way of their world. Titles and estates passed down the male line. Besides...his gaze swept over her and he felt his pulse kick: she really was *most* striking... he had no need to feel guilty. An attractive young woman like her would have little trouble finding a husband to provide for her.

Mama continued to introduce Aaron's brothers and sisters. 'This is Frances and Isabel—who is twin to Harry here—and the other boys are George and Joseph.'

'And this is my daughter Diana,' Lavenham said, half-turning and taking Diana's arm, urging her forward.

She did not crack so much as a smile when Mama greeted her with a warm kiss to the cheek. Aaron made his bow and Diana responded with only a grave nod of her head.

Would it hurt her to be a little more welcoming? Her dislike of his family invading her precious home could not be more obvious and Aaron hoped his sisters, in particular, were not hurt by her unfriendliness. Both Eliza and Frances had been looking forward to

meeting their distant cousin for the first time. They would be so disappointed to find this starched-up miss.

Aaron's resentment over this visit resurfaced. How much fun could they expect this Christmastide if they must rely upon these people to organise the festivities? He could not imagine a drearier time ahead if he tried.

Chapter Two

Diana followed their guests and her father into the house. It was not only her thoughts that were weighted with dread, but every single nerve in her body appeared to have gone numb in sympathy. How could she bear the next few weeks? She swallowed past the lump of hurt in her throat. It was bad enough this other Fleming family had invited themselves to stay, but to choose this time of year, when Mother was even more demanding than usual, made their visit even less welcome.

Movement on the staircase attracted her attention and every muscle tensed as her mother drifted down the stairs, her natural pallor accentuated by the head-to-toe black she wore every December to remember Simon, even though it was eight years now since he died. Eight long years since Diana had not only lost her younger brother and playmate, but also left behind her childhood. How different might the lives of the whole family be now had Simon lived?

She slid a look at Aaron, her third cousin—or was it her fourth?—and Simon's replacement as Papa's heir: the next Viscount Lavenham. Resentment bubbled behind her breast bone. His visit would never be welcome to her or her mother, but to come in December, so soon after the anniversary of Simon's death, proved he was no less arrogant and unfeeling than she remembered.

Aaron was the only one of this branch of the Fleming family Diana had ever met. He had visited in the summer after Simon died—a newly commissioned cavalry officer, more interested in chasing giggling housemaids than in noticing his shy eleven-year-old cousin. Diana had suffered the pangs of a young girl's infatuation as she was completely overlooked by her handsome cousin and that hurt had mingled with the pain of Simon's death and the confusion of her mother's inconsolable grief for a long time afterwards.

Now, Aaron was here again…just as attractive as she remembered, with the same dark lustrous hair and eyes the colour of river water, clearly a family trait as every one of his family had identical colouring.

Her mother neared the foot of the stairs and Diana eyed her anxiously, recalling the prolonged bout of wailing with which she had greeted the news of the impending visit. Papa—with his usual knack for avoiding his wife's tantrums—had retreated to his library and his weighty tomes of ancient Greek. Diana later found him there with a blanket over his head to drown out Mother's shrieks. No amount of Diana's

cajoling and begging had moved him. It was time Aaron learned about his inheritance and the workings of the estate, and now was as good a time as any, Papa had told her.

'My dear, come and greet our guests,' Papa said as Mother reached the hall.

Diana slipped her hands behind her back and crossed her fingers that her mother—unused to being thwarted and resistant to change—would prove gracious in her defeat—a defeat only conceded when Papa announced that Cousin Sally and her family would have set off on the journey already and it was therefore too late to put them off.

Even Diana's objection that the servants would never cope with the extra work caused by eight additional people had been given short shrift. 'Cousin Sally is sending her own servants ahead to help with the additional workload,' her father had said. 'They arrive tomorrow.' Leaving Diana to wonder just how long her scatter-brained father had known about this forthcoming visit.

The hairs on the back of Diana's neck stood up as her mother and Cousin Sally exchanged greetings and she glanced round in time to catch Aaron's curious gaze rising from her crossed fingers to meet her eyes. He raised one dark brow in a silent query and Diana's heart gave a funny little flip in her chest as long-suppressed girlhood dreams of knights on white chargers cantered into her thoughts. She stiffened and

whipped her attention back to their mothers. She had
long ago dispensed with those stupid fantasies.

Her mother smiled vaguely at Cousin Sally's *brood*,
as she had taken to calling them, and beckoned to
Diana.

'Help me back to my boudoir, Diana,' she said, in
a long-suffering voice. 'I declare I am quite overcome
by this hustle and bustle. I can feel one of my megrims
coming on. I am sure you will excuse us, Sally…'

Mother's voice faded into silence as Cousin Sally,
with a determined smile, grasped her arm.

'Let us leave the young people to become acquainted, Venetia,' she said. '*I* shall help you upstairs
and we can have a cosy chat.'

Before Mother could respond, Diana's father said,
'Splendid notion, Sally. Diana, show your cousins into
the drawing room and ring the bell. Cook is ready to
send up refreshments as soon as you wish.'

Sally had already urged Mother to the stairs. Diana
stared at her father in bewilderment, scarcely able to
recognise him, with this new-found decisiveness. He
never gave orders and most particularly not within
Mother's hearing.

'Perkins?' She gestured to their butler, who was
hovering in the hall, ready to direct the new servants.

'Miss Diana?'

'Show my cousins into the drawing room, please.
I should like a private word with my father.'

The instant the words left her mouth Diana realised
how unfriendly she sounded and she glanced behind

her, to catch Aaron glowering in disapproval. Her stomach churned, but then she conjured up anger to quell her nerves. What did she care what he thought of her? She would not bow and stoop before him, even if he were Papa's heir. Or, more particularly, *because* he was Papa's heir.

'You should welcome the chance to meet your cousins and to have some fun, Diana,' Papa said reprovingly as her cousins trouped into the drawing room. 'Heaven knows, you get little enough between caring for your mother and with me being so engrossed in my work.'

Her initial shock that her vague and unworldly father had even noticed the tedium of his daughter's life soon gave way to an unaccustomed bitterness. Fun? She'd forgotten what the word even meant. But this visit only heralded more duty, between caring for the visitors and indulging Mother and her inevitable bouts of ill-health, both real and imagined.

'I doubt I shall find the time for fun,' she said quietly. 'Mother will need me.'

Papa gestured at the stairs and the two women slowly climbing them.

'It is all arranged. Sally has agreed to keep your mother company to give you the time to entertain your cousins.'

Diana eyed this newly practical version of her father with suspicion. Papa *never* involved himself in such trivial matters. Once again, it begged the question of how long, precisely, he had known about this

visit. Demanding an answer to that question would change nothing, however, so she did not waste her breath.

'Very well, Papa.'

She crossed the hall to the drawing room where she paused, suddenly reluctant to enter. But she must. She sucked in a deep breath, straightened her spine and pushed the door open. Seven faces looked at her and her nerve faltered, but she stretched her lips into a smile and forced her legs to carry her into the room.

After a fraught silence, which surely was not as lengthy as it seemed, Diana said, 'I shall ring for refreshments.' It was not much but it was better than saying nothing. She swallowed and continued, 'I am sure you are all hungry after your journey.'

She rang the bell and moved to sit in a chair to one side of the room, slightly apart from the others.

'It was exceedingly dull.'

It was the youngest of her female cousins who spoke. The twin. Isabel.

'I should imagine it was, Isabel.'

Diana was gratified to see Isabel's face light up.

'You remembered my name.'

'I did.' She recalled the tension between Isabel, her twin brother and the youngest of the boys on their arrival as both boys mocked their sister. 'I remember thinking how wise you were to travel inside the carriage instead of on top with your brothers in the freezing cold.'

'I *am* wise; too clever to bother with *you* pair.'

Isabel pointed at her brothers in turn. 'Even Diana says so.'

Too late, Diana realised that in her attempt to build a rapport with Isabel she had inadvertently insulted the boys. Two pairs of reproachful grey eyes fixed on her and her cheeks heated.

'I do not believe Diana meant it in quite that way, Isabel,' a deep voice said.

Far from comforting her, Aaron's interjection made Diana feel even more foolish. Her brain might tell her she had dispensed with her former infatuation, but her heart seemed to have missed that message: tumbling into a breathtaking swoop as his attention fixed upon her. Her mouth felt like it had been sucked dry and she was relieved when three maids came in carrying trays of cakes, lemonade and tea.

She stood up and went to pour the tea, saying, 'Please come and help yourselves to whatever you like.'

There was a rush of feet as Harry and Joseph stampeded to be first.

'Walk!'

Aaron's roar rattled the windows and Diana's heart leapt into her throat. Her hand trembled, the teapot clinking against the china cups, as she continued to pour.

'What will Diana think of you, acting like heathens?'

He sounded so cross. Butterflies invaded Diana's stomach at the harshness in his voice.

Those poor boys.

'All you have achieved,' Aaron continued, 'is to prove her right when she said Isabel was better off with her sisters.'

Diana felt an arm slip around her waist. 'I do hope we will not prove too trying for you, Cousin,' Eliza said in her ear. 'You are unused to such disorderly children, I know.'

Diana smiled tentatively. 'I am sure I shall become accustomed.' But she wasn't sure she spoke the truth, and it wasn't growing accustomed to the children that she feared.

Soon afterwards, Diana's father sent for Aaron to attend him in the estate office and Diana spent the remainder of the afternoon getting to know her younger cousins. She showed them around the Hall, including her beloved conservatory, where she cultivated all manner of plants, relishing the challenge of coaxing them to flower out of season. She found it easier to relax in the absence of Aaron, with his stormy grey eyes and his deep voice that seemed to vibrate through her body, and she had to admit that she had quite enjoyed this change to her normal routine.

'But you must understand Diana's point of view, my darling son.'

'Must I?'

Aaron peered through his mother's bedchamber window into the gathering gloom outside. December—

with its promise of family fun and frolics—usually held no power to dampen his mood, despite the short daylight hours and the sun's struggle to penetrate the grey clouds. This December, though, all was spoilt. He wondered what the others were doing. Were they as bored as he? After their arrival, Aaron had spent the afternoon closeted with Lavenham and his bailiff, Walker, discussing estate matters, and no sooner had he been released from that obligation than Mama had sent for him to task him with ensuring Diana was made to feel part of the family during their stay at Lavenham Hall.

'She does not want us here any more than we wish to be here. After all, she hardly gave us a rousing welcome, did she?' he said, his still-simmering anger over the disruption to their traditional Christmastide tipping him into indiscretion. 'Why, she could not even summon a smile. A marble statue would offer more warmth.'

'Aaron! This has been her home all her life and it will pass to you upon her father's death so she will be forced to leave it.'

Aaron glanced over his shoulder at his mother, then stared through the window again, setting his jaw. He felt uncomfortable enough being here as it was—as though he were rubbing his hands over what would belong to him one day. He did not need Mama's reminder that he'd be making Diana homeless as well.

A glimmer of light below caught his attention and he leant forward, propping his knuckles on the sill.

What is that?

He could see now. Someone carrying a lamp moved through the conservatory that jutted out from the house wall. A second lantern was lit and he recognised Diana as the light accentuated the curve of her cheek and the delicate line of her jaw. He watched her as she threaded her way through the luxuriant foliage. When *had* his mouse of a cousin grown into such an attractive young woman? It was a pity she was so cold and standoffish.

'She is, surely, entitled to be wary of our intrusion,' Mama continued. 'It is unfair of you to judge her upon one brief meeting.'

He faced his mother—who was resting on her bed before it was time to change for dinner—and folded his arms across his chest.

'Then she should inflict her disapproval upon her father, for it was he who insisted upon this visit.'

His mother dropped her gaze to her fingers as she fiddled with the fringe of the shawl that draped her shoulders.

'She is an only child, Aaron, who lost her beloved brother. Can you not believe her reserve is due more to shyness than to displeasure? Consider how it must feel to be invaded by a large family such as ours. Much as I love you all, I cannot help feeling poor Diana must be somewhat overwhelmed.'

Aaron did not reply, but his conscience stirred, whispering that his mother made a good point.

His mother sighed. 'I know you, Aaron—you feel

hard done by because I did not consult you over the decision to come here and you are stubborn enough to cling to your resentment. But do not, I beg of you, place the blame on poor Diana's shoulders. If anyone should be blamed, it is Cousin Arthur and I, for it was we who made the arrangements. Please, give Diana a chance before you condemn her.'

She is right. I am being stubborn and if I am not careful I shall spoil Christmas for everyone.

Aaron crossed the room to sit on the bed next to his mother. He patted her hand. 'Very well, Mama. I shall try harder, I promise.'

Chapter Three

Diana wanted nothing more than to remain in her bedchamber until they all went home again. But that was impossible. They were here for three weeks and she must become accustomed to every last noisy, boisterous member of this other Fleming family. More particularly, she must become accustomed to Aaron, with his tall, manly good looks and his glares of disapproval. Her misgivings loomed as large as ever, despite having enjoyed showing her younger cousins around the Hall.

She had not seen Aaron since their arrival and the thought of seeing him again—of being obliged to *speak* with him and of having his attention directed at her—that thought made her dizzy with nerves. He was so different from any of the young men she met at church at Sunday services: his military bearing; his innate confidence; his appearance. Even Diana could recognise a man of fashion when she saw one.

And then there were those girlhood fantasies fol-

lowing his last visit to Lavenham—flights of fancy in which Aaron had been cast as the knight of her dreams despite her disappointment in his character. She had believed those daydreams deeply buried in the past where they belonged, but they had resurfaced with Aaron's arrival, rendering Diana as tongue-tied and awkward as she had been at the age of eleven.

Perhaps he will be so occupied with Papa and estate matters I shall barely see him.

But that was surely a forlorn hope. Papa would soon become bored and would bury himself once again in his beloved Greek translations. It would be impossible to avoid Aaron—Papa had impressed upon her that her cousins adored Christmastide and its old traditions and that she, Diana, must help them enjoy the festive season as much as they would if they were at home.

That edict from Papa had troubled Diana as much as everything else put together.

What do I know about Christmas festivities?

More importantly, how would her mother react when, above all, she hated any change to her routine?

Diana dressed in her best gown—an azure-blue crepe over a white satin slip—for dinner. Not that her appearance was of any consequence…all that really mattered was that she did not make an utter fool of herself. She leaned forward and examined her appearance in her mirror, tidying a wayward strand of hair. Brown. And not even a rich lustrous brown like that of every last one of Cousin Sally's family, but a dull, muddy sort of colour. And boring hazel eyes, in con-

trast to her cousins, who all boasted large, clear grey orbs that sparkled as they chattered and laughed. They all seemed to know what to say and to understand intuitively what the other meant. They frequently completed one another's sentences and collapsed into giggles when, no matter how she tried, Diana could not understand the funny side.

With a huff of impatience, she turned from the mirror. They might very well be company for her for now, but the arrival of her cousins had also underlined the solitary nature of her life. Had he lived, would she and Simon have become so attuned to one another's thoughts that they, too, would have had no need to finish a sentence before the other understood its meaning? Had he lived, would Mother—like Cousin Sally— watch her children with quiet, maternal pride and a glow of loving approval, instead of with discontent and reproach? The ache of his loss lay heavy in her heart.

Diana cast a final glance around the sanctuary of her bedchamber and squared her shoulders. She could not linger. Mother had demanded that she attend her before dinner, in order that they might go downstairs together. She left the room, closing the door behind her, and then gasped to see her father lurking in the corridor outside. She thought she caught the flash of shimmering orange out of the corner of her eye, but when she looked there was nothing there.

'Papa? Is anything amiss?'

'Ah…no, my dear. Nothing. Nothing whatsoever. I merely came to instruct you to go *straight* down-

stairs, if you please, to be ready to greet our guests before dinner.'

'But Mother specifically asked me to go down with her.'

'*I* shall escort your mother, Diana. Run along now, there's a good girl. We cannot have Cousin Sally thinking we do not know how to treat our guests, can we? Hmmm? Yes. Very good.'

He clasped his hands behind his back and paced slowly in the direction of his wife's bedchamber. Diana stared after him. After about ten paces, Papa turned.

'Go.' He waved his arm at her, as though he were shooing a fly. 'Make haste.'

Diana shook her head, still puzzled, but did as he bid. She descended to the drawing room in some trepidation. It was not that she was shy, precisely, but there were so many of them and she felt a little like an interloper in her own home—a discomfiting feeling. She entered the room and stopped short. The sole occupant was Aaron Fleming. He turned his gaze upon her and her insides performed a somersault. She hauled in a deep breath and gathered her courage. Mayhap she *had* cast him in the white-knight role of her dreams, but she had been young and impressionable then. It had been his strong features she had dreamt of: the square jaw, the lean cheeks, the sharp profile. Not him. Not the person…the character. And so far the character had not impressed her, no matter how hand-

some he looked in his blue tailcoat, cream waistcoat and pantaloons.

'Good evening, sir.'

She concentrated on walking sedately to one of the pair of sofas, the hairs rising on the back of her neck to tell her that his gaze tracked her across the room. She tried to tamp down her fluttering nerves and the snide inner voice that reminded her Aaron was accustomed to the most fashionably dressed ladies in society.

'Is Cousin Sally on her way down?'

His brows bunched across the bridge of his nose. 'She was, but she must have been delayed. We were on our way down when she returned to her bedchamber for a handkerchief. She told me to come ahead of her.'

Diana sat down, but Aaron remained standing, darting occasional glances at the door. He looked as uncomfortable as she felt. That thought settled her nerves. After a period of silence, he cleared his throat.

'As we are cousins—albeit very distant—might we dispense with the formalities?'

'Formalities, sir? I… I am not sure I take your meaning.'

'Sir. You are calling me sir. Could you not call me Aaron and I will call you Diana—or Cousin Diana if you insist.'

He smiled, revealing strong, even teeth, his eyes crinkling at the outer corners. Diana's breath caught. He was so…*masculine*. No man in the neighbourhood came close to equalling him in looks or stature.

'I understand,' he added, 'that you are already on Christian name terms with my brothers and sisters so there should be no objection to it.'

Diana considered his request. She imagined her mother might object but, for herself, she found she was in agreement with him. There was no logic in not treating him in the same manner as she did the rest of his family.

'I have no objection, s— Aaron. I am happy for you to call me Diana.'

Silence reigned once more, until Aaron, with the look of a man speaking against his better judgement, said, 'I realise our visit must be difficult for you, Diana—'

'Difficult?' She gripped her hands in her lap. 'How so?'

'Well…' Aaron paced across the room before returning to sit opposite her '…because I am your father's heir.'

His penetrating gaze fixed on her face and Diana found she could not meet it, concentrating on his mouth instead.

Difficult? She swallowed a bitter laugh. *Arrogant devil.*

But she could not help noticing the beautiful shape of his lips and how they softened his otherwise hard features.

'I should not wish you or your mother to feel… vulnerable…should your father—' His lips compressed, almost disappearing. 'I apologise. That was

insensitive. But I understand he has been in somewhat poor health in recent months.'

His words snatched her attention from his mouth and she frowned. 'Poor health? Why should you think that? He is very well, despite spending too much of his time hunched over his books.'

'I beg your pardon. I… I must have misunderstood. I thought…that is, my mother…' His chest expanded as he hauled in a deep breath. 'I hope my brothers and sisters did not overwhelm you this afternoon? I understand you gave them the grand tour?'

A strained smile stretched his lips as Diana deliberated over her reply, a touch fearful of saying the wrong thing.

'I was not *totally* overwhelmed,' she said eventually, plumping for truthful rather than a platitude. 'Although it did take me some time to learn who was who.'

'It becomes easier when you realise their names are in alphabetical order.' He grinned, his eyes warming as he spoke of his family. 'Eliza, Frances, George, Harry, Isabel and Joseph.'

'Oh!' Diana leaned forward. 'I had not realised that, even though I have known of your family and the children's names all my life. How very…' Appalled by what she almost said, Diana allowed her sentence to peter out.

'How very odd?' Aaron suggested.

'I did not mean to be impolite. Your mother—'

'My mother,' he said, 'is in full agreement. It was

my father's idea. He claimed it would help him re-
member us all. Mama longed to name one of the girls
Rachel but, once Papa got an idea into his head...'
Aaron's eyes dimmed. 'The children with the initials
B, C and D all died in infancy.'

Diana's heart went out to him. 'I am sorry.'

'I have little memory of them,' he said, 'but I was
very happy when Eliza came along. Although, naturally, I was less happy that she was a girl.'

He hesitated and again Diana was aware of him
studying her. She concentrated on her hands, now
loosely clasped in her lap.

'You must miss your brother.'

Diana swallowed hard. She did, but she had no
wish to discuss Simon, or her feelings. And particularly not with Aaron. She was saved from answering
by the door opening. Eliza and Frances entered, followed by George.

'Diana! Here you are. *There*, Eliza. I told you
she would be down here by now. I *knew* Mama was
wrong.'

Frances, dressed in a pretty pink poplin gown,
flounced across the room and plumped down on to
the sofa beside Diana.

'Please do not criticise Mama, Frances. It is un-
becoming.' Eliza glided in her sister's wake. 'And do
remember we are not at home now. We are guests. If
you are serious about making your come out in the
spring, you *must* curb your unfortunate tendency to
speak first and think later.'

Frances pouted. 'You are worse than Mama for scolding.' She turned to Diana. 'I have a gift for you, Diana.' She held her hand out and opened it to reveal a pretty tortoiseshell hair comb.

'Oh, but I could not possibly accept—'

'But you must.' Frances deftly inserted the comb in Diana's hair. 'There! I just knew it would suit you far better than me. My hair is so dark and boring and *common*. The comb can hardly be seen when I wear it, whereas your hair is so warm and rich and...like... like cinnamon! It sets off the comb beautifully. Do you not agree, Aaron?'

Aaron—who had retreated to the far side of the hearth, where he conversed quietly with George— frowned.

'Do I not agree about what, Frances?

Diana's face flamed hot and she wished she could disappear behind the sofa. She'd been delighted by Frances's compliment, but she did not relish being the centre of attention. Neither did she care to hear Aaron's opinion of her hair.

'Frances! You are embarrassing Diana,' Eliza hissed. Then she raised her voice. 'It is nothing, Aaron. Merely Frances and her childish games.'

'*Childish—?*'

Eliza bent over her sister and grabbed her wrist. 'Do you wish me to support you in your ambition to come out next year or do you not?'

Frances glared at her. 'You know I do.'

'Well then, I suggest you be quiet. *Now.*'

Eliza rolled her eyes at Diana, who flashed her a smile, grateful for her intervention. She felt much as though she had been caught in a whirlwind, but a glimpse of Frances's glum expression stirred her compassion and she patted the younger girl's hand.

'Thank you very much for the comb, Frances, and for the compliment about my hair.'

'Come and look in the mirror.'

Frances leapt up and pulled Diana to her feet and across to the fireplace. Diana moved her head this way and that to inspect the comb in the mirror above the mantel. Frances was right. The colour of her hair did contrast well with the random dark brown blotches of the tortoiseshell and it was an exact match to the smaller, lighter brown areas.

'Diana!'

Oh, heavens. Trust Mother to catch me preening in front of the mirror.

She spun round, noticing in passing that Aaron was watching her with an expression of…she would prefer to think of it as sympathy rather than pity.

Chapter Four

Aaron watched a delicate pink wash over Diana's cheeks, brightening her complexion and turning her from an attractive girl into one who was quite stunning. How had he not noticed when they were talking earlier? It had been hard work, keeping the conversation going with someone who appeared to weigh every single word she uttered. He had been reminded of his earlier impression of her as a cat: aloof and hard to cajole into making friends. With a mother like hers, however, maybe she should be forgiven for her caution.

'Mother.' Diana was by her mother's side in an instant, guiding her to sit in a chair next to the fire.

'Not there, Diana. The heat will ruin my complexion.'

Aaron battened down the urge to leap to his cousin's defence. Lady Lavenham—Cousin Venetia—had, if anything, grown more demanding since his visit several years ago. The relationship between mother and

daughter was not really his business, but how he wished Diana would show some backbone and stand up to her mother. The woman would put some commanding officers he had come across to shame with her orders and her exacting requirements.

His own mother had entered the room with Diana's parents and Aaron caught her eye. Her sweet smile made him thank the Lord that she, and not Cousin Venetia, was *his* mother.

'Where were you, Diana?' her mother demanded once she was settled in a chair further from the fire and her shawl arranged around her shoulders. 'I particularly told you to attend me before you came downstairs.'

Lavenham, standing behind his wife's chair, put his hand on her shoulder.

'I asked Diana to come down early, my dear, in order that our guests should not find themselves neglected.'

'I do wish you would not change my arrangements without consulting me, Lavenham. It is vastly unsettling to find you at my door instead of Diana.'

Mama crossed the room to sit next to Cousin Venetia, who was once again dressed in black. Aaron's valet, Giggs, had told him she wore black for the whole of December every year, to mourn Simon. Next to Venetia, Mama looked positively radiant in her favourite orange silk evening gown.

'Diana is making us all most welcome, Venetia,'

Mama said. 'You should be proud of having raised such a lovely young lady.'

A blush again lit Diana's cheeks and her hair gleamed in the light of the candles. Frances was right, Diana's hair did set off the comb beautifully. Aaron had pretended not to hear his sister's earlier appeal for his opinion—he was not yet ready to pay his cousin compliments, but he *was* ready to admit he must not be so quick to judge. Diana had spent the afternoon with his sisters and her wariness had noticeably lessened when Eliza and Frances had come into the drawing room. Mama was right: he must allow her time to lose her inhibitions with him, too.

Harry, Isabel and Joseph burst through the door at that point, drowning out any further exchange between the Lavenhams and Mama with the hubbub of their arrival. All three looked uncommonly clean and tidy, with hair neatly brushed. Both Harry and Joseph sported identical expressions of resignation, but Isabel was beaming. Aaron wandered over to find out what she was up to.

'I am not up to anything.' Isabel gazed up at Aaron, her wide eyes brimming with innocence.

Hearing a muffled snort from her twin, he grasped Harry by the ear. 'Share the joke, why don't you, Harry?'

'Ow!' Harry exclaimed in a loud whisper. 'Let go.'

Diana was watching, her eyes huge. Surely she didn't imagine he was really hurting Harry? How ri-

diculous. Aaron ignored her and bent to put his mouth close to his brother's ear.

'Only,' he said, 'when you tell me what is going on.'

'Isabel fancies she's a lady,' Joseph piped up. 'She's *happy* to dress up and eat dinner in the dining room and to mind her manners, but me and Harry—'

'Harry and *I*,' Aaron interrupted. 'What *do* they teach you at that school?'

'Harry and I would rather eat upstairs.'

Is that all?

Satisfied there wasn't serious mischief afoot, Aaron smiled at Isabel.

'You look very pretty tonight, Issy,' he said. 'Pretty enough to grace any fine dinner table.'

He was gratified to see his compliment bring a blush to his sister's cheeks. She had shot up since he'd last seen her. In fact…he looked from Isabel to Harry and back again…she already topped her twin by a couple of inches. It would not do to say so, however. Poor Harry would be mortified: Aaron well remembered those awkward years between childhood and manhood.

Aaron returned to stand by his mother's chair, curious to observe more interaction between Diana and her mother. Did she have any spirit at all, or did she always capitulate to her mother's demands without protest?

'Thank you,' Mama whispered. 'Isabel is feeling excluded by your brothers.' She sighed. 'She will be a young lady before we know it.'

He did not know how she had remained sane, raising the young 'uns on her own since his father died. His conscience stirred, and with it that niggling guilt…maybe he *should* have spent more time at home and done more to help, rather than living his life purely for pleasure since he left the Guards.

He dropped a kiss on her dark hair, noticing with a pang the widening streaks of silver.

'Oh!'

The high-pitched gasp tore Aaron's attention from the plate of sweetmeats from which he was about to make his selection. At the far end of the dining table, Cousin Venetia had raised a delicate hand to her brow. Her eyelids fluttered.

'Diana,' she quavered. 'Help me to my room.'

Aaron's mother rose to her feet. 'I will help you, Venetia. We should allow the young people every opportunity to get to know one another.'

'Should we?' A hectic streak of colour stained Venetia's cheeks. 'I thank you for your consideration, Sally, but Diana knows my precise needs. Come, Diana.'

Aaron watched as Diana, her expression inscrutable, rose to her feet and rounded the table to her mother's side. He saw the look of exasperation his mother cast at Lavenham, whose gaze remained riveted to his plate, seemingly oblivious to his wife's manipulation of their daughter. How many times had a similar scene been enacted? Despite his earlier irritation with Diana's cool

reserve, sympathy stirred in Aaron's gut. What chance did she have to withstand her mother's demands when her father totally ignored the dramas unfolding around him? And, in fairness, if Aaron were in Diana's shoes, would he not also opt for the quiet life rather than risk continual confrontation? This had been her life since she was eleven. He recalled his dismissal of her as a little brown mouse when they first met and once more guilt trickled through him. Her brother had died barely six months before, her mother—he remembered—was still distraught and her father had simply withdrawn into himself.

What gave me the right to be so judgemental about the behaviour of an eleven-year-old girl?

It was no excuse that he had been little more than a boy himself—he was a man now and still he had been ready to condemn her instead of trying to understand her life. Remorse prompted him to offer an olive branch.

'I hope you will join us again soon, Diana,' he said. 'My mother is correct, we should all become better acquainted if we are to enjoy Christmastide and its festivities.'

Diana shot him an enigmatic look. 'Thank you, Aaron. I shall return as soon as I am able to, once Mother is settled.'

She helped her mother from the room. Aaron's mother dabbed at her mouth with a napkin, murmured 'Excuse me' and followed, leaving Aaron to wonder

why she appeared so determined to spend time with Cousin Venetia.

'Diana!' Venetia's complaint drifted back into the dining room. 'Do watch what you are about. You almost steered me straight into the banister.'

'I am sorry, Mother.'

Aaron mentally shook his head. She was a child no longer; why did she accept the blame when Cousin Venetia, blessed with two perfectly functioning eyes, could easily see for herself where she was walking? He sighed, casting his gaze around the dining table, recalling an earlier conversation in the drawing room. Venetia had not hidden her displeasure at the inclusion of the younger members at the meal, voicing her belief that children—and she had included George in that description, much to his disgust—should be consigned to eating their meals in the nursery. Between them, Lavenham and Mama had convinced her that the family should dine together, particularly at this time of the year. Diana had not ventured an opinion one way or the other and, at the time, Aaron had considered it a miracle she had not sided with her mother.

If he wished his family to enjoy their normal Christmas, it seemed he had no choice but to take the initiative and organise the festivities himself. If it was left to their hosts, he feared Christmas would consist of nothing more than a church service, a roast goose and the distribution of gift boxes to the staff on St Stephen's day.

Lavenham clearly would not stir himself; Cousin

Venetia would resist any change to their normal routine; and Diana—judging by what he had seen thus far—would meekly submit to her mother's edicts.

Well, that would not do for Aaron. Lavenham—according to Mama—had said in his letter that they must celebrate Christmas as normal and, by God, that was precisely what they would do.

'Aaron?'

Aaron spun on his heel and returned to the open door of Cousin Venetia's boudoir, which he had just passed on his way downstairs to meet with Lavenham and Walker in the estate office. His mother and Venetia were sitting in a pair of chairs next to a south-facing window, their embroidery in their laps. Both had paused in their work, but, whilst Mama's attention was on Aaron, Venetia was frowning at Mama.

'Yes, Mama?' He bowed his head. 'Good morning, Cousin. How are you today?'

'I am as well as can be expected, thank you.' Venetia spared him the most fleeting of glances before returning her attention to Mama. 'Really, Sally, there is no need to involve Aaron. I am sure he has more pressing concerns than Diana's whereabouts.'

Pressing? Ha!

Not as far as he was concerned. It was only their second full day here and already he was bored with the minutiae of estate management. He understood the fundamentals well enough and he was confident the rest, with Walker's help, would fall into place when the

time came. Which, from what he could gather, would not be anytime soon. And he really must tackle Mama about that. Why had she told him Lavenham was in ill health when it was clearly untrue?

Fortunately Lavenham appeared to be losing interest in business matters as well and Aaron was certain he would soon return to his studies, leaving Aaron free to spend time with his family.

'It will only take Aaron a few minutes to find Diana and send her to you, Venetia.' Mama caught Aaron's eye. 'Diana promised to mix a tisane for Venetia and—'

'That was an hour ago,' Venetia said, peevishly. 'I declare, that girl has changed and not for the better. Shirking her duties—'

'Now, Venetia. She has not been gone that long. The tisane will take time to infuse and you *did* ask her to replenish the flowers in here as well.' Mama caught Aaron's eyes and rolled her eyes. 'You go and find Diana, Son. Mayhap she is in the conservatory? It was obvious when she showed me around the Hall how she enjoys spending time there with her plants and flowers.'

'Hmmph! She is always idling around in there, avoiding her responsibilities—'

'She is a dutiful daughter to you, Venetia. You ought not to begrudge her an interest of her own.'

'I will go and find her, and send her to you,' Aaron said.

Even such a mundane errand was a welcome delay

to spending yet more hours cooped up in the estate office.

He bowed and withdrew, and headed downstairs.

The sweet sound of song guided him through the warm, moist air of the conservatory. Diana had her back to him as she wandered along the path, selecting an occasional flowering stem which she snipped and placed in a basket. Aaron's gaze travelled the length of her willowy frame from her delicate shoulders to the glimpse of one ankle as she leaned over to reach a more distant bloom.

In her own domain, and private, her normal stiff self-consciousness—the careful watchfulness; the consideration of, it seemed, every word she uttered; the imperceptible withdrawal into herself whenever he spoke directly to her—had disappeared. This was the most relaxed he had ever seen her and she exuded a restful calm that coaxed forth an answering peacefulness from within Aaron.

The lilting song ended. Diana halted, tilted her head back to gaze at the ceiling and breathed in a deep sigh, her shoulders lifting as she inhaled and then dropping as she exhaled. A sudden awkwardness invaded Aaron, as though he were spying upon her in an intimate moment. He turned to leave and, in so doing, his boot scuffed the flagged floor. Diana pivoted, the sudden pallor of her skin enhancing her huge, hazel eyes.

'Oh! You startled me.'

For a moment, she was all vulnerability. But then,

as though a veil had been drawn across her features, her expression was once more inscrutable and she was still. Tension shimmered in the air between them and she reminded him more than ever of a cat as it faced another on its territory, uncertain whether the stranger might be friend or foe.

'I am sorry. I should have spoken when I first came in, but…' He hesitated, but then realised he didn't need to invent an excuse for remaining silent. 'But I enjoyed your singing too much to interrupt.' He smiled at her, keen to put her back at her ease. 'You have a lovely voice.'

Her throat rippled as she swallowed. 'Thank you.' She smiled, tentatively, and then reached for another bloom and snipped the stem. 'Were you looking for your sisters? They have gone for a walk.'

'Did you not wish to join them?'

She looked at him and her eyes appeared to glow from within; they were a definite green today, blending with their surroundings. A trick of the light, Aaron told himself, even as he registered their hypnotic pull.

'It was not that I did not wish to, but…' A fleeting frown creased her forehead. 'So, if you are not looking for your sisters, why *are* you here?'

'I was looking for you.'

'Me?'

'Your mother sent me. Well, to be exact, it was my mother who asked me to look for you. Something about a tisane?'

He thought she suppressed a smile as she cut a stem of foliage and placed it gently on top of the flowers.

'Ah, Mother's tisane.' She shot him a quick glance before focusing again on the plants. 'The herbs are infusing and I shall take it up to her as soon as I have finished in here.'

She snipped another stem, apparently in no hurry to obey her mother's demand.

'Mother,' she continued, 'finds it hard to believe that a tisane cannot be conjured up the instant she conceives a desire for one.' Her mouth curved with an unexpected hint of mischief. 'And *I* consider it my duty not to encourage her by fostering unrealistic expectations.'

Aaron grinned. 'Why, Cousin Diana,' he said. 'You surprise me. Is this an admission that you are not quite the dutiful daughter I believed you to be?'

She blushed, tilting her head to one side. 'Oh, I think I am dutiful enough, but I also have responsibilities in running the household. I cannot neglect them completely, no matter how—'

She snapped her mouth shut, a look of guilt crossing her face, and Aaron was convinced she had been on the brink of criticising her mother.

'Why *did* you choose not to go for a walk with the others, Diana?'

'Mother had need of me.'

He could almost picture the scene—Cousin Venetia playing the poor, neglected martyr and piling the guilt upon her daughter.

'But my mother is there to keep her company. Does she really need you there as well?'

'Mother is...*unsettled* by change.' A rueful smile crossed her face. 'And I am used to her ways. It is how it has always been. Well, how it has been since Simon died.'

Without volition, he brushed the backs of his fingers across her cheek, registering her jolt of surprise. 'Maybe now is a good time to change how it has always been?'

She shook her head. 'I cannot see her ever changing. Now, if you will excuse me, I must fetch Mother's tisane and take these flowers to her.'

He stood aside to allow her to pass. Her lavender scent lingered in the air after she had gone.

Chapter Five

Lady Lavenham's displeasure at having to share Diana's attention and company had given rise to more than one fit of the vapours in the first few days after the other Fleming family's arrival. And, at first, it was only Diana who could settle her down again and who could calm her bitterness at having her beloved Simon's replacement under her roof.

Diana discovered that pacifying her mother's resentment had the unforeseen effect of soothing her own. She might still wish the other Flemings had not chosen Christmas to visit Lavenham, but when Mother complained—as she so often did—that Aaron had come to gloat over his inheritance, Diana could, quite truthfully, say that she had detected no hint of such gloating in either his talk or his behaviour.

Over the next few days, Cousin Sally's calm good sense and practicality little by little brought about a change in Diana's mother, who slowly began to rely less on Diana, leaving her more time to spend with their guests.

And Diana gradually grew to love spending time with her noisy cousins. Her increasing closeness to Eliza, in particular, awoke within her a long-buried desire for friendship, but she worried it was at the cost of her peace of mind. She marvelled at how readily she had locked away all her hopes and dreams and she began to dread the time when her cousins would return home and leave her to readjust to her former dull existence. She did not dare to believe Mother's change might be permanent, but was instead convinced she would revert to her normal demanding self without Cousin Sally's calming presence.

She often wondered if would have been easier not to have her eyes opened in this way.

She had not grown fully accustomed to Aaron—he still spent much of every day with her father—but she *was* more relaxed in his company, their meeting in the conservatory having done much to ease her awkwardness. In its place, however, she was horrified to realise her former infatuation with him had resurfaced and, far from wishing to avoid him, she now keenly anticipated seeing him every day.

Several days after her cousins' arrival, Diana and Eliza were discussing—over a copy of *La Belle Assemblée*—the plans for Eliza's forthcoming wedding when Aaron wandered into the drawing room.

'I am surprised to see you at this hour, Aaron. Why are you not with his lordship?' Eliza said as he saun-

tered across the room to peer over their shoulders at the open magazine.

Diana felt a whisper of warm breath on her neck, sending delicious tingles radiating across her skin.

Aaron rounded the sofa to face them. 'I think he is *finally* bored with discussing business—he disappeared into the library, muttering something about not monopolising my time. And most relieved I am, too.' Aaron smiled and rubbed his hands together. 'Diana...'

Her stomach swooped and her mouth went dry at being the focus of his attention.

'...have you selected your Yule log?'

'Yule log?' Her gaze skittered around the room, searching for inspiration. 'Wh-what is a Yule log?' Two pairs of identical grey eyes stared at her in amazement.

'You do not know what a *Yule log* is?'

Diana felt a touch aggrieved at Eliza's tone. 'Well, it is clearly to do with Christmas,' she said indignantly, 'but, no. I do not know.'

'Come along then. No time to waste.'

Aaron grabbed one hand of each of the girls, hauling them to their feet, and Diana's breath almost seized at the sheer strength of his pull.

'Go and put on some old frocks and warm coats and I will round up the others,' Aaron said, striding for the door. 'We are going on a sortie.'

By the time Diana changed her clothes and joined her cousins outside, they were all assembled. Eliza,

standing next to Aaron, beckoned Diana over and gave Aaron a little shove.

'Aaron…give Diana your arm and then you will be able to tell her all about the Yule log.'

Diana glanced at Aaron, embarrassed at him being coerced into escorting her even though the prospect thrilled her. He, however, appeared happy enough with the suggestion.

'Good idea,' he said cheerfully as he proffered his arm. 'Come along, Diana, and let me tell you all about it.'

Diana, after only a second's hesitation, tucked her gloved hand into the crook of his elbow and they strolled in the wake of the others, towards Lavenham Wood. Eliza and Frances appeared determined to re-gress to childhood, skipping along arm in arm, whilst George, Harry and Joseph—jostling and joking—pushed a handcart containing a saw of around four feet in length with a handle at either end, two sledgehammers and a number of wedge-shaped pieces of wood. Isabel ranged between her sisters and her brothers as though unsure to which group she belonged, but she eventually settled with the other girls.

'Did you bring all those tools with you from Shep-cott Place?' Diana asked Aaron, only half-joking.

'Of course not, what a foolish notion,' Aaron said with a grin. 'You saw our carriage when we arrived. There wasn't enough room left for a mouse, let alone woodcutting tools. Your head gardener provided everything we need.'

'Surely he could have loaned you a couple of men to carry out any sawing required?'

Aaron laughed. 'That, my dear cousin, is tipping perilously close to an insult. The Fleming men need no assistance to harvest our Yule log. Shame on you.'

His happiness was infectious and Diana laughed, a warm feeling of belonging enveloping her.

The three Fleming sisters joined hands, skipping and twirling, as they all trooped along the path that led down into the wood. It was hard to believe Eliza was the same age as Diana and her exuberance made Diana aware of her own limitations. She might take pleasure in watching her cousins, but she was far too self-conscious to join in.

'The Yule log,' Aaron said, 'is a tradition from the Middle Ages. They had massive hearths in those days—far bigger than the ones at Lavenham Hall, unfortunately—and in the summer months they would identify a fallen log and then, just before Christmas, they would bring it up to the house. On Christmas Eve, it would be lit—preferably with a saved remnant of the previous year's log—and it would be expected to last until Twelfth Night. It was thought to be bad luck if the log burned out before then.'

'But we have never had a Yule log, so how can we light it?'

'Harry!'

Harry spun round at the sound of his name, then loped back to his brother, grinning.

'Tell Diana what you brought with you,' Aaron said.

'A piece of the Yule log we saved from last year,' Harry said before, with a whoop, he sped off to catch up with his brothers.

'It is fortunate the weather has been dry. All we must do is find a suitable fallen tree. Our biggest problem will be that the fireplace in the drawing room is not really big enough for a log the size we would use at home.'

'How big is your fireplace?'

'Enormous. Shepcott Place was a medieval manor and it still has the original fireplace in what was the great hall.'

Diana's mind immediately conjured up images of knights and ladies and jousting.

'How romantic,' she breathed. 'Are there suits of armour?'

'One or two,' Aaron said with a laugh, 'although romantic is not a word I should choose to describe it when the wind is blowing through the gaps in the windows and the doors. It is dark and gloomy and the old chimney smokes like the devil, too, when the wind is in the east.'

'I should love to see it.' Diana's face scalded as soon as the words left her mouth and she recalled who she was with. She had forgotten all about feeling uncomfortable or intimidated. Aaron really was very easy to talk to.

'Well, you never know—maybe the opportunity will arise sooner than you think,' he said, his voice warm with amusement.

'But… What do you mean?'

'Oh, dear. I fear I have spoilt Eliza's surprise.' Aaron chuckled and squeezed her hand with his arm, his heat radiating through the fabric of his greatcoat and her kidskin gloves. 'Eliza told Mama how much she likes you and asked if you can visit us in the spring and stay for her wedding. Mama promised to speak to your parents about it.'

Diana digested this information. Her pleasurable flurry of excitement subsided. 'I should like nothing better,' she said. 'But Mother would never allow me to go.'

'But she will have to lose you eventually,' Aaron said, pausing to face her. 'What about when you marry?'

Again, Diana was aware of the heat flooding her face. She pulled her hand from his arm and continued in the wake of the others. 'I shall not marry.'

The scrunch of leaves under Aaron's boots sounded from behind her. He grabbed her hand, hauled her to a stop and then he gripped her upper arms, giving her a little shake.

'What do you mean?' His voice was harsh. 'How can you know you will never marry?'

His gaze sliced into her, sharp as steel. She averted her face, fabricating a smile and a nonchalant shrug.

'Mother is not well enough to attend balls or assemblies and Papa… Papa is content with his books. We do not socialise.'

She was never likely to meet any eligible men and

her few childhood friends had gradually drifted away after Simon's death.

Aaron's fingers tightened, vice-like. She looked up into smouldering grey eyes—reminiscent of storm clouds gathering—and saw a muscle leap in his jaw. Then he muttered something fierce-sounding under his breath and abruptly released her. He grabbed her hand and placed it once again upon his arm. The others had by now dispersed amongst the trees and were lost from sight and Aaron set off in their wake, his long-legged stride forcing Diana to concentrate on keeping pace with him. Her insides tangled with nerves as she tried and failed to understand his re-action. Was he angry with her parents, or with her?

'I'm sorry, Diana.' He slowed his pace as they reached the edge of the wood. 'I spoke out of turn. How you decide to live your life is not my business.' He gave her a rueful smile. 'Reprehensible, I know, but I forgot for a moment that you are not my sister. It is not my place to judge you.'

'There is no need to apologise.' Diana smiled at Aaron, feeling awkward, but with a glow inside that he had—even if only for the shortest moment—thought of her as a member of his family. 'My life is…' She frowned. How could she explain without criticising her parents? 'I am content. I am more fortunate than many: I do not have to earn my living and I want for nothing.'

Except friendship. Except the promise of children. Determinedly she silenced that voice. 'Mother and

Papa love me. And Mother's health has been fragile since Simon died. She is, I think…' and it had never occurred to her before to wonder at her mother's behaviour '…afraid of losing me, too.'

Papa—though Diana loved him dearly—was far too preoccupied to provide the companionship Mother craved. She hated being alone. No wonder she demanded so much attention from Diana.

'You are not lonely, with no friends of your own age?'

Diana held her breath, considering his question. She had not been lonely. Not until now when, in a few short days, her cousins had lifted the veil from her eyes, forcing her to view her life differently. But Christmas would come and go, her cousins would leave and life at Lavenham Hall would return to normal.

'No.' To admit to anything else would be to smash open the lid on her locked-away dreams and to invite in the dissatisfaction and pain that would inevitably follow. She would enjoy this interlude with her cousins and tuck away the happy memories for the future. 'Mother needs me. She has suffered enough.'

Aaron battened down the urge to shake Diana again. Once had been enough. He had only admitted a part of the truth. Yes, he had forgotten momentarily that it was not one of his sisters he was talking to, but the instant he had grabbed Diana his male instincts had reared up and reminded him in no un-

certain terms that she was *not* his sister. And that reaction had prompted him to follow in the path of the others as quickly as possible lest he act upon that unexpected and urgent compulsion to kiss her. How on earth had a woman he was not sure he even liked prompted such a visceral reaction in him?

'Well…' he strove to remain detached '… I still hope your mother will release you for a few weeks at the time of Eliza's wedding. Perhaps there is another relation who might stay at Lavenham to keep her company?'

They were now amongst the trees, the naked branches of oak, ash and sweet chestnut intermingling with the evergreen swags of firs and the stiff salute of hollies. As they walked deeper into the wood, Aaron glanced at Diana at the exact time she looked up at him. Her eyes shifted mysteriously from brown to green as a shaft of sunlight lit her face and his heart tumbled in his chest as he fought another impulse to taste her lips. Thankfully, she appeared innocently oblivious to his turmoil.

'Papa's sister, my Aunt Honoria, has always loved Lavenham Hall.' Her words came slowly. Thoughtfully. 'She grew up here, you know.' Diana's fingers suddenly tightened on his sleeve. 'You may be right.' Her voice was touched with breathlessness. 'Perhaps Mother *will* allow me to visit Shepcott Place.'

She gave a little skip, and it was so unexpected a bubble of laughter escaped Aaron's lips. His opinion of his stiff and unfriendly cousin was altering by the

day. By the minute. It was almost as though… His thoughts faltered. How could he describe it? Almost as though her personality had stirred and stretched after a deep sleep.

Chapter Six

A shout, followed by a shriek, grabbed Aaron's attention.

Grateful for the distraction, he said, 'Come. Let us see what the young 'uns are up to. No doubt Isabel and Harry are at loggerheads again.'

'Poor Isabel.'

Aaron paused. 'What do you mean, poor Isabel?'

A blush washed over her cheeks and Aaron found himself noticing the delicacy of her brows and her fine cheekbones. And the soft fullness of her lips.

This will not do.

He dragged his gaze from her face, surveying instead the nearby woodland for signs of his brothers and sisters.

'Well?' The word came out more harshly than he intended.

'I am sorry, it is not my place to comment on your family.'

He immediately felt like a brute. It was not Diana's

fault he had suddenly—tantalisingly—become aware of her as a woman.

'Don't apologise, I did not mean to bark at you. Come,' he urged her onwards, 'and tell me what you meant whilst we search for the others.'

'I remember what it is to be Isabel's age: no longer a child, but not yet a woman. She is torn between clinging to childhood and playing with Harry and Joseph as she has always done, and embracing her future... following her sisters and leaving those silly, squabbling boys behind.'

'Those are wise words from a woman who has no brothers or sisters.' He wished the words unsaid as soon as they left his mouth, but it was too late. 'Now it is me who is sorry. That was an insensitive thing to say.'

She touched his hand. 'It is a fact, nevertheless. Do you suppose we might agree not to tread so lightly around one another? I have no wish to measure my every word for fear of causing offence.'

He threw her a smile. 'And neither do I wish to spend my entire Christmas apologising to you, Diana. Let us instead agree that, should one of us cause the other distress, we may be adult enough to inform the other of it. We are not children any longer...unlike, I am afraid to say, the twins and Joseph.' He raised his voice. 'You three! Stop that.' He started in their direction, then paused to look back at Diana. He raised a brow. 'You were saying about Isabel? It would ap-

pear that, today, she is firmly in a "clinging to child-hood" mood.'

Diana laughed and he felt another laugh bubble in his chest in response. He inhaled, keeping it in its place as he turned again to the squabbling trio—pushing and shoving over who might begin cutting a fallen tree that lay on the ground—and saw that Isabel, with her two brothers ranged against her, was close to tears.

'Enough!' he roared and, looking sheepish, the three of them immediately obeyed.

He peered around. Only George was in sight. He had been standing apart from the rough and tumble, but now he strode across to stand at Aaron's side.

'Where are Eliza and Frances?' Aaron asked.

'They went that way—' George pointed deeper into the wood '—looking for holly berries and mistletoe whilst we searched for a suitable Yule log. I told them not to go too far and get lost.'

'And will that tree yield a log of the correct size?' Aaron knew George had measured the fireplace in the drawing room to ensure they cut the perfect-sized log.

'It will.'

When had his young brother become so serious? Aaron had sensed a change in him as soon as he had arrived home for Christmas. Now, following Diana's comments about Isabel, Aaron recognised George's eagerness to spend time with him and his constant seeking of his older brother's approval as a sign that he, too, was growing up fast. He clapped George on the shoulder.

'Excellent idea of yours, to measure the hearth,' he said. 'You have saved us much hard work.'

George beamed.

'Now. What were you three arguing about?'

He eyed Harry, Isabel and Joseph in turn. They shuffled their feet and exchanged looks of loathing.

'They won't allow me to help saw the log,' Isabel said. 'It's not fair. Why shouldn't I—?'

'You're a girl,' Joseph shouted. 'And girls are too... Ow!'

Aaron twisted his young brother's lobe before releasing it. 'It is bad manners to interrupt, Joseph. And...' he encompassed Harry in his glare '... I expect you both to remember you are guests here at Lavenham Hall. What Diana thinks of your behaviour I shudder to think. I believe all three of you owe her an apology.'

Poor Mama, having to contend with this on a regular basis.

It was fortunate Harry and Joseph were away at school for much of the year whilst Isabel attended a school in their local town as a day pupil. He couldn't recall Eliza, Frances and George causing such ructions— it must be because Harry and Isabel were twins, making their relationship close and yet more volatile at the same time.

The three of them muttered, 'Sorry, Cousin Diana', in unison.

'Isabel,' Diana said. 'Would you help me find Eliza

and Frances? Then I will show you where to find the best holly and mistletoe berries.'

She walked over to Isabel, put her arm around her waist and tipped her head close to the younger girl's. Aaron strained to catch her words.

'They are looking in the wrong place, you see.' Diana glanced up, catching Aaron's gaze, her smile warming her eyes. 'The best holly berries are on a tree that grows on the edge of the wood. And mistletoe…' her lids lowered, a light blush again enlivening her complexion '…does not grow in the wood, but on some trees near to the river.'

Diana might not know the tradition of burning a Yule log, but that blush confirmed she was aware of the significance of mistletoe and Aaron found himself wondering again what she might taste like. Perhaps the mistletoe would give him the chance to find out and to conquer this unexpected fascination he had developed for her.

Isabel's scowl transformed into a grin and Aaron nodded his thanks at Diana.

'Come along, then, lads. Let us get this log cut, then we can load it in the cart and take it home. Harry and Joseph, as you found the trunk, you may start sawing. Then George and I will take over.'

He knew the novelty of using the saw would soon wear thin.

'George, you have the measurements—show the others where to begin cutting, will you, please?'

As the younger three gathered around the fallen

tree, Aaron overheard Diana's words as she and Isabel walked away, arm in arm.

'We shall leave the boys to the dirty work, Isabel—there, is no need for us to blister our hands or soil our clothes when you have four strapping brothers. It will be no fun pushing a heavy log all the way home to Lavenham…there are *some* advantages to being female.'

Diana and Isabel soon met up with Eliza and Frances, both looking glum.

'We found three hollies,' Eliza said, 'but two of them had no berries at all and the other one was very small and only had about a dozen. What shall we do if we cannot find more?'

Diana was delighted to be able to share her knowledge. 'There is a large holly on the edge of the wood that usually produces an abundance of berries. Follow me.'

The sisters were thrilled to see the holly tree from which they could cut enough berried sprigs to brighten the garlands with which they planned to decorate the Hall.

'But we cannot take any greenery indoors until Christmas Eve,' Frances warned Diana. 'It is unlucky.'

'We shall come back again on Christmas Eve to cut the branches. With four of us working, it should not take long to make the garlands and decorate the Hall,' Eliza said.

Diana then showed the others the place, next to the

River Wye, where a trio of large poplars grew. They sported green balls of mistletoe, their white berries glistening in the afternoon sun. The mistletoe grew high up out of reach, but Diana's suggestion of ladders and gardeners was scoffed at by her cousins.

'Our brothers would be furious were you to suggest such a thing,' Frances said. 'They pride themselves on being able to cut what we need themselves without the use of ladders.'

'Male pride,' Eliza said, with a wink at Diana.

Diana eyed the tall trees uncertainly. They were very tall but well-branched so should prove easy enough to scale, but…

'*All* of your brothers?' The thought of Aaron climbing so high churned her stomach. It would be a long way to the ground. The younger boys were so much smaller and more nimble than their oldest brother.

'And me,' Isabel declared. 'I've always done it before. I'm excellent at climbing trees.'

Eliza's brows twitched as she caught Diana's eye. Diana had quietly told her of Isabel's earlier upset, whilst Frances and Isabel had run ahead to the poplars.

'Isabel, do not forget you are to be my bridesmaid in the spring. I cannot risk you breaking a limb or injuring yourself. It would ruin my wedding. And think how the bark will roughen your hands.'

'Besides,' Diana added, with a smile, 'climbing trees is a pastime for children, is it not? You, surely,

are too grown up for such things even if Harry and Joseph are not.'

'*I* gave up climbing trees years ago,' Frances declared. 'Only hoydens climb trees after childhood.'

Isabel elevated her chin. 'You are right. I shall leave such childish activities to my brothers.'

They returned to the wood, following the sound of sawing until they emerged into the small clearing that had been created by the fallen tree. Two cuts were needed to create the log—Harry and Joseph had already sawed through the narrower end and Aaron and George were now sawing through the thicker end, closer to the roots. Their coats and waistcoats lay discarded on the ground and Diana stared, mesmerised by the to-and-fro motion of the sawing and the way in which Aaron's muscles strained his shirt as he worked with his back to her.

Quite fascinating.

A swell of heat swirled deep inside her and then flared to flush her skin as her gaze dropped to the taut roundness of his buttocks. Confused, she tore her gaze from Aaron and glanced at her female cousins, apparently unperturbed by their brothers' activities. Eliza had crossed her arms over her chest and was tapping her foot whilst Frances gazed vacantly into the distance. Isabel chatted with Harry, their former squabble seemingly forgotten.

Diana moved, subtly, to alter her viewpoint. Sweat glistened on Aaron's brow and his sleeves were rolled up, exposing hard, sinewy forearms dusted with dark

hair. Her stomach clenched oddly as she recalled the rock-like feel of that arm beneath her gloved hand. As she watched, Aaron signalled to George, who was beetroot red and even sweatier than his brother, to take a break.

Aaron swiped his left arm across his forehead as he straightened with a low groan that seemed to vibrate right through Diana. She watched as he put his hands on his hips and arched backwards, stretching. He then straightened, nodded to George and they settled once more into a steady rhythm of push and pull. Again, she wrenched her gaze away.

'This is dull indeed.' Frances touched Diana's arm. 'Shall we return to the Hall?'

Diana did not wish to leave. Delicious fragmented pictures, with Aaron once more cast as her knight in shining armour, floated inside her head. When her cousins had first arrived at Lavenham, she had dismissed Aaron as a handsome face with no substance to his character. Gradually, though, her perception of him had changed. He no longer seemed arrogant, she enjoyed his company and her feelings were hopelessly muddled.

'You go on back if you wish to, Frances, but I should prefer to stay if you do not mind. I have never seen a Yule log being brought in before.'

Eliza grimaced. 'There will be nothing new to see, Diana, merely more of the same. Back and forth, back and forth…and that noise! It sets my temples throbbing.'

Nothing new to see… Diana's eyes were drawn back to Aaron. More of the same sounded utterly tempting.

'But,' Eliza added, 'you need not feel obliged to go with us. Aaron will see you safely home.'

And with that, she whisked Frances and Isabel away, leaving Diana with Aaron and his three brothers.

The saw jammed and Aaron called for Harry and Joseph to knock in a couple of wedges, to hold the cut open. He sauntered over to Diana as his brothers enthusiastically wielded the sledgehammers. With him came radiated heat, the sound of quickened breathing and the smell of the outdoors and of sweat…not the stale, offensive sweat of the farmhands after they had laboured in the fields all day in the heat of summer, but a fresher scent of hot male…musky, with a hint of spice.

Diana smiled at him, praying her cheeks were not as pink as they felt. 'That looks like hard work.'

He grinned. 'It is. And hot. Excuse me…' He began to unknot his neckcloth, then paused and raised a brow. 'I trust you do not object?'

Diana shook her head. He pulled his neckcloth from around his neck and then used it to fan his face. Diana could not tear her gaze from the hint of dark hair made visible by the open neck of his shirt. Her heart felt as though it were lodged in her throat. Heavens, but he was attractive. And all male, unlike the youth she recalled. She had not, until now, considered what changes might have been wrought by his

years of military service. A soldier did not remain a boy for long and Aaron had fought at Waterloo; had performed acts of bravery, so Cousin Sally had written in her letters to Papa.

'This will not take much longer.' A vertical line grooved above the bridge of Aaron's nose as he studied her face. 'Are you quite well, Diana? You look a little flushed yourself.'

Diana swallowed. 'I am quite well, thank you. I dare say it is the surfeit of fresh air.'

Their eyes fused for several moments as their surroundings seemed to fade away. Aaron's frown deepened and then, of a sudden, it cleared.

'Fresh air,' he murmured. 'Quite.' His gaze dropped, a knowing smile tugging at his mouth. 'I must go and help George.'

He pivoted on his heel and strode back to the trunk, leaving Diana wondering if he had somehow guessed at the turmoil raging in her breast. Aaron and George soon finished cutting the log. The younger three jostled for position to heave the log on to the handcart whilst Aaron put his waistcoat and jacket back on.

'Ouch!'

It was Joseph. In a flash, Aaron was by his side, examining his hand as his youngest brother battled to hold back tears.

'It's only a scratch,' Harry scoffed. 'What a fuss. You're just like a girl.'

'Enough, Harry. George…you and Harry start pushing the cart back to the Hall, please.'

Aaron turned back to Joseph, his forehead furrowed with concern as he used his handkerchief to dab at the blood. Diana joined them, impressed by this change in him. She had thought him brusque in his previous dealings with his brothers, but this revealed a different side to him—a caring side. The thought came unbidden that he would be a good father.

'Can I help?' Diana took Joseph's hand to examine his thumb. Not only had he cut his thumb, but half the nail had torn away, exposing the nailbed.

'It hurts.' Joseph's bottom lip jutted.

'I'm not surprised,' Diana said. 'Injuries like that are most painful. I have some salve at home that will help.' She smiled up at Aaron. 'I often make up potions and lotions in my still room, to treat the servants and the estate workers.'

'Well, it's fortunate we have someone with medical knowledge, isn't it, Joseph?' Aaron tousled his brother's hair. 'And it's also fortunate it's not your toe that's injured. I shouldn't fancy carrying a great lad like you all the way home. Come along. The sooner we get back, the sooner Diana can treat it.'

Later, after Diana had treated and bandaged Joseph's thumb, Aaron stayed Diana with a hand on her arm as she went to leave the still room. She halted, and turned to him, her brows raised.

'Thank you.' He smiled into her eyes. 'I hope you enjoyed your first experience in fetching the Yule log, despite the surfeit of fresh air.' He bent his head, put-

ting his lips close to her ear. 'I have enjoyed getting to know you better, Cousin.'

All the way upstairs to her bedchamber his words echoed in Diana's head. Was he just being nice? Cousinly? Or had he intended to convey some other message?

Whatever *Aaron's* intention, Diana was in no doubt of the tentative hope unfurling in her heart.

Chapter Seven

Christmas Eve was the busiest day Diana could remember for a long, long time and she relished every bustling, noisy minute of it: cutting and loading boughs of fir and laurel in the woods; gathering armfuls of ivy; watching—heart in mouth—as Aaron and his brothers clambered up trees in pursuit of the most richly berried sprigs of holly and mistletoe; and raiding the garden for sweet-smelling bay and rosemary. Finally, the four girls laboured to fashion the garlands, enhancing the greenery with bows of scarlet ribbons, candles, paper flowers cut from gold and silver paper, apples and nuts.

The boys and Aaron joined them to help decorate the downstairs rooms, draping garlands over mantels and windowsills, and hanging decorative balls of greenery from wall sconces and chandeliers. They had enough left over to decorate the servants' hall, too, and the younger element—up to and including Frances—clamoured to be allowed to deliver them,

enticed by the wonderful, mouth-watering smells of baking that had scented the entire house as the afternoon wore on.

'I envy them,' Aaron said, his voice a little wistful as the youngsters disappeared, laughing and singing, towards the kitchen. 'Do you remember, Eliza, how we used to haunt the kitchen on Christmas Eve, begging to scrape out the mixing bowls and squabbling to be the first to sample Cook's gingerbread when she took it from the oven?'

Eliza laughed. 'Yes, and burned our mouths more often than not, so impatient were we.' She sighed. 'It will never be the same, after this year.'

'But you will have your own family soon, Eliza, and you will create your own traditions and memories,' Diana said, feeling a little wistful herself.

'I suppose I shall,' Eliza said. 'It will seem strange at first, but…' She sighed again and shrugged. 'We cannot cling on to childhood for ever, much as we might like to. I hope you do not mind us doing all this, Diana? Mama told me you do not celebrate Christmas since Simon died, but do you have happy memories of when you were children?'

Diana's heart twitched at the reminder of all she had lost, the memories she had buried deep because to remember would mean she must mourn not only the loss of her brother and her friend, but also of her own childhood. Now, the door to that past was wide open and long-suppressed memories of happiness and laughter flooded through.

'Yes. Yes, I do.'

She tamped down a surge of emotion and turned away, bending her head to fiddle with the last remaining decoration to be hung—the kissing bough: mistletoe bunched with sprigs of scarlet-berried holly and tied with red ribbon bows.

She vaguely heard a whispered exchange and then Eliza said, her voice over-bright, 'I promised Mama I would tell her as soon as we finished decorating down here. I shall go and find her whilst you hang the mistletoe, Aaron.'

Her footsteps receded up the stairs. A gentle hand touched Diana's shoulder, soothing as it caressed.

'Eliza did not mean to upset you, Diana.'

She forced herself to meet Aaron's concerned gaze. 'I know. It is all right; I am not upset. It just brought back memories.' She inhaled. 'And it brought home to me how different my life would be if Simon was still here.'

One dark brow rose. 'Well, you would not have been invaded by my family for a start,' he said, wryly.

'Oh! I did not mean that. I have loved meeting you all.'

Aaron tipped his head to one side and smiled, his eyes warm. 'I am glad. Christmas should be a time for family and it should be a time of hope, not of sorrow.' He brushed her cheek with one finger, his touch featherlight. 'Relive the happy times, Diana; do not dwell on the sadness.' He straightened then, his hand falling away. 'I must hang this mistletoe, so

all is ready when our mothers come to make their inspection.'

He fetched a chair from the side of the hall and stood it beneath the chandelier suspended from the centre of the ceiling. Once he had tied the kissing bough to one arm of the chandelier, he replaced the chair, then went back to stand beneath the kissing bough.

'I need to be sure I can reach it.' He stretched up one long arm.

Diana crossed to the middle of the hall and tilted her face up to stare at it. 'Why do you need to reach it?'

Aaron grinned. 'Surely you know the custom of removing a berry for every kiss, Diana? Here. I shall demonstrate.'

He bent to kiss her quickly on the cheek. Her breath seized in her throat and she felt her cheeks flame.

'And now,' he said, with a wicked grin and a teasing twinkle in his eyes, 'I remove a berry, like so—' he plucked a berry from the kissing bough '—until all the berries have gone.' His voice deepened. 'Consider the consequences if the mistletoe is hung out of reach, Diana. The kissing might *never* stop.'

A hot flame flared in his eyes and was as quickly gone, leaving Diana to wonder if she had imagined it as a rush of feet from the direction of the kitchen heralded the return of the rest of the Flemings, led by Harry and Isabel.

'Your cook is the best, Diana,' Harry said. 'She gave us all gingerbread and it was scrumptious.'

'*And* she is sending the maids to the drawing room with mulled wine and fruit cup and mincemeat pies!' Isabel added breathlessly.

Diana smiled at their excitement and their simple pleasure.

'What do I see here?' George struck a pose, pointing dramatically at the kissing bough. 'No maiden is safe now!' and, laughing, he grabbed first Frances and then Isabel and kissed them soundly on their cheeks, to the accompaniment of squeals and giggles.

Diana had no time to feel awkward or like the outsider, for George grabbed her hand next and tugged her beneath the mistletoe before, a little shyly, he pecked her on the cheek. Then Aaron kissed Frances, followed by Isabel and, finally, Diana again, his warm lips lingering in a way they had not before, his cologne—subtle and spicy—teasing at her senses. As he drew away, he caught her eye and her stomach swooped and knotted as heat sparked between them.

Maids carrying trays now appeared whilst voices from the direction of the stairs suggested Eliza was returning with their mothers. The entire family went to the drawing room, which filled with happy voices and much laughter as they ate and drank and planned the coming evening's entertainment.

Even Mother's disapproval could not crush Diana's joy.

'Mistletoe? A Yule log? I never heard such non-

sense,' she had grumbled when she saw the decorations. 'Such heathen practices died out centuries ago and quite rightly, too. Why you cannot be satisfied with a church service and a roast goose I fail to comprehend.'

'Now, Venetia, do not say so.' Cousin Sally smiled encouragingly at Diana as she steered Mother to her chair. 'It is harmless fun. The village folk have always partaken of the old traditions and, from what I read in the newspapers, those traditions are enjoying a revival amongst our sort of people. I think it looks splendid, children—you have done well.'

Mother scanned the room again. 'Hmmph. Yes… well… I dare say it will not hurt anyone. And you won't forget to light the Christmas candle, will you?'

Everyone stared in amazement, before Frances hurried away to find the biggest candle she could. Searching her memory, Diana recalled the ancient tradition of placing a lit candle on a windowsill to signify that the Christ child—and any weary traveller—would find a welcome in their home. The candle would be left to burn right through to Christmas night.

Mother's words might have been uttered in a grudging tone, but they lifted everyone's spirits for the remainder of the afternoon and well into the evening.

On Christmas morning Diana arose early, before dawn. The maid had already been in to kindle her fire and Diana had asked for warm water to be sent up immediately. She dressed in a simple woollen dress,

wrapped her shawl around her shoulders and hurried silently downstairs to wander through the downstairs rooms, committing the festive decorations to memory and reliving the warmth, fun and laughter of Christmas Eve. She had never felt such joy and contentment. Whatever happened after this Christmas, she would always have these happy memories to sustain her. She left the drawing room and crossed the hall. The sight of the kissing bough, hanging below the chandelier, tripped her pulse and set her cheek tingling at the place where Aaron's lips had lingered.

'Diana.'

Her heart leapt at that deep voice and she halted, her hand pressed to her chest as her eyes shifted to the tall figure on the stairs. Aaron. At the very moment she had been thinking about him and reliving... She swallowed past a sudden constriction in her throat. He had paused halfway down the flight, a smile playing around his lips as his eyes traced her from her head to her toes, sparking prickles of awareness wherever they touched. Would he kiss her again? Unconsciously, she pulled her shawl tighter around her. She had no need to look up to know she stood directly beneath the mistletoe. Without volition, one hand rose to her cheek, remembering the soft touch of his lips.

Aaron descended the remaining treads, the intent in his gaze pinning Diana to the spot. Her heart thudded in her chest as he reached the tiled floor of the hall. She could not have moved away if her life depended

upon it. He stopped immediately in front of her, his eyes burning into hers.

'Good morning,' he murmured.

She felt her lips tremble as she curved them into a tentative smile. His gaze lowered to her mouth.

'And Merry Christmas…' His voice deepened. He cradled her face and dipped his head. 'Diana…'

His breath whispered across her lips. She parted them and then his mouth covered hers…softly moving, slick and sensuous and skilled, sparking pulses of energy that melted her bones with the fire of her need. She clutched his shoulders and followed his lead, shyly returning the caress of his tongue, losing all track of time and place. She sighed her pleasure and his answering hum of appreciation rumbled through her.

It felt like for ever—although it could have easily been mere seconds—before he abruptly tore his lips from hers and muttered a curse beneath his breath, jerking Diana from the sensual haze in which she drifted.

What did I do wrong?

She stepped back, her throat tight with repressed emotion as she strove to conceal her confusion, smoothing her skirts and rearranging her shawl. Aaron's expression had blanked, his grey eyes curiously opaque. Was she supposed to understand—?

The sound of footsteps from above penetrated Diana's dazed thoughts and, seconds later, a housemaid appeared at the head of the stairs, carrying a bucket.

'It's lucky I heard her,' Aaron whispered. 'If she'd seen us, I dread to think of the consequences.'

So now I know.

It would have winded her less if he'd curled his hand into a fist and punched her in the stomach. A snatched kiss under the mistletoe, and she—*fool that I am*—had kissed him back as though…as though…

Stubbornly suppressed tears stung her nose and burned behind her eyes.

As though it was for real. Such a gullible fool.

She'd fallen once again into that trap of daydreaming about him as a white knight. Diana pressed her lips tight as she fought to conceal her humiliation, but on the heels of that emotion came disillusionment. In him. She'd thought—*or was it just a forlorn hope all along?*—that he'd changed and yet, here he was, behaving no differently to that careless lust-filled youth who had chased after giggling housemaids.

What the hell was I thinking?

Aaron cast about desperately for something to say to allay any suspicions the approaching maid might have. The last thing he needed was to be forced into a marriage because he had been overcome by…what? Curiosity? Lust?

All he knew was since that moment in the woods—when he had responded to the dawning of desire in Diana's eyes and had been forced to battle his urge to kiss her—he had fantasised about quite how she would taste. His eyes had been drawn to her, time and

again, as he enjoyed her pleasure at taking part in his family's Christmas traditions and his fascination with this distant cousin had deepened.

When he had seen her, perfectly positioned under the kissing bough, he had only intended another chaste peck on the cheek. But, as he drew closer, her evocative scent weaved through his senses and, before he knew it, his lips were on hers.

So now he knew how she tasted: sweet and fresh and...tantalising. And all he could think was he wanted more.

Diana's clear voice cut across his thoughts.

'Yes, of course I shall cut some flowers for your mama's bedchamber, Cousin Aaron,' she said. 'I shall send them up directly.'

She really is as cool as a cat.

And quick thinking, too. Unlike him. She betrayed not a hint of the fluster that, surely, she must be feeling after such a kiss. Was that a trait to admire, or one to resent? It made her impossible to read. He silently cursed himself again for taking such a careless risk.

'Thank you.' His voice matched Diana's for nonchalance. 'I am sure Mama will appreciate them.'

A swift glance at the maid as she reached the foot of the stairs revealed no hint of suspicion. Relief crashed through him. He knew one thing for an absolute certainty: there was far more at stake here than a passing flirtation. His position as Lavenham's heir meant he must be extra cautious around Diana, no matter how enticing he found her. The last thing he

wanted was to find himself treading a path to matrimony simply because a servant had witnessed a passionate kiss under the mistletoe. He understood his own character well enough to know he would resent and resist any attempt to force him into marriage, and his recent escape from the clutches of Caroline Caxton had made him doubly cautious.

He had always known he must eventually marry, but that had been a long way in his future: he was only five-and-twenty. Still young. But the complex emotions aroused by this alluring yet enigmatic cousin of his had started him questioning that view of his future and they were questions to which he still had no definitive answers.

He needed time to explore what he truly wanted and how he felt about Diana and, even more importantly, how she felt about him.

He watched her glide down the hallway in the direction of her conservatory. She had not been able to disguise her response to his kiss: she had kissed him back, melted against him. No matter how well she disguised her feelings now, he was certain that kiss had affected her as much as it had affected him.

Later that morning, the Flemings *en masse* attended the local church for the Christmas Day service. Aaron's silent prayer that the Caxtons would not attend was in vain…they entered the church as the final peal of the bells faded, sitting towards the back of the congregation as the vicar ascended to the pulpit.

Aaron was sitting in the pew directly behind Diana, whose hair…

How had Frances described the colour of her hair again? Cinnamon, that was it.

Whose cinnamon-coloured locks were pinned up, topped by a dark blue hat with a white feather, exposing the slender column of her neck. She turned her head a little and the curve of her cheek came into his view. He shifted uncomfortably as his fingertips recalled the silky smoothness of her skin and he felt himself harden. He wrenched his gaze from her and tried to concentrate on the vicar's words, but he found his thoughts constantly straying back to Diana and that morning's kiss.

The vicar droned on, the message of his Christmas Day sermon mingling with assorted coughs and sneezes and the occasional snore from the congregation.

After the service the villagers and the surrounding gentry congregated outside the church to wish each other a 'Merry Christmas' and to exchange items of news and titbits of gossip. The Lavenhams and Mama, together with Diana, Eliza, Frances and George, paused to talk to the vicar whist Harry, Isabel and Joseph rushed away, down the cobbled path and out through the lych-gate. Aaron followed them—hoping to avoid the notice of the Caxtons—and paused just outside the gate, where he could keep

an eye on the young 'uns and make sure there was no mischief afoot.

'Mr Fleming!'

The shrill voice set Aaron's teeth on edge. He plastered a smile on his face and turned back to greet Miss Caxton and her brother, who were bearing down upon him.

I might have known I wouldn't escape that easily.

Again, he regretted not confronting them when he had discovered their plan to entrap him, because it now meant he could not avoid acknowledging them.

Aaron bowed. 'It is a pleasure to see you both again. Merry Christmas.'

'Well met, Fleming.' Caxton thrust out his hand, which Aaron shook, thrusting down his resentment at this fellow officer who had so cynically betrayed their friendship. 'You staying at Lavenham? Jolly good. It's been devilish dull at home, I can tell you. You joining the hunt tomorrow?'

'No, not this time.'

Aaron's anger at his erstwhile friend simmered anew, but he was conscious that Eliza and Diana had followed the Caxtons to the lych-gate. He must not forget he was a guest at Lavenham Hall and that the Caxtons were the Lavenhams' neighbours. And friends, too, for all he knew.

Miss Caxton, seemingly unperturbed by his brusqueness, fluttered her lashes at him and pouted.

'You did not tell us you were spending Christmas-

tide in our neighbourhood, Mr Fleming. Shame on you.' She tapped him playfully on the arm.

Aaron set his jaw. 'I was unaware of it myself when last we met, Miss Caxton. Had I known, you would have been the very first to know.'

Eliza and Diana had by now joined them and Diana's gaze flicked to his, inscrutable as ever.

'Good morning, Mr Caxton, Miss Caxton,' she said, inclining her head. 'I did wonder if you were already acquainted with my cousins and I see that you are.'

Miss Caxton returned Diana's greeting with a tight smile and it was clear to Aaron the two were not friends.

Caxton bowed. 'How d'ye do, Miss Fleming? It is too long since we last met. I need not enquire after your health, for I can see you are in fine form.'

His gaze slid over Diana from her face to her toes and back again, appraising her as though she were a prize filly. Aaron fought the urge to plant his fist in the man's face for his insolence. Then Caxton bowed to Eliza and greeted her.

'Good morning to you both,' Eliza said, both her voice and smile chilly. She had been vocal in her condemnation of the pair when Aaron had told her what happened. 'I had not realised you lived near Lavenham.'

'Oh, yes, indeed,' Miss Caxton gushed. 'We have always lived in this area…such a wonderful place to live.' She edged closer to Aaron and peeped up at him

through her lashes. 'I should be *exceedingly* loath to have to move away.'

Aaron stiffened. It was one thing throwing broad hints at him in London, quite another to cast her bait within hearing of his family. He saw Eliza give Miss Caxton a coldly haughty stare, but he recognised a touch of mischief in the smile that flickered on Diana's lips.

'I am sorry to hear you may have to leave the district, Miss Caxton.'

Miss Caxton tossed her head. 'I did not say I was *leaving*, Miss Fleming; merely that I should be loath to do so.'

Diana regarded her gravely. 'It will do your nerves no good to dwell upon eventualities that may never come to pass, Miss Caxton. Might I suggest you instead direct your thoughts to your good fortune in continuing to reside in such a beautiful part of the country?'

Chapter Eight

Aaron bit back his grin at Diana's gentle mockery
and his admiration for her grew as she met the other
girl's glare with composure. Her dignity—in contrast to Miss Caxton's affected behaviour—was like
a breath of cleansing air.

And I had thought her without spirit.

'My nerves, Miss Fleming, are perfectly sound,
thank you so much for your concern.'

Miss Caxton's eyes glittered dangerously and—his
protective instincts aroused—Aaron moved closer to
Diana. She, however, appeared unconcerned. Once
again, she had surprised him. Miss Prim-and-Proper—
as she had first appeared—had hidden depths.

That kiss was hardly prim and proper.

His pulse quickened at the memory.

'As we are old friends, can I entice you to dine
with us at Caxton Manor whilst you are in the area,
Mr Fleming?' Miss Caxton said. 'And your family
and your hosts, of course. Although…' and she di-

rected a kindly smile at Diana '... I do understand Lady Lavenham's reluctance to socialise, particularly at this time of year. You must not feel obliged to leave her on her own if she declines to come, Miss Fleming. I do sympathise, but you will hardly miss a thing, I promise you.'

'I thank you for the invitation, Miss Caxton,' Aaron said, 'but I must decline on behalf of us all. Please excuse us—it is time we went home.'

'But...when shall we see you again, Fleming?' Caxton said. 'You have become something of a stranger of late.'

'We *might* meet again at church next Sunday, I suppose,' Aaron said. 'If, of course, your sister is still resident in the area.' He smiled and bowed, then turned to Diana, effectively dismissing the Caxtons. 'Would you allow me to drive you home in my curricle, Diana? Mama found it a little chilly on the way to church and I should prefer her to return home in the carriage.'

'Nothing would give me greater pleasure,' Diana said, smiling sweetly at Miss Caxton, who scowled as Diana tucked her hand into the crook of Aaron's elbow. 'Goodbye, Miss Caxton; Mr Caxton. *Such* a pleasure to see you again.'

The remainder of the Fleming party, having taken their leave of the vicar, approached the lych-gate as the Caxtons walked away.

'Aaron?' Mama's voice was sharp. 'Where are the children?'

'They are only a little way down the street, Mama.

There is no need to fret. They've been keeping out of trouble.'

George strode forward. 'I'll go and round them up, Mama.'

'Frances and I will come with you, as we are all travelling together in our carriage,' Eliza said.

Mama watched them go with a smile. 'Dear George,' she said. 'He is such a help.' She turned to the Lavenhams. 'Whenever I worry about losing Eliza, the knowledge that George is so dependable eases my mind. I don't know what I would do without him. In fact, the younger boys listen to him far more than they do Eliza or Frances.'

'You are so very fortunate to have so many fine sons,' Venetia said with a sigh.

There was a fraught silence and Aaron felt Diana's fingers clutch his sleeve. Did the woman have no thought for the hurt she inflicted on her daughter? Was it not enough that her reclusive ways had isolated Diana and made her an easy object for ridicule and false sympathy from the likes of Miss Caxton?

'I know you were cold on the way here, Mama,' Aaron said, to divert attention from Venetia's thoughtless remark, 'so I suggest you travel home in the carriage with Arthur and Venetia. Diana has agreed to keep me company in the curricle.' His arm flexed involuntarily, squeezing Diana's hand into his ribs.

'But…no! That is unacceptable.' Venetia glared at Aaron. 'I need Diana with me.'

He thought Venetia had improved—she had even

worn a lilac pelisse and hat today, rather than her ubiquitous black—but it seemed not. There was a touch of panic in her eyes as she looked from Aaron to Diana and back again and Aaron recalled Diana's comment that her mother was afraid of losing her as well as Simon. Well, that might be true, but it did not give her the right to exploit her daughter like this.

Aaron cast a sidelong glance at Diana, wondering what her reaction would be. Would she give in to her mother, or would she stand up to her?

A muscle bunched in Diana's jaw. 'Cousin Sally will be with you, Mother, as well as Papa, and we shall be at home in less than half an hour.'

Mama tucked her arm through Venetia's. 'These young people do not notice the cold like we do, Venetia; I am certain Diana will enjoy the drive and we will be home before you even notice her absence, I promise. You can fill me in on all the gossip about your neighbours.'

Venetia's lips thinned so much they were barely visible in her pale face. 'Diana. I—

'Do you know,' Mama added, 'the vicar swears it will snow before the week is out.'

Lavenham clasped his wife's other elbow and together he and Mama turned her in the direction of the waiting carriage. 'Yes, yes, let us leave the youngsters to enjoy each other's company. Snow, you say, Sally? What about that, Venetia? That will be fun for the children, will it not? Come now, let us away home and get you and Sally into the warm by the fire.'

Venetia allowed them to lead her away, but she called over her shoulder, 'Diana! I expect you to attend me the *minute* I arrive home, do you hear me?'

'Yes, Mother.'

Diana watched her mother being led away, her thoughts whirling. There was something...she could not quite put her finger on it, but there was definitely something going on that she was not a party to. She glanced up at Aaron. He did not appear puzzled. Mayhap she was imagining it...she'd always been prone to vivid imaginings.

Aaron clasped her hand; his strength as he helped her into his curricle and the scent of his cologne combined to send her senses reeling. She fought to suppress her reaction. Vivid imaginings? What could be more vivid than imagining a kiss under the mistletoe meant anything more than a pleasurable way to spend a few minutes?

At first, Diana had been hurt by Aaron's reaction to their kiss and had wondered if he was angry with her or if he somehow blamed her for that kiss, but his protectiveness during their encounter with the Caxtons had reassured her. He had positively bristled when Gordon Caxton had leered at her in his usual objectionable way and he had been quick to shield her from the worst of Miss Caxton's spite.

The fact remained, however, that he clearly dreaded the consequences if they had been caught. There could be only one outcome... She would be compromised

and he would be forced to marry her. And no matter how much she longed for him, she couldn't bear the thought of being married to a man who did not love her.

'I owe you an apology for kissing you,' Aaron said, as soon as the horses were in motion.

She could not escape this conversation. Her only hope was to act as though the kiss meant as little to her as it did to him. She took her courage in both hands, desperate to hide her burgeoning feelings.

'I thought we agreed we would not spend our time apologising to one another?'

'We did. But I still should not have kissed you…at least, not in the way I did.'

'I did not stop you.'

There was a brief silence.

'Why did you not stop me?'

She half-turned on the bench seat and studied his strong profile. After half a minute, he looked at her and quirked a brow.

'Do I infer from your silence that you do not know the answer?'

She searched his eyes. 'I do know the answer. I was debating whether I dare to say it out loud.'

His brows lowered, but then his frown cleared and he shouted with laughter, shaking his head. 'You never cease to amaze me, Diana. Here was I, expecting you to blush and go all maidenly on me and you sit there, cool as can be, and tell me exactly what you are thinking. Do you never prevaricate?'

She worked hard to keep any trace of amusement from her expression.

'I try not to,' she said. 'I do find it easier when the person to whom one is talking knows exactly what one means, don't you? Prevarication can lead to so many misunderstandings. If I cannot speak the truth, then I should prefer to say nothing at all.'

'And that makes you a rarity amongst women,' Aaron said. 'And amongst men, come to that. It is an admirable trait.'

'Thank you.'

'And have you reached your decision? Do you dare to say out loud why you did not stop me kissing you?'

She caught her bottom lip between her teeth, and saw his gaze drop to her mouth. *Now* she blushed. He looked up again and his eyes were dark and unfathomable.

'Yes. I *shall* dare to tell you. I did not stop you kissing me because I *wanted* you to kiss me. I have never been kissed before, you see. And I may never be kissed again.'

She paused. She had relived that kiss, over and over, whilst the vicar had droned on. And she *knew*— inexperienced as she was—that Aaron *had* enjoyed kissing her, as much as she had enjoyed kissing him. And so now she could not resist teasing him a little by adding, 'I regret I was too inexperienced for you to derive any pleasure from it.'

'Pleasure?' His voice was gruff. 'You surely are not serious?'

He was staring at her, but she kept her attention firmly on the horses' ears, struggling again to prevent a smile from showing. He hauled in an interminable breath, but then released it with a whoosh, a low laugh riding on it.

'You little tease! And you just told me if you cannot speak the truth you prefer to say nothing at all.'

'Ah…but you must ask yourself: can you *ever* trust the person who claims to always tell the truth?' she asked gravely. 'For they may as easily be lying.'

'And you were lying?'

She cocked her head and smiled sweetly at him. 'I did not say that. I have heard it said a lady must retain *some* mystery.'

'Very well, Mysterious Lady. And now, I shall be honest with you. I did enjoy kissing you, very much. But…' His voice tailed into silence.

'But we must take care?'

'I am sorry, but, yes. I hope you understand.'

'Heavens! So serious!' She patted his gloved hand. 'Is that not what mistletoe is for? Kissing?'

She understood more than Aaron realised. No matter how much she yearned to be in his arms and to kiss him again, the very real risk of being seen and being forced into marriage did not appeal. She had too much pride for that.

She cast about for a safer subject for discussion. 'You seemed a touch abrupt with the Caxtons. Are you not a friend of Mr Caxton's?'

'I am not, not any longer.'

Diana studied his grim profile. 'You used to be friends? I know you were both officers in the Guards. I felt certain you would accept their invitation.'

'We *were* on amicable terms. All I can say is... Caxton presumed too much on our friendship.'

'In what way?'

He glanced at her as he steered the curricle expertly between the stone pillars that marked the entrance to Lavenham Hall.

'I discovered they planned to trap me into marriage with Miss Caxton, by catching us in a compromising position.'

Diana gasped. 'But...that is dreadful. You mean to tell me that Mr Caxton would deliberately put his sister into such a position? Why ever would they do such a thing?'

Aaron huffed a laugh. 'Caxton's pockets are seriously to let. A wealthy brother-in-law—particularly one who stands to inherit a neighbouring estate— must have seemed a convenient solution.'

'But you would not be responsible for his debts. Would you?'

Aaron shrugged. 'Under the law, no. But they seemed to believe my...er...code of honour would not allow me to sit by and see my wife's brother thrown in debtors' prison.'

No wonder he was so concerned the maid had seen us.

'Thank goodness you realised what they were up to.'

'And now you know why it was no hardship to refuse the Caxtons' invitation.'

'But it must be dull for you at Lavenham, when
you are used to the social whirl of London,' she ventured.

They had arrived in front of the Hall and Aaron
brought the curricle to a standstill. A groom ran to
take charge of the horses and Aaron rounded the vehi-
cle to help Diana to the ground. She placed her hands
on his shoulders and her gaze captured his. Tension
shimmered in the air between them as he encircled
her waist, his grip firm. He lifted her, but did not step
back. He lowered her and she relished the feel of his
hard, muscled body against hers during that achingly
slow, sensual slide. Heat erupted from deep inside her
core as she was consumed by want and by need. She
could not tear her gaze from his.

'As it happens,' he said slowly, the crease between
his brows deepening, 'it is not dull. Not near as dull
as I feared.'

Hope flamed deep in her heart as she studied his
face. Read the intent in those penetrating grey eyes.
Could she… *Dared* she…hope?

Chapter Nine

Diana tapped lightly on the door to her mother's bed-chamber and entered. The room was empty. Diana frowned. She'd expected her mother to be resting after the church service—going anywhere always seemed to exhaust her. In the far corner, the door that joined this room to Mother's boudoir was ajar and, as she approached it, she caught the murmur of voices from beyond.

'You must know I cannot countenance such a scheme, Sally.'

Diana peered around the edge of the door to see Mother and Cousin Sally seated on chairs on opposite sides of the hearth, in which a welcoming fire blazed.

'I fail to understand why you find it so objectionable, Venetia, when it will benefit you as much as Diana.'

Diana halted at the mention of her name. Neither of the other women had noticed her presence. Cousin

Sally's attention was fully on Mother, who had turned her head to stare into the flames.

'There is nothing wrong with how we live our lives now,' she said in a peevish tone. 'I do not know why you and Lavenham needs must conjure up this ridiculous notion and, as for keeping me in ignorance all this time…*well!* I am sure if Diana knew your plans she would think the same as me. She has no thought of marriage.'

Marriage?

Nausea bubbled up into Diana's throat, leaving a hot, sour taste. This could only mean one thing and, after what Aaron had just told her, she knew it would enrage him.

Cousin Sally fixed Mother with a stern look. 'Even if you will not support our efforts to match Aaron and Diana, surely you realise it would be to your benefit if you were less confrontational in your dealings with Aaron, Venetia. You should think of the future for you and Diana should anything happen to Arthur.'

'Oh, I shall be dead long before Arthur.'

'I do not doubt it, Venetia, if you continue to wallow in the past.' Diana had never heard Cousin Sally sound so grim. 'But in that eventuality there would still be Diana's future to think about. Or do you not care what might become of her?'

Mother gasped. 'Of course I care, Sally. How dare you suggest otherwise?'

'You have a peculiar way of showing it. Why do you think Arthur wrote to me in the first place? He

is twenty years your senior and, although he may not admit this to you, he is deeply worried over what will become of you both when Aaron inherits Lavenham.'

'I shall have my widow's portion; that will go to Diana afterwards.'

'But…forgive me, my dear.' Cousin Sally's voice gentled. 'Arthur has been quite frank with me. Your portion is not large and he has little else to bequeath to you or Diana. Everything is entailed. Venetia, if you continue to alienate Aaron, what is there to stop him casting both you and Diana adrift when he does inherit?'

'It is so unfair. Not only did I lose my precious Simon, but to see such a distant relative—a virtual stranger—inherit our beloved Lavenham Hall… There is no justice! All my memories are here!'

Cousin Sally sighed. 'But that is the law, Venetia. And Aaron does not need to remain a stranger. Just think, if our plan succeeds you would have no need to quit Lavenham and leave those memories behind. It is the perfect solution. It is time Aaron settled down… I do so worry about the life he leads… It is so *aimless*.'

Her heart thumping in her chest, Diana willed her trembling legs to carry her backwards out of the room. She paused outside the adjoining door to catch her breath and then crept silently to the bedchamber door. She cursed herself for a coward, but she dared not confront Cousin Sally and her mother, for what could she say to them?

A black cloud engulfed her as she hurried back to

her own bedchamber. The darkness settled, smothering her, sinking in through every pore until it coalesced into a heavy weight of dread in the pit of her stomach.

What am I to do?

How could she tell Aaron? Not only would he be furious, he would also be devastated to discover his own mother had schemed behind his back.

She dreaded seeing Aaron again, for how could she hide the truth from him?

Lavenham wielded the well-honed carving knife and sliced down through the breast of the goose. The butler and several footmen hovered, ready to serve the slices of roast meat to the family, all of whom were seated around the huge dining table, which groaned with the weight of china, lead crystal glassware, silver cutlery and food. The candles flickered and the fire roared, and the chatter and laughter around the table was happy and full of anticipation as the members of both Fleming families waited to tuck into their Christmas dinner.

Aaron gazed around the table in contentment and, while the food was being served, his mind wandered over the events of this Christmastide, remembering its unpromising start. He was not afraid to admit he had been wrong. He had enjoyed their stay at Lavenham Hall, despite his initial reluctance.

'Harry! That was *my* potato!'

'Isabel. Moderate your voice, if you please,' Mama

said. 'Harry—that was rude. There is more than enough food to go around. If you cannot behave in a civilised manner, you will be sent to eat on your own in the nursery.'

Mama caught Aaron's eye and rolled her eyes in exasperation at the twins' antics and he smiled at her, shaking his head. It was ever thus. His big, noisy, lively family—give him dinner with them over any number of elegant, *tonnish* dinner parties.

Eliza was seated opposite him and his pleasure was tempered by sorrow. Christmas would never be quite the same again after she married. And it would not be long before the others began to fly the nest, one by one, as well. He looked around the table again, committing each and every one of them to memory. Spending this time with his family in different surroundings had somehow crystallised a longing in him that he had been unaware of until now: the longing for a big, happy, loving family of his own. And it struck him—*here*, with his beloved family, was where he was happiest. Not taking part in the frivolous nonsense of London society, with its petty rules and its stuffy etiquette.

Once—after the horror of war—that life had been all he craved, but now it had begun to pall, although it had taken this Christmas for him to realise it and to understand what was truly important. He glanced to his right. To Diana, by his side, and he felt the tug of desire he experienced now every time he looked at her.

'Would you care for creamed parsnips?' He proffered the dish.

'Thank you.'

He took the opportunity, as he spooned the vegetable on to her plate, to study her. He felt a frown pucker his forehead. She was subdued, in marked contrast to the lively girl he had driven home in his curricle, and disquiet twisted his heart as he recalled that, in the drawing room before the meal was announced, she had studiously avoided his gaze. Was their kiss still bothering her? He was aware he could have handled the aftermath better, but he had thought she'd forgiven him. Certainly, the way she had teased him during their drive home had given that impression.

Her obvious unease unsettled him. He did not want her to be uneasy. He wanted her happy, always, and he wanted to be the man to make her so. Always.

He spooned some parsnip on to his own plate, and passed the dish on, responding by rote to any remarks sent his way, as the greater part of his brain grappled with an idea that was so new...so unthinkable up to now...that he could barely believe he was even considering it.

He ate his food and sipped his wine without tasting any of it, his gaze resting on his mother. Wondering. Had her frequent hints about him settling down made more of an impression on him than he realised? The thought did not fill him with the horror he would have felt this time last year.

Which led his thoughts inevitably back to Diana,

and the idea that had begun to take shape—the idea that maybe, just maybe, he was ready to marry. And there was only one woman for him. Diana. He watched her surreptitiously, from under his lashes, mesmerised by those sweet lips he now knew tasted divine and filled him with the urge to kiss her again and again.

He leaned to his right. 'You are quiet this evening, Diana. Is there anything wrong?'

She jumped, as though she had been bitten.

'No. No. I am quite all right, thank you, Aaron.'

Her cheeks glowed bright red and although her face turned in his direction she did not quite meet his eyes. He felt his brows lower and she looked even more nervous.

'Truly. I am well.'

She bent her head to her plate and, with an inner sigh, Aaron abandoned the conversation, caution whispering deep in his gut. He was still unsure how Diana felt about him. That kiss had led him to hope but, now, he did not know what to think. But there was one thing he was damned sure of: for the same reason he would not choose a wife merely out of duty, neither would he want any woman to accept him out of duty or practicality. Or simply because he was better than nothing.

He expected more than that from a wife and from marriage.

Maybe she could think straight if only she hadn't been forced to sit next to Aaron, but Papa had been

embarrassingly insistent. Diana, knowing what she now did, was mortified…convinced Aaron would suspect what her father was up to. She picked at her food. It looked delicious, but it turned to ashes in her mouth.

She forced herself to take another bite in an attempt to divert Aaron's attention from her change in mood. He was already puzzled, she could tell. She could feign illness…return to her bedchamber…but how would that help? She could not be ill for the remainder of Aaron's visit. Besides, she did not want to stay closeted away. She wanted to spend time with him, while she still could.

And, of a sudden, her head cleared of that all-pervading sense of dread that had fogged her mind ever since she learned of their parents' plot. And she grew angry: with their parents, yes, but also with herself.

Why should *she* feel guilty when she had done nothing wrong? She glanced sideways at Aaron, drinking in his dark good looks, listening to him joking with his brothers, and she knew the choice she faced. She could either withdraw into herself—and spend the rest of her life wondering what might have been—or she could fight for what she now knew she wanted above all else.

Aaron.

The knowledge hit her with the force of a lightning bolt. She loved him and she could not bear to lose him.

Could he love me, too?

She remembered his words when they had arrived

back home; pictured the look on his face; felt again the way he had held her…and she knew there was hope. She touched his arm, to get his attention. His head snapped around and she smiled at him. The relief in his eyes was palpable.

'I am sorry I've been quiet,' she said. 'I had a slight headache. It has gone now.'

'And has your appetite returned?' He indicated her plate, still half-full.

'It has.'

'I am very pleased.' His grey eyes were warm as he smiled into hers. 'And just in time for the plum pudding.'

Perkins, their butler, approached the table with the round pudding—topped with a sprig of holly— balanced on a salver. He placed it in the centre of the table and a footman poured warmed brandy over it. The candles nearest the pudding were extinguished, and then Perkins used a taper to light the brandy. A shimmering ball of blue flame engulfed the pudding, and cheers and applause erupted.

Diana gazed around the table, her heart full of love for her family…even Mother was smiling, her hands together as though she had so far forgotten herself as to clap along with the others.

The rest of Christmas Day passed in a blur. Aaron was attentive, but not in such a way as to attract attention and for short periods Diana even managed to forget the truth. The knowledge would resurface all

too soon, however, reminding her that she must at all costs avoid being alone with Aaron.

How awful if they kissed and were caught. Because now she knew, without a shadow of a doubt, that their parents would insist upon a wedding.

That evening, urged on by her mother, Frances sat at the pianoforte and began to play, her nimble fingers making light work of pieces by Mozart and Vivaldi. She then progressed to playing folk songs and some carols, and they all gathered around the instrument to sing. Diana's heart skipped a beat as Aaron stepped into the narrow gap between her and George, forcing his brother to move aside to make room. Aaron's deep baritone thrilled right through her, and her heart swelled, feeling as though it might burst, for not only was it full of love for Aaron, but also with the happiness and the sense of belonging that her cousins took for granted.

And then, during a lull in the singing whilst Frances and Eliza squabbled over the next song, Aaron's hand touched hers. Such a fleeting touch she could almost have imagined it. But there it was again, the merest brush of his fingers over hers and a surge of... What? Energy? Joy? cascaded through her and over her, making her heart pound and her breath catch. She glanced sideways at him, through her lashes, and their gazes met. And held. Then his lips pursed, ever so slightly, as though suppressing a smile, and he looked away, leaving Diana almost afraid to dare to hope that she might win his heart.

Chapter Ten

The following day was St Stephen's Day with its tradition of distributing Christmas boxes to tenants and staff and Aaron consequently spent the entire morning with Lavenham and his bailiff, Walker, meeting the Lavenham tenants, whilst Diana and her mother gave the servants their gifts.

After luncheon, Aaron tracked Diana down to her still room.

'There you are. Come for a walk with me.' He took her hand, lacing his fingers through hers. 'It is cold outside and starting to snow, so you will need your cloak. I've asked your maid to bring it downstairs.'

She smiled, somewhat puzzled. 'You are very certain I will accept.'

'I am hopeful.'

'Then how can I refuse? Are the others coming?'

'They have already left,' he said. 'We can catch them up.'

Aaron already wore his greatcoat and a muffler

and was carrying his hat and gloves. Outside the still room, the maid was waiting with Diana's favourite cloak—scarlet and fur-lined—and her fur hat, her scarf and gloves. They set out along a path that led down towards the river.

'It is enchanting.' Diana tilted her face to the sky and tried to catch snowflakes on her tongue. 'I love the snow.'

'If it settles, we could go sledging,' Aaron said. 'That would be fun.'

'Ooh, it's years since I went sledging. I wonder if we still have the sledges.'

'You do,' Aaron said. 'As soon as the vicar mentioned snow yesterday, the boys made it their mission to check. All we need is for it to keep snowing.'

He tucked her hand more securely under his arm and kept walking.

'I was concerned about you yesterday,' he said. 'You were very quiet.'

Her insides went very still. She looked at him, but he kept his attention on the path ahead.

'I had a headache. I told you.'

'You also told me it had gone.'

She swallowed nervously. 'It did.'

'But I was watching you. There were times when you became very subdued, but then it was as though you donned a mask so no one could tell.'

She forced a laugh. 'Then it was a poor effort on my part, if it was so obvious to you.'

He stopped and she saw him cast a quick look

around. Diana knew without looking that they were out of sight of the house. The snow was falling faster, settling on her lashes and on the tip of her nose and her top lip. He tugged her to face him and gently brushed the flakes away.

She started to pull away, suddenly nervous in case they were seen.

'It's cold. We should go back.'

'Wait.'

He cupped her chin, tilting her face to his, searching her expression. Then his eyes softened and his lips curved and she felt her own lips relax and part.

Quickly, he unbuttoned his greatcoat and then pushed his hands beneath her cloak, wrapping his arms around her and pulling her in close, fitting her curves into the solid contours of his body. He nuzzled her earlobe, just visible below the brim of her bonnet.

'Let me warm you,' he whispered and a shiver that had nothing to do with the cold raced across her skin.

Her hands came between them. He tensed, but as she raised them to frame his face, he relaxed again. Their gazes fused, his lit by a beguiling gleam that made her heart sing.

I may never have another chance...

She pushed on to her tiptoes and their lips met with passionate intensity. His tongue found hers, his hands roaming the curves and hollows of her back and her buttocks, and she melted into him as his tongue stroked hers with tantalising promises of pleasure.

With each breath she drew in his clean, masculine scent and as her body heated, her corset grew tighter.

With a soft groan, he took his mouth from hers and held her captive with his clear grey gaze. He moved his hands to her shoulders, and Diana clung to his lapels, entranced; craving more. As her thoughts slowly reassembled, she pushed him away.

'What if someone should see?'

He laughed. 'No one will see.'

'But…your family. What if they had seen us? They are out here somewhere.'

He bit his lip and concentrated on straightening her cloak, pulling it across her front. Then he buttoned his greatcoat. 'They went the other way,' he said, finally.

'But…'

'Let us go home. You will catch a chill.' He removed one glove and caressed her cheek with his fingertips, then traced her lips. 'I wanted to be alone with you.' He dipped his head and brushed her lips with his. 'Do you mind?'

'I…no.' She shivered, still fretting about the risk and the possible consequences. 'But I should like to go back now.'

They began to retrace their steps, Diana worrying about what could have happened—even though it hadn't—and wondering if she dared to read anything into his actions this afternoon. He kept his arm around her waist until they came within sight of the house, then he took her hand and placed it on his arm.

'No point in inviting trouble,' he said, with a grin, and her heart sank.

As they entered the house, Perkins approached them and bowed. 'His lordship has asked that you attend him in his study as soon as you return, Mr Fleming.'

'Very well,' Aaron said. 'Have my brothers and sisters come back yet?'

'Yes, sir. A few minutes ago. They have gone upstairs to change out of their wet clothing.'

'I suggest you do likewise, Diana,' Aaron said. 'I shall see you later.'

'You sent for me, sir?'

Lavenham stood up and came around his desk, gesturing towards the pair of chairs set either side of the fireplace in which, Aaron was pleased to see, a fire blazed. He sat and stretched his hands to the flames, rubbing them.

'I'm sorry I kept you waiting,' he continued. 'We have been for a walk.'

'So Perkins said. Would you care for a glass of wine?'

'Thank you.'

As Lavenham poured the wine, Aaron's thoughts drifted pleasantly, reliving his walk with Diana, and their kiss. Lavenham handed him a glass before settling in the other chair.

'Well, m'boy. I know you were not keen on spending Christmastide here at Lavenham, but I venture to

suggest you have not found your visit to be a waste of time, eh?'

'No, sir. I have learned much about the estate and the running of it from you and from Walker. Although, of course, I hope it will be many years before I need to put such knowledge into practice.'

Lavenham waved a dismissive hand. 'Oh, you will manage the estate without much trouble. Walker will steer you right on that score.'

Aaron waited. Lavenham clearly had something on his mind. If it was not about the estate he could not imagine what else it might be. He could not suspect any attachment between himself and Diana for, other than those two stolen kisses, he had acted with the utmost caution. It was not only that he wanted to be sure of both himself and Diana, but he could not abide the thought of having to run the gauntlet of knowing looks and arch comments if anyone else happened to guess at his burgeoning feelings.

At least now he had the satisfaction of knowing this was his decision and that Diana would welcome his offer.

Lavenham gulped at his wine, then set the glass decisively on a small table by his side.

'Yes…well…you know you can ask me anything, lad, do you not… If you have any questions…any *specific* questions… Yes…quite…'

Lavenham snatched his glass again, and swigged another large mouthful of wine.

An uneasy feeling unfolded in Aaron's gut. 'And

what *specific* question do you imagine I might wish to ask?'

'I thought… That is…you… Diana…' Lavenham swallowed more wine, draining his glass. He inhaled. 'Your intentions, m'boy.'

'My *intentions*?'

Nobody saw us. I know they didn't. What is going on… Did Diana tell Lavenham? No! I will not believe that.

'We hoped…we thought…your mother and I…'

Aaron straightened, frowning. 'What do you mean by "your mother and I"? What involvement has my mother with this?'

'I'm sure she meant no harm. You rub along together well enough, you and Diana, just as we hoped when we arranged for you all to spend Christmastide here at the Hall.' Lavenham smiled, rubbing his hands together. 'And you need not fear she will refuse you, m'boy.' Lavenham leaned over and clapped Aaron on the knee. 'I know what it's like for you young men, with your pride. No, Diana will accept you. She knows when she's well off and she's a dutiful daughter, as I'm sure you have seen. This is the perfect solution: you are of an age to settle down and Dia—'

'I think you have said enough, sir.'

Aaron stood, anger surging through him. Lavenham might on occasion amuse with his absent-mindedness and lack of the social niceties, but Aaron could not make allowances for this.

And as for Diana! Does she know? A dutiful daugh-

ter indeed! Surely *she cannot know. And* Mama*! How* could *she betray me like this?*

'I do not know what you hoped, sir, but I regret to inform you that you are sorely mistaken if you believe I can be...*ambushed*...into making an offer for your daughter.'

He stalked across the library and out of the room, only just stopping himself from slamming it behind him. Instead, he closed it with meticulous care and then stood stock still, eyes screwed shut and fists clenched as he willed his breathing to slow and struggled to control his rage.

'Aaron? What is wrong?'

It was the very last thing he wanted...to talk to Diana whilst anger and betrayal burned in his gut. He forced his eyes open. She stood before him, worry etched on her lovely face, and his rage slowly subsided. She did that to him: calmed and soothed and delighted him. Surely she was not party to this...this *debacle*. He would not let his anger loose upon her, but neither would he be forced into such a life-changing decision. He dashed aside the voice in his head that whispered he had been on the verge of declaring himself anyway. He refused to be manipulated like this and Diana, surely, would be as horrified as he at their parents' plotting and scheming.

'I have just learned—' he sucked in a breath, willing himself to remain calm '—that this visit...this plan to spend Christmas here in order that I may learn

about the estates…was merely a subterfuge for a plot cooked up by your father and my mother.'

A light flush coloured Diana's cheeks and she caught her bottom lip between her teeth. Sick realisation stole through him. There was no surprise, merely a hint of guilt in her slanting eyes.

'You *knew*!'

How dare *they all conspire against me?*

The bitter feeling of betrayal swelled. He could not keep still—he strode a few paces down the hall, then returned to confront her.

'Were you in on their plan from the start?'

He could not bear to look at her. He turned from her, fury pumping his blood hard and hot, but he did not walk away. He waited, rigid with the effort it took to remain, waiting to hear her excuse.

Diana stared helplessly at Aaron. He was almost vibrating with fury. What could she say but the truth? It would not be enough…she knew how much he resented being forced into anything. Were there any words that would change his mind if it was made up?

'Aaron, please.' She touched his elbow. 'Can we talk about this? I only found out yesterday.'

'And you did not think to tell me? To *warn* me?'

She grabbed his hand, pulling him to face her. 'How could I do so? How could I say those words to you, after what you told me about the Caxtons? After that kiss? I was afraid…afraid you would think…as you do now…that I, too, wish to force you into mar-

riage.' His livid features blurred as her eyes filled with tears. 'Aaron, I love you. *How* could I tell you such a thing? I thought…if you made up your own mind… then there was no harm done.'

'No harm done? *No one* has the right to try and rule my life for me. I make my own decisions.

'Giggs!'

His roar echoed through the Hall and his valet came running from the back of the house.

'Order the curricle and then pack my bag. Quickly, man!'

Giggs hurried away.

'Aaron.' She must try to get through to him. 'Don't go. Not like this. Please.'

'I'm sorry, Diana, but I'm leaving today, right after I speak to my mother.' He stormed off up the stairs two at a time and did not look back.

Diana watched him go. She had read of hearts breaking, but she had never imagined the pain, the utter feeling of helplessness as he disappeared from her view.

Chapter Eleven

Aaron found his mother with Cousin Venetia in her boudoir. They both looked up as he entered. Mama took one look at his face and stood up.

'Excuse me, Venetia, whilst I speak to Aaron.'

She swept past Aaron into the corridor outside.

'What is it, Aaron?'

'I know,' he growled.

She opened her mouth, but before she could speak, he continued, 'And do not even consider denying it. Lavenham let the truth slip. Or, actually, he did not let it slip…that would be beyond a clumsy fool such as he. No, he blundered right in and tried to force me to the point.'

His mother's nostrils flared as she inhaled. 'Oh, dear,' she said. 'Come, we cannot discuss this here. Come to my bedchamber.'

Once inside the room, Aaron paced to the window and stared out at the gardens below. The snow still

drifted from the sky. It no longer appeared magical but bleak, much as Aaron felt.

'How could you do this to me, Mama?'

'I will not speak to your back, Son. Please have the courtesy to face me.'

He hauled in a breath and turned, folding his arms across his chest. His mother stood before him, her foot tapping...a sure sign she was annoyed. Well, so was he...and he had far more right to be angry than she did.

'How *could* you?'

Mama frowned. 'What have I done that is so reprehensible, Aaron?'

'You lied to me. You betrayed me.'

'Betrayed? Oh, come now. How, pray, is it a betrayal to introduce you to Diana? For that is all we have done.'

He didn't want to listen to words of reason. 'You tricked me, then. Do you deny you lied to me, to get me to come here? You told me Lavenham was in poor health.'

'But he *is* very worried about what will become of Diana when he—'

'I do not want a wife because it is *convenient* for her. Or for Lavenham. I am leaving. *Now.*'

He stalked from the room and slammed the door. As he strode for the stairs, he heard the door open behind him.

'Aaron...please...don't be so stubborn. Stay here the night. It is snowing. You will get stranded.'

She is right. Come now, give yourself time to cool down.

He swatted away the whisper of reason inside his head. 'Then I shall stay at an inn. Anywhere is preferable to here.'

He ran downstairs. Perkins, his face poker straight, helped him on with his still-damp greatcoat. Aaron was aware Mama had followed him downstairs and that Diana and her father were both in the hall, but he ignored them all—as well as the growing misgivings in his heart—as he strode past them and out of the front door.

Giggs was already by the curricle, stowing their bags under the seat. Aaron leapt on board and picked up the ribbons. The groom at the horses' heads watched him for the signal to release them.

Aaron paused, Diana's words hammering in his head. He believed her. Even as she had spoken, he had recognised the truth in her words. She had been in an impossible position. But his obstinacy had driven him on. His heart thundered, pumping his blood around his body, and his chest heaved with every painful breath, only now it was Mama's words that echoed through his head.

Stubborn.

It was in his nature, but that didn't mean he could not fight it. He looked back at the Hall at Diana and Mama, standing side by side on the top step, and love for both of them flooded his heart. Lavenham's stooped form stood behind them, his hand protec-

tively on his daughter's shoulder. The faces of his brothers and his sisters—their distress discernible even at this distance—stared at him from an upstairs window. His gaze returned to Diana, drawn to her as if by a magnet.

The desolation…the *defeat*…in her expression tore at his heart.

What the bloody hell am I doing?

And the answer came from deep, deep within his soul. He was allowing his cursed stubbornness to deny him happiness.

All I love is here: Diana, Mama, the young 'uns.

All my hopes for the future: a large and loving family and a wife I adore.

Why would I allow one bumbling but well-meaning old man to drive me away?

He swallowed. Hard. His future happiness hung by a thread and only he could stop it snapping.

There goes my pride.

He tied off the reins with an inner, rueful smile.

'Unpack the bags, Giggs. We're going nowhere.' And he climbed down from the curricle and paced slowly back to the front door, his eyes riveted to Diana's.

'I am sorry. Mama's right. I'm a stubborn fool.' He reached for her hand and he raised it to his lips, pressing them to her chilled skin.

'I love you, Diana.'

Her eyes spilled over and he wiped the tears with

his thumb, then dropped to one knee, heedless of the wet and the cold.

'Will you marry me?'

It was New Year's Eve. Diana awoke to the sensation that the light was brighter than usual. She had either overslept, or... She leapt out of bed and ran to the window, throwing open the curtains.

'Snow!'

Ever since she was a child she had loved the snow— seeing the world all pristine and white and glittering, the sharp edges all smooth and plump. She shivered in the chill air and, leaving the curtains wide, she hurried back to bed and snuggled down. The snow was still falling but later...when it stopped...

It will be so much fun with my cousins here. With Aaron...my husband-to-be.

Those words still made her heart pound. They were to be married in a little over two weeks. Aaron would move to Lavenham Hall to live with her and— to everyone's surprise—Mother had quickly accepted the match once she realised it meant Diana would not have to leave her after all. She was even eagerly— if prematurely—anticipating the arrival of her first grandchild.

How Diana's life was about to change...no longer just herself and her parents to think of, but another person... Aaron, the man she loved with all her heart, but the man who would also have ultimate control of her life. Of her.

* * *

'Come on, sweetheart. Sit here in front of me.'

Aaron patted the sledge, shifting back to leave a space in front of him, between his thighs. There were only two sledges, plus a plank of wood the boys had found in one of the barns, so they had to share as they slid down Abbotts Hill—the steepest land on the estate. Diana felt a shiver of nervousness chase down her spine. She'd sledged down the hill many times in her childhood, but always alone. She had been in control. Now she must put her trust in someone else to steer her safely to the bottom.

Her doubt must have shown in her expression, for Aaron laughed and beckoned to her.

'You will be safe with me. Come on, it'll be fun.'

Diana flicked a glance at Frances, who had settled on to the other sledge in front of George—against whom they were going to race—and copied her position. Aaron's solid thighs cradled her as one strong arm wrapped around her waist. For one blissful second she basked in the warm support of his vital strength, then she shrieked, grabbing his thighs as Harry and Joseph shoved them over the brow of the hill and they shot down the slope.

The sledge seemed to fly, faster than she had ever known, the bottom of the hill hurtling ever nearer. She tensed. They were going so fast…how would they ever stop?

'Diana!' The yell was in her ear. 'Don't lean— you'll—*arggghh*!'

The sledge tipped to one side and they rolled over into the snow. But Aaron kept her safe, catching her to his chest and cushioning her fall with his body. George and Frances shot past them, yelling and jeering. Breathlessly giggling, Diana wriggled around until she was lying on her belly on top of Aaron. His hand curved around her head and he brought her mouth to his, kissing her soundly.

'Mmm...' she murmured, as she returned his kiss.

'Wretched woman,' he grumbled against her lips when they finally came up for air. 'I can't believe you upset us. We'll never hear the last of it, letting them win like that.'

'But I wanted a kiss,' she whispered and was rewarded by a flare of heat in his eyes.

He kissed her again and she felt his arousal even through their thick clothing. Her hair had fallen around her face and he brushed it back with the edge of his gloved hand.

'How much longer must I wait?' he murmured.

'Only fifteen days. Then we will be together for ever.'

'Fifteen days too many.' His eyes narrowed slightly and she caught the flicker of a smile. 'I trust you have learned your lesson, Wife-to-be.'

She pushed her hands against his chest, straightening her arms. 'Lesson?'

'That you must trust your husband to steer you straight, in life as well as on a sledge.'

Diana bit back a smile.

'And what makes you think, Husband-to-be, that I want to keep to the straight and narrow?' She leaned down and kissed his lips. Hard. 'A little diversion now and again does have its rewards.'

* * * * *

*If you enjoyed these stories,
you won't want to miss these other
Regency collections*

*ONCE UPON A REGENCY CHRISTMAS
by Louise Allen, Sophia James
and Annie Burrows*

*IT HAPPENED ONE CHRISTMAS
by Carla Kelly, Georgie Lee
and Ann Lethbridge*

*WISH UPON A SNOWFLAKE
by Christine Merrill, Linda Skye
and Elizabeth Rolls*

MILLS & BOON®

HISTORICAL

AWAKEN THE ROMANCE OF THE PAST

MILLS & BOON®

EXCLUSIVE EXTRACT

Read on for a sneak preview of
A SECRET CONSEQUENCE FOR THE VISCOUNT
by Sophia James
the final book in the daring and decadent series
THE SOCIETY OF WICKED GENTLEMEN

'I was more than surprised to see you tonight. I don't know why you would wish for all those years of silence and no contact whatsoever, but—'

'It was not intentional, Lady Eleanor. My memory was lost.'

Her eyes widened at this truth and she swallowed, hard.

'I must have been hit over the head, as there was a sizeable lump there for a good time afterwards. As a result of the injury my memory was compromised.'

She now looked plainly shocked. 'How much of it exactly? How much did you lose?'

'Everything that happened to me before I disappeared was gone for many years. A month ago I retrieved most of my history but still…there are patches.'

'Patches?'

'The week before my disappearance and a few days after have gone entirely. I cannot seem to remember any of it.'

She turned at that, away from the moonlight so that all her face was in shadow. She seemed slighter than she had done a few hours earlier. Her hands trembled as she caught them together before her.

'Everything?'

'I am hoping it will come back, but...' He stopped, because he could not know if this was a permanent state or a temporary one.

'How was your cheek scarred?'

'Someone wants me dead. They have tried three times to kill me now and I doubt that will cease until I identify the perpetrators.'

'Why? Why should you be such a target?'

'I have lived in the shadows for a long time, even before I left England, and have any number of enemies. Some I can identify, but others I can't.'

'A lonely place to be in.'

'And a dangerous one.'

'You are different now, Lord Bromley.' She gave him those words quietly. 'More distant. A harder man. Almost unrecognisable.'

He laughed, the sound discordant, but here in the night there was a sense of honesty he had not felt in a long, long time. Even his friends had tiptoed around his new reality and tried to find the similarities with what had been before. Lady Eleanor did not attempt to be diplomatic at all as she had asked of his cheek and his circumstances and there was freedom in such truth.

He felt a pull towards her that was stronger than anything he had ever known before and stiffened, cursing beneath his breath.

DON'T MISS
SECRET CONSEQUENCE FOR THE VISCOUNT
BY SOPHIA JAMES

Available December 2017
www.millsandboon.co.uk

Join Britain's BIGGEST Romance Book Club

50% OFF your first parcel

- **EXCLUSIVE offers** every month

- **FREE delivery direct** to your door

- **NEVER MISS a title**

Call Customer Services
0844 844 1358*

or visit
millsandboon.co.uk/bookclub

* This call will cost you 7 pence per minute plus your phone company's price per minute access charge.

KCB4